C000176067

Taken to the Hills

S J Richards

TAKEN TO THE HILLS

Published worldwide by Apple Loft Press

This edition published in 2023

Copyright © 2023 by S J Richards

S J Richards has asserted his right to be identified as the author of this work in accordance with the Copyright, Design and Patents Act 1988.

All rights reserved. This book or any portion thereof may not be reproduced or used in any manner whatsoever without the express written permission of the author, except for quotes or short extracts for the purpose of reviews.

www.sjrichardsauthor.com

For Penny

Chapter 1

It was his smile that hurt the most. It stretched from his boxed beard to his deep brown eyes, the whole of his face filled with bonhomie. That smile had drawn her in and she had trusted him. It was always there.

Until it wasn't.

"Nearly done," he said, and cocked his head to one side. "You're doing really well. Come on, my darling, keep going."

She stared at the piece of paper, afraid for herself and also for the others, then put the pen down, not wanting to look him in the eyes and see that cheery disposition. She knew only too well how quickly he could change. "Why are you making me do this?" she whispered, unable to keep her voice from quivering.

"It's a precaution," he said.

"But it's nonsense, a pack of lies."

He bent forward, put his hand under her chin and gently lifted her face so that she was forced to look him straight in the eyes. "Don't worry, you know I wouldn't hurt you." He let go and stood upright. She turned away and put a hand to her sore cheek.

"I can't do it," she said, her voice stronger now. She started to stand but he put his hands on her shoulders.

"Don't be silly, dear," he said, gesturing to the paper. "You've added two, one to go."

"But I…"

He hit her. It was the left cheek this time, and it wasn't a slap but a full-bodied fist to the face. Her head was thrown backwards and she screamed with the shock and the pain. He grabbed her hair and pulled her forward so that she was forced to look him in the eyes. The smile had vanished and he was sneering. He put his hands around her throat and she felt his thumbs press hard, constricting her airways. She tried to scream again but nothing came. He pressed harder still and the blood began to rise up her neck. She felt herself fading.

He released his hands and stood back, watching as she flopped forward to the table. "Are you okay darling?" he said, his sing-song-happy voice returning.

She took in great gulps of air.

He lifted her head by the hair again. "Finish it," he said.

Trembling, she picked the pen up and started to write.

Chapter 2

Chloe had cooked the meal, Luke's favourite, and she and Ben had regaled him with stories from their first few months at University. Chloe had also told them about Tristram, a boy she had started to see regularly, and had coped remarkably well when her brother had continually asked her if she fancied a shandy.

"That was delicious, Chloe," Luke said.

"Not bad, sis,' Ben teased. "Not as good as my own chilli but you're getting better."

She punched him playfully as they made their way to the sitting room. It was a typical farmhouse lounge, with exposed wooden beams, pale cream walls, aged pine flooring and a mix of furniture that was practical but with a weathered, worn look. Fortunately, for both Luke and his son, the ceiling was vaulted which made ducking unnecessary.

The three of them sat back, kicking off their slippers at more or less the same time. Luke settled into the grey armchair, or 'Dad seat' as the twins had labelled it, while Chloe stretched out on the cream linen sofa and Ben took the mustard wingback.

Wilkins leapt onto Luke's lap, rotating twice and trying to grab a sneaky lick of his face before curling up. He stroked the cocker absent-mindedly. This was the first time his children had been home from University at the same time since Christmas and he was absolutely loving it. Yes, they bickered, but no more than you would expect. What was great was that they supported each other and him, and that support had been oh-so-important over the previous six months. The twins had struggled initially, but they had come to terms with what had happened much more quickly than he had.

He glanced at Chloe, who was sipping her white wine. Every day she grew more and more like her mother. At five foot eight inches, she was only an inch taller than Jess and her hair was the same strawberry blonde, stretching down to just below her shoulders. However, with her high cheekbones and blue eyes it was in her face that the resemblance really showed.

Ben, on the other hand, took after his father. He was a lot leaner, lanky in fact, but Luke knew his shoulders would broaden when he got into his twenties.

Luke noticed a serious expression had come over his son's face. "What's up, Ben?" he said. "Is something worrying you?"

"You won't like it, Dad."

"What?"

"I rang Granddad on Wednesday."

Luke grunted. "I bet that was a delight."

"I wanted to tell him about my course, and about all the new friends I've made"

Chloe sat up. "How was he, Ben? What did he say?"

"He let me talk for a bit but I could tell he wasn't interested. In the end, I just kind of fizzled out and asked him about Grandma. He dodged the question and started talking about all his posh friends, Lord this and Lady that."

"Did he ask about me?" she asked.

Ben looked over at his sister and Luke could see he was upset. "He didn't ask about any of us," he said.

"Try not to take it personally," Luke said. "He's selfish and self-centred, always has been."

It was true. His father's world had always revolved around his own achievements and anything he could boast about. He wasn't interested in other people, even his own family, and never had been. It was upsetting but Luke had learned to live with it. Unfortunately, it seemed that his children hadn't.

He decided to change the subject. "I'm right out of cheese," he said. "Do you two fancy a trip to see Roger tomorrow?"

"Cheese?" Chloe said with a big smile on her face. "Who are you trying to kid, Dad?"

"And some trout. Perhaps some of his pickled eggs. They're lovely in a packet of crisps."

"I'll drive," Ben said.

"Are you sure?" Luke asked.

"Definitely."

"Thanks, Ben."

"Cheers Bruv," Chloe said. "I might have a bit of 'cheese' myself." She giggled, and once again Luke was reminded of her mother. "Might even have a pint of it."

*

Luke was up bright and early the next morning and decided to take Wilkins for a walk before the twins emerged.

"Come on, boy," he said, as he released him from his crate. The spaniel immediately leapt in the air and pulled his lead down from its hook before offering it to his master. "Clever bugger," Luke said with a grin.

He led Wilkins out of the kitchen door and down the garden to the gate that led straight onto the field at the back of the house. Once through he let him off the lead and the dog immediately raced towards a jackdaw which ignored him until he was a few feet away then flew off insouciantly. He followed the cocker clockwise around the field as he darted from hedgerow to hillock, savouring the smells and odours that only a dog could sense.

Luke sighed as his thoughts turned to Jess. He would give anything to see her again, to feel her hand in his, to talk together and to share memories. Of course, it wouldn't happen, couldn't happen. She was lost to him forever, and yet he still sensed her presence. Not just through the children, who had inherited her strength and her indomitable nature. No, it was more than that. Somehow, Jess was in his very core, offering advice and guidance.

And right now she was telling him to stop wallowing and get on with his life, which was exactly what he planned to do. He wasn't going back to Avon and Somerset Police though. He couldn't face that, not after the sentence Thompson had been given. The man had killed someone and the judge had sentenced him to 18 months in prison. It was bloody ridiculous, a mockery.

He had to admit the force had been great to him though. He had received endless messages of goodwill and support from everyone up to and including the chief constable, and been given compassionate leave, initially for a month then extended to three months. He hadn't used it well though, and had allowed thoughts of anger and revenge to stew him up and mess with his brain. It was only when the three months were up, and he took the decision to resign, that he began to come to terms with his loss. It was still hard, and would be for a long time, but he needed to move on and stop stewing in his own juices.

Chloe was up at just after nine but it was gone eleven when Ben finally emerged.

"Are you ready?" Chloe said. She had already showered and was sitting at the breakfast bar reading the latest David J Gatward novel.

Ben stared at her through half-closed eyes, his wild morning hair doing its own thing on top of his head.

"Uh?" he said.

"Give him a chance," Luke said. "Coffee, Ben?"

Ben gave him a thumbs-up and dropped onto the stool next to his sister.

Luke poured his son's drink and placed it in front of him. "You ready for our trip out?" he said, and received another thumbs up as Ben took a sip of his coffee.

"He smells, Dad," Chloe said. "He needs a shower first."

"I don't smell," Ben said.

"Aah," she said. "It can speak."

"Will you be ready for 11:30?" Luke said.

"Yeah," Ben said.

"Including time for a shower?" Chloe said.

Ben gave her a look that could have wilted a cabbage. "Yes sis," he said, "including time for a shower."

True to his word Ben was ready for 11:30, his hair now carefully moussed into shape and his chin bristle-free.

"Right," Luke said as he got behind the wheel of Ben's Ford Focus. "The container's in the back. I'll drive there. Are you still happy to drive back, Ben?"

"Sure, Dad," Ben said.

It was nearly an hour's drive to Roger's place but it was a journey Luke enjoyed, taking in as it did some of the county's best scenery and also Wells, England's smallest, and in his opinion most beautiful, city.

As they approached Mudgely the road narrowed until it was little more than a car's width. There were tall hedges on either side and Luke drove slowly as the lane weaved between the fields. When they reached Land's End Farm he reverse-parked next to a battered old Land Rover and the three of them climbed out. He threw the keys to Ben and led them into the cider barn at the side of the farmhouse.

Roger's gentle Somerset accent could be heard as soon as they entered. He was chatting to a middle-aged couple, all three holding glasses of cider, the man and woman half-pints and Roger a large tankard which was about half-full. He turned when he saw them enter.

"Afternoon, Luke," he said and shook his hand. He turned to the twins. "Sorry, I forget your names."

They re-introduced themselves and Roger gestured to the couple by his side. "This is Alan and Rosie," he said. "Come over from Avebury. Cider, Luke?"

Luke nodded. "Dry please."

"And you, Chloe? Ben?"

"Medium please," Chloe said.

"Not for me," Ben said. "I'm driving."

"Right you are," Roger said. He grabbed a couple of glasses and went around to the massive cider tuns, each of which Luke knew held over 200 gallons.

"Got any cheese?" Luke called.

"Only the best strong cheddar you'll ever eat," Roger said, and Luke could hear the pride in his voice. "Grade 1 Stilton too. I gets it from Melton Mowbray. Proper good stuff it is."

"£5 worth of each please, Roger. I've brought my 10-litre container too. Can you fill it with dry?"

"Be pleased to." Roger emerged with full glasses of cider. "This one's for you, young Chloe," he said, passing one of the glasses to her, "and this one's yours, Luke. Help yourselves to a top-up when you need one. I'll go and get that cheese."

They sat around the only, rather battered, table and Luke took a sip of his cider. As ever it was delicious and although it didn't taste strong he knew it was 6.8% but, as Roger was apt to say, 'My cider never gives you a hangover, not like that modern watered-down stuff these kids drink'.

Luke took one more sip and decided it was time to tell them.

"I've got an interview tomorrow," he said.

Chloe put her glass down. "Really, Dad?" she said. "Avon and Somerset?"

"As I've said before I'm not going back to the police."

"Who's it with then?" Ben asked.

"It's for Filchers, an outsourcing company. You won't have heard of them but they're pretty big. Successful too."

"Outsourcing?" Chloe said. "What's that?"

"They take responsibility for parts of a business, like finance and human resources, and streamline them to save money."

"Heady stuff," Ben said.

"Ben!" Chloe said.

"Sorry Dad," Ben went on, "but are you sure you'll enjoy working for them? You need something that stretches you. What's your role going to be?"

"I'll be Head of Security," Luke said. "Security is a big thing for an organisation like Filchers. I'm sure it'll be challenging."

Luke sat back and looked first at his daughter and then at his son. They meant well, he knew, but it wasn't as if he had a wealth of job offers to choose from. He hadn't got this one yet for that matter.

*

Chloe fussed like a mother hen before Luke left for his interview, retying his tie for him and brushing his suit clean. He had to admit he liked the attention though, and knew he would sorely miss her when she returned to Portsmouth.

"You look great," she said. "Just like Dwayne Johnson, but with hair."

"And without the muscles, or the acting ability," he said.

"You've got the smile, Dad, and your scar adds a certain…"

He put his finger to the thin line that ran from below his left eye to just short of his upper lip. "…ugliness?" he said.

She punched him gently on the shoulder. "I was going to say charm. You look great, Dad, and I'm sure you'll get the job. Who's interviewing you?"

"Ambrose Filcher. He founded the company and he's the Chief Executive. I'm meeting him in one of their offices in Bath. It's between Pulteney Bridge and Sydney Gardens."

"Good luck." She gave him a peck on the cheek.
"Thanks. I'll see you later."

Chapter 3

Luke looked through the annual report while he was on the bus into Bath, but it told him little about security. Ambrose Filcher would undoubtedly enlighten him later.

It was a short walk from the bus stop to Pulteney Mews. Number 16 was halfway up and a bronze plaque to the side of the entrance read '*BOODLE'S*' and underneath '*For Gentlemen of Distinction*'. It wasn't one of their offices, it was a gentlemen's club. This was a whole new world, more akin to his father's interests than his own, and he wasn't sure he was ready for it. He rang the bell and a man in his mid-sixties pulled the door open. He wore a hat and tails in black with gold trim and a red waistcoat.

"Yes sir," he said, his accent reminiscent of King Charles. "How may I help you?"

"I'm here to see Mr Filcher," Luke said.

The doorman disappeared inside and reappeared a few seconds later.

"Mr Sackville?" he asked. Luke nodded. "Come this way sir."

Luke followed him down an oak-panelled corridor. They passed an opening on the left through which he saw a seated middle-aged heavily-moustached man buried deep in a copy of the Financial Times. The man looked briefly his way before returning his gaze to the newspaper.

At the end was a door bearing the sign '*Roderick Room*'. The doorman opened the door and gestured for Luke to go in.

"Be careful sir," he said.

"It's okay, I'm used to it," Luke said as he ducked through the opening.

The room was a small library, the four walls filled from

floor to ceiling with bookshelves into which were crammed leather-bound tomes that looked to be Victorian or earlier. Two checked club chairs sat facing each other over a small mahogany coffee table.

Filcher sat in the right-hand chair. He was in his mid-fifties, Luke guessed, and had a full head of salt and pepper hair. However, it was his hooked nose that made him stand out, with the bushy moustache only serving to draw attention to its size. His eyes widened slightly as he took in Luke's height.

Luke gestured to the other chair.

"May I?" he said.

Filcher grunted his agreement. "Bidwell," he said, a deep timbre to his voice. "Tea and biscuits."

"Coffee for me," Luke said.

Filcher breathed in through both nostrils. "And coffee," he said, disapproval evident in his tone.

"Very well sir," Bidwell said.

Luke waited for the doorman to leave. "It's a pleasure to meet you Mr Filcher," he said.

"Mmm," Filcher said, ignoring Luke's outstretched hand. He clasped his hands over his chest and leant back in his chair. "I understand you haven't worked for six months."

"Yes, I decided to take a break."

"Why?"

"It was for personal reasons."

"Were you dismissed?"

Luke felt his hackles rise. He took a deep breath. "As I said, it was personal." He looked pointedly at Filcher, who swallowed and picked up a manilla file from the table.

"Moving on," he said, pulling a stapled document from the folder. "Your experience is limited. One employer for twenty years and you've never worked in Security. What relevant skills do you have?"

Luke almost laughed at this. "I assure you, Mr Filcher,

that security has been central throughout my two decades in the police."

"Mmm." Filcher scratched his chin. "What about teams? Have you been responsible for large groups of people?"

"Certainly. When we were working on a large case I might have as many as…"

"Yes, yes," Filcher interrupted. "But it's not the same."

"The same as what?"

"The people working for you were police, government employees, public sector." He almost spat the last two words out.

Luke bit his tongue. "I am sure," he said, "that my skills and experience can bring a lot to the company you founded."

Filcher held his hand up. "Do I look in my seventies, Mr Sackville?" he said.

"Of course not, but…".

"I am Edward Filcher. Filchers was founded by my Uncle Ambrose. Did you really think that for a job of this level he would conduct the interview?"

"I was told my interview was with a Mr Filcher and I assumed…"

"Mmm." Filcher made a note on his pad.

There was a knock on the door and Bidwell entered bearing a silver tray which he placed carefully on the table between them before leaving. Luke leant forward to take the cup of coffee but Filcher held his hand up to stop him.

"I think we're finished, Mr Sackville," he said. "I've heard enough." Luke couldn't believe what he was hearing but was even less prepared for what he heard next. "I am prepared to offer you the job as Head of Security."

"May I ask a few questions?"

Filcher harrumphed and looked at his watch.

"Very well, but be quick."

"Why is my role important?"

"Security."

"Yes, I appreciate that, but why is security important in an organisation like Filchers?"

"We deal with sensitive matters," Filcher said condescendingly. "Information is valuable. Industrial espionage is rife."

"Really? How often has that happened in Filchers?"

"Never."

"How can you be so sure?"

Filcher hesitated. "We have had excellent security so it hasn't."

Luke could tell Filcher was on uncomfortable ground and decided to change tack.

"Why do you need a new Head of Security?"

"That is irrelevant." Filcher looked at his watch again. "I must go. I'm sure your other questions will be answered in the formal offer." He pressed a bell fixed to the top of the coffee table.

"Can I ask…"

"I'm a very busy man. The private sector is pressurised, intense, demanding. Quick decisions needed. Very different from what you are used to. I have many responsibilities and I have seen enough."

Bidwell opened the door.

"Yes sir," he said.

"Show Mr Sackville out, Bidwell," Filcher said. He looked away, his phone already to his ear, Luke dismissed.

Chapter 4

The rain splashed and splattered against the window, the weather only adding to Angie's misery. She was tired, upset and emotional. Her mind was in turmoil and her eyes burned to hell. Coming in was a mistake. No way could she put in a decent day's work. What's more, the morning was starting with a team meeting which meant she'd have to face Olivia. The thought was unbearable.

She had made a bacon quiche, Rob's favourite, and was pleased with her make-up and especially with the way her red mini dress still clung in all the right places. She had been determined to make the evening a memorable one.

And memorable it certainly was.

In he had walked, one hour later than promised, head down, eyes glued to his mobile. She decided to make light of it and grabbed the phone from him.

"What's got you so gripped, Rob," she said, holding it away from his grasp. "Is it Candy Crush or…"

She glanced down and was shocked by what she saw. He reached out but she backed away, looked up at him then back at the phone. The words made sense, but they didn't make sense. This was Rob. He loved her.

"I was going to tell you," he spluttered.

It had all come out then. Almost three months of lies and deceit. He had been seeing Olivia after work, at weekends when he was 'at the gym', on Tuesday evenings when he supposedly went to football training. The list went on and on. She had packed a bag and left, told him she never wanted to see him again, spent the night in a hotel room, screamed at herself in the mirror, cried into the pillow and not slept a wink.

There was a creak and she turned to see the door open

and the diminutive figure of Tom walk in, thick-framed glasses over his nose, coffee in one hand and laptop in the other. He nodded hello and took a seat at the table. Immediately behind him came June and Olivia, or 'that bitch' as she now thought of her.

June also nodded as she sat opposite Tom. As ever, she was power-dressed and sported a navy jacket with broad lapels over a pale blue silk blouse and navy slacks.

Olivia sat down next to June. Her clothes were rumpled and her make-up had been put on a shade too hastily. What's more, she wouldn't meet her eyes and it dawned on Angie that Rob must have been straight on the phone to her after she had stormed out.

The room was the one they usually used for their team meetings. It was bland and characterless but sufficed for a round-robin of what everyone had achieved followed by a run-through of next steps. Angie debated whether to sit but couldn't bear to be any closer to Olivia than she had to.

Last in was Eric, dressed in a brown tweed jacket and brown and white striped tie. He had never been a geography teacher but she was sure that was his true calling. He moved to the head of the table and looked at Angie, an expression on his face that fell somewhere between pity and outrage.

"Sorry, Angie," he said.

"What?" she said incredulously. "How did you know about…"

He interrupted before she could finish. "I need to have a private word with you. Could you come outside for a moment?" He moved back to the door. She followed him through and he took a deep breath as he closed it behind them.

"I know," he said.

"How?"

"I've seen the emails."

"Emails?"

This wasn't making sense.

"The emails you exchanged with Danny Ogletree," he said. "I'm sorry, Angie, but they paint you in a very bad light. I've passed them to HR who are going to do a full investigation." She stared at him, lost for words. "In the meantime, you're suspended on full pay for two weeks."

"What, I…"

She opened her mouth for a moment then closed it again. Turning, she walked back into the meeting room.

"You need to go home," he said, but she ignored him.

"Did any of you know about this?" she said.

"About what?" Tom said.

"I've been sacked."

Tom gave a little yelp of surprise and Olivia bent forward over the table with her head in her hands. Only June looked up at her, the corners of her mouth turned slightly upwards in a smirk she was struggling to conceal.

Angie walked slowly back to the window. She tried to focus on the spatters of rain hammering against the glass, but her vision was blurred and her hands were shaking. She needed to calm down and be rational, but it was hard to think straight. She turned, rage transforming her thoughts into words before she had a chance to stop herself.

"I've done nothing wrong," she said. "You," she pointed a trembling finger at Eric, and she realised that she was shouting now, "have no right to sack me."

"It's suspension," Eric said. "You haven't been sacked. I'm sure everything will be okay."

She looked back at him and he attempted a smile, but she could see her outburst had shocked him. She was normally quiet, not a mouse by any means but polite and respectful.

"Why don't you accept what's happening," he said, "and we can all move on?"

"How can I move on when I'm fucking suspended?"

"Calm down, Angie. It's only for two weeks. You had a

week's holiday booked from this weekend anyway so only a week really. June has agreed to cover for you as my deputy and when you return, fully exonerated I'm sure, you can take up the reins again."

Angie turned her attention to June, who now found it vital she tidy the papers she had brought to the meeting.

"You knew about this?"

June looked up. "Well, I, ah…" She glanced at Eric, who gave a slight nod of his head. "Eric told me yesterday afternoon."

"So you knew when we were in the pub after work?"

"Yes, but…"

Suddenly Angie put two and two together.

"You told him about the emails." It wasn't a question and the lack of response told Angie she was right. "Was it pillow talk?"

Tom gave a little gasp and Eric stood up, all traces of a smile gone now.

"Listen, Angie," he said.

"Listen, Angie," she mimicked, then took a step around Tom to stand in front of Eric. God, he was tall. She'd forgotten how big the man was. She stood on tiptoe and waved a finger, wanting to assert herself by shouting in his face but conscious that his chest would have to do. "You have a cheek telling me to listen," she said, conscious that she had raised her voice again but unable to stop herself. "When have you ever listened to me? All you do is ponce around, making the ladi-dah, all 'I am the big Bid Director look at me', when you're nothing but a jumped up little asswipe, promoted before his time." She turned to June. "And if you're screwing him then good luck to you and I hope it's worth it."

She knew she'd gone too far, that she'd blown her position in the team, whether she was found guilty or not. Hell, she'd be lucky if she had a future in Filchers after this.

There was a noise as a chair was pushed back, then

Olivia stood up, hands raised, ever the peacemaker.

"Don't," Angie said.

"Ah right, yes, ah…" Olivia sat down again.

"What about you, Tom?" Angie said. "Do you want to calm me down? Or do you think I'm the guilty party here?" He didn't speak. "Anyone think I'm in the right?"

She looked at Tom and then at Olivia. Silence.

"Well, thanks a bunch."

She strode away from Eric, opened the door, stepped out, and slammed it behind her. She almost collapsed then, her chest heaving as she tried to control her breathing. My god, what had she just done? The week had started off badly, got worse, and now, well now it was just mind-numbingly awful. But what to do next? Could she make things better? Did she want to make things better?

After a few seconds, she opened the door again and the murmuring that had started up immediately dissipated.

"One more thing, Eric," she said.

"Yes, Angie," he said, his voice an octave too high.

"You can stick your fucking job where the sun doesn't shine."

And with that, she left.

Chapter 5

The layout of the Salamander had changed little over the years. A bow window faced the street next to the entrance door. Inside the pub was narrow. To the left were distressed plank tables and sympathetically plain oak chairs while opposite was the small bar. The walls were a pale blue-grey that matched the tables and chairs perfectly.

There were only three occupants: a middle-aged guy serving drinks, a suited business type bashing away at a laptop in the back corner, and Angie, perched on a bar stool and cradling a brandy glass in both hands.

She looked up from her drink and waved one hand to signal for the barman to come over. He ignored the gesture since he was already standing directly in front of her.

"I think you've had enough," he said.

He was wrong. Another drink would help, but she had something else to say. What was it? Was it about the pub? Then it came to her, but she knew she had to speak slowly. The barman was English, but he seemed to struggle to understand what she said. Perhaps it was her accent.

"Sit - always - iss - quiet?" she said, emphasising each syllable.

"Sorry?"

She waved her hands at the vacant tables and chairs, losing her balance as she did so and almost falling off the stool. "No one here…iss quiet."

"It's half past three," he said.

"Really?" Angie looked down at her arm to check the time. After two failed attempts she managed to slide the sleeve of her blouse back and stared at her wrist in horror. "My watch," she said. "Iss gone."

"Left wrist," he said, pointing to her other arm.

She looked at her left wrist. "Silly me," she said and belched. She stared at her watch, trying to focus but failing. Had the hands always been that small? And what was that red one doing moving so quickly? Or were there two red ones?

She became aware of someone on the stool next to hers.

"What can I get you?" said the barman.

She started to answer but the newcomer beat her to it.

"Peroni please," he said, and even through her fuddled haze, Angie recognised a pleasant voice, perhaps someone who would listen to her problems, someone who might empathise.

"Are you all right?" he said.

"She's been here a while," the barman said. "Bad day at the office. God knows how she'll get herself home."

"Might've had too much," Angie said, then hiccuped. "Need to soberise." She covered her mouth with her hand. "Oops, thas wrong. Soberise. Not a word. Need to…" The correct word was in her brain, she knew it. Not 'soberise' but similar. Then it dawned on her. "I need soberano," she said.

"Definitely not," the man said. "You mean 'sober up'."

She found herself staring at his mouth, loving the way the corners were turned up. She moved her focus slowly up to his eyes. "Thassit," she said. "Sober up."

He held his hand out. "I'm Mac."

"Hi, Mac." She shook his hand. "You sound like a coat." She giggled. "I'm Angie."

"Hi, Angie. Why don't we sit in that booth over there." He smiled again and it really was a lovely smile she thought. "It will give you a chance to soberise."

She tried to giggle again but snorted instead.

"Have we met before, Mac?" she said.

"No, I don't think so." He asked the barman for a black coffee then guided Angie to the booth and helped her to sit down. "I think a strong sweet coffee will help."

"Iss horrible," Angie said. "Yukkedy yukkedy."

"Nonsense," Mac said. "It'll do wonders."

After a couple of minutes, the barman brought the coffee. Mac took an envelope out of his pocket and emptied the contents into the mug. "Sweeteners," he said as he stirred. "This will do you the world of good. You'll feel better in no time."

Angie raised the cup to her lips. "Nosso bad," she said as she took her first slurp. "Nosso nasty after all."

Chapter 6

"Wake up, Angie. I've got to go to work."

She tried to open her eyes but they were glued together. And boy did her head hurt. There were a hundred little people in there bashing at her brain with hammers.

"Come on darling, wake up."

She recognised that voice. But where from? It was a nice voice, a comforting voice. Then she remembered. That friendly man, what was his name? Sounded like a coat. Mac, that was it. He'd helped her. She'd been drunk and he'd sorted her out, given her a coffee, listened to her moans and mumbles and then, and then…

And then what? She couldn't remember anything after the coffee. And what was with the 'darling'? Filled with sudden fear she forced her eyes open in time to see his hand move back then forward with force against her face.

"Sorry," he said, his voice still gentle, still soothing. "I'm in a hurry."

She tried to put her hand to her cheek and realised she couldn't move her arms. Looking down, she saw they were tied to a metal bed frame. Her eyes flew from side to side. She was in a room with bare stone walls. It was roughly square, about twelve feet by twelve feet, with a corrugated metal roof. There was a table, on which was a jug of water and a basin, a wooden chair and in the far corner a bucket.

She looked up at him, and he stared back. He was a few years older than her, probably late thirties, with stylishly short brown hair, brown eyes and a boxed beard that accentuated his cheekbones. In any other circumstances, she would have thought of him as attractive.

"What's going on?" she said.

"Don't be afraid, Angie," he said. "You're safe here.

You won't come to any harm if you follow the rules."

"What are you going to do to me?"

He ignored her question. "The rules are simple. There are only three. First, you need to do as I ask, always and without hesitation. Is that clear?"

She looked at him in shock, struggling to take everything in.

He raised his voice. "Do you understand?"

She nodded.

"Second, under no condition will you try to escape." He winked. "Not that any attempt could possibly work. I've spent weeks ensuring this place is secure, and even if you did get out we're miles from anywhere." He pointed at the studded blue door. "That door served its time at a prison and is incredibly solid."

She shuddered.

"And finally, do not attempt to communicate with anyone other than me." He waited a moment before bending forward so that his nose almost brushed hers. "Are the rules clear?" he whispered, "or do I have to repeat them?"

"They're clear," she said, her voice trembling. But why did he have that last rule? How could she communicate with anyone if they were miles from anywhere?

He stood upright again. "Can you hear that low humming?" he said, gesturing to the door.

She nodded.

"It's a generator." His full-on smile returned. "I installed it myself and it means you have light, heat and power." It was evident he hadn't taken her on impulse. Everything had been planned to the last detail. But why? He gestured to the corner of the room, his voice still light and almost sing-song in its irritating cheeriness "There's a microwave too so you'll be able to heat up the food I bring you."

"Why…" She swallowed and tried to speak, squeezing

her eyelids together to hold the tears back. "Why have you brought me here?"

Again he ignored her question. He was in a world of his own and enjoying every moment. "How tall are you, Angie?" he said.

"I'm 5 foot 3, but…"

"I thought so. Not ideal but I've got a solution for that." He winked again, then reached into a carrier bag and retrieved a long blonde wig. "Isn't this lovely?" he said, turning the wig around to show all sides of it.

"What's that got to do with…"

He slapped her across the face again, harder this time. "Oh, Angie," he said, still smiling, "please don't forget rule number one. Now lie still." He bent forward and placed the wig on top of her head, wiggling it slightly until her black bob was hidden beneath it. "Excellent, really excellent." He reached across to push the hair off her shoulders and she flinched automatically. "That's much better." He cocked his head to one side. "Yes, yes, yes. It really suits you. Makes you look more feminine, much softer. I like women who are gentle and kind. Are you kind, Angie?"

He didn't wait for an answer but reached into the carrier bag again and pulled out a pair of black stiletto shoes. "These are a size five," he said. 'What size are you?"

"I'm a five."

"Terrific. I'll put them here." He placed them on the floor at the foot of the bed. "You don't have to wear the wig or the shoes when I'm not here but when you hear me knock you must put them on. Is that understood?"

She nodded.

He reached into the carrier bag and retrieved a large butcher's knife. Angie screamed. "You'll get used to me having this," he said. "It's an extra precaution to ensure you don't get ideas."

"No. I…" Angie looked wildly from side to side, more scared than she had ever been in her life. She thought of screaming, of spitting in his face, of pleading for mercy.

Watching her carefully he raised the butcher's knife to her neck. Instinctively she tried to pull her head back. "Be still," he shouted, "or I swear I'll cut your throat."

She tried to hold her head still but she was shaking too much.

Slowly he took the knife from her throat and used it to cut the rope binding her right hand, then walked to the other side and cut the other one before moving to the end of the bed, still brandishing the knife, the ever-present smile plastered to his face. That smile was going to haunt her every waking moment.

"Sit up," he said.

She did as he asked.

"Now be good, Angie. Get used to your new home and enjoy yourself."

The man was delusional.

"There's food and drink in the microwave. I'll be back this evening."

He left and she heard a bolt being drawn. He raised the flap of the door's vision panel to look at her for a few seconds before closing it again.

Chapter 7

Luke bounced Tigger-like off the bus and looked at his watch. Twenty to nine. It was only a five-minute walk to the office so he was fine. More than fine. For the first time in six months he had energy, felt almost like running.

He stood by the bus stop to get his bearings. Filchers was on Broadbank Avenue. Or was it Brookbank Avenue? Whichever one it was, he was pretty sure the turning was a little further towards the old Windsor Castle pub. He headed at almost jogging pace in that direction and reached inside his trouser pocket for his phone to check the address. As he did so he found his gaze drawn to his left foot. He had his happy socks on, vivid yellow with zebras all over them. Nothing unusual about that. But his shoe was brown, which was odd. He could have sworn he'd put on black shoes. He looked at his other shoe. It was black.

"Shit," he said and stopped abruptly, feeling someone collide with his back as he did so. He turned to see his wife bending forward, her hair falling over her shoulders, hand covering her nose. The breath went out of him and he staggered back a couple of paces. "Jess…" he said.

The woman pulled her hand away from her nose and inspected it, evidently relieved there was no blood. She stood upright and looked up at him and he could see now that she wasn't Jess. She was much the same height, five foot seven or so, and her eyes were also deep blue, the blonde hair almost exactly the same length and shade, but her cheekbones were less pronounced and her lips not quite as full.

He held his hand up. "Sorry," he said. "You must think I'm mad."

"Mmm," she said.

"I've got two odd shoes."

"Pardon."

"That's why I stopped." He gestured to his feet. She looked down, and the corners of her mouth turned up slightly. "And you look a little like my wife," he went on. "It's the strawberry blonde hair."

"My hair is a light shade of red," she said, before looking him in the eyes and smiling.

He swallowed and smiled back. Since Jess had gone he'd found it incredibly hard to talk to women, especially attractive women. But he was forty-three for goodness sake. He needed to get over it, make an effort, act his age. Christ, he wasn't on a date. This poor woman was just someone he had bumped into, literally as it happened.

"Are you okay?" she said.

"Sorry, I, ah…I don't suppose you know if there's a shoe shop around here do you?"

"What?"

"I start a new job today and it's hardly the best first impression." He gestured to his feet again.

"There's an M&S around that corner," she said indicating the next road along.

"Thanks. One other thing. Do you know where Filchers is?"

"That's easy. It's the very large blue and white monstrosity just past M&S on Brookbank Avenue. You can't miss it."

"Thanks again," he said as she walked past him and headed away.

*

Filchers did indeed occupy a very large building. It was five stories, unashamedly modern and trying too hard to be original at the expense of taste. Some windows were clear glass, others tinted and between them were a variety of different-sized blue and white rectangles. As a whole, it scored ten out of ten on the as-ugly-as-possible scale.

Once Luke walked through the automatic doors the reception area made the outside look reserved. It spoke of a company striving, and perhaps struggling, to project an image of superiority and high status. The walls were a deep blue and the large wooden reception desk was curved and adorned with gold filigree. It faced a large gold sofa either side of which were two flowering bird of paradise plants that had to be eight feet tall. Taking pride of place on the wall behind the desk were large capital letters, also in gold, spelling out 'F I L C H E R S'. Underneath them a set of smaller black letters read 'Providing Business Services since 1987'.

"Someone will be down for you in a minute, Mr Sackville," the receptionist said when he had checked in. She had a striking Jamaican accent and despite her shocking white hair looked to be not much more than forty.

"Thanks," he said. "But please call me Luke. I start work here today, so we'll probably see a lot of each other."

"Well, hi Luke." She shook his hand. "I'm Angelica. It's a pleasure to meet you." She lowered her voice. "And nice that you acknowledge I'm a real person. Not everyone here does that." She looked beyond him. "And here he is," she said and winked.

He turned to see a man in a pin-striped navy suit marching towards them. Luke had thought Edward Filcher pompous at his interview, but he had been seated throughout their meeting, so his almost comical military gait came as somewhat of a shock, and spoke much about a man trying to project authority.

"Luke," Filcher said, the deep resonance of his voice a perfect match for his sergeant major movements. "Welcome to my company."

Your uncle's company, Luke thought, but said, "Happy to

be here sir."

"None of that nonsense, Luke. You're not in the police now you know." He laughed at his own joke. "We don't believe in that level of formality here."

"Sorry, ah…"

"Mr Filcher. You can call me Mr Filcher. Come with me. We'll take the lift to my office. It is of course on the Executive Floor."

"See you later, Angelica," Luke said, and she gave him a little wave and another wink.

"It doesn't do, you know," Filcher said, as they waited for the lift, "to fraternise and be personal and pally with people you might be investigating." He turned and gestured back to the reception desk. "Like her."

"Angelica, you mean."

"Yes, that coloured woman."

"She's not a box of crayons," Luke said. He didn't raise his voice but there was something in his tone that made Filcher move away a little.

"No, but she's… ah…"

"She's black, Mr Filcher."

"Yes, indeed, quite." He paused for a second before continuing. "However, the point remains that in your role it's important to keep your distance."

"As Head of Security?"

"Yes." He paused. "Although there's been a slight change."

"To my job title?"

"That, and… well, you'll see."

The lift pinged and Filcher marched down the corridor towards a door signed 'E Filcher - Director of Internal Affairs'. Next to the door was a desk behind which sat a suited young man in his early twenties, matt black hair slicked back over his head and shaved to an inch above his ears.

"Where's Gloria?" Filcher barked.

"She's popped out, Mr Filcher, and asked me to cover

for her. Answer any calls, take messages, that kind of thing."

"Yes I know what 'cover for her' means, Josh. Have there been?"

"Have there been what, Mr Filcher?"

Filcher sighed. "Any calls or any messages?"

"No… well yes."

"Which is it?

"There's been one. One call and he left a message. So two, if you count them both."

"And?"

"And? Oh, I see. Yes." Josh shuffled through some papers on the desk before emerging triumphantly with a post-it note.

"Mr Baxter rang," he said, waving the note in the air. "He's going to be a few minutes late."

"Right. Do you think you could manage tea, Josh?"

"I've just had one." Josh paused and then saw the scowl on Filcher's face. "Oh, I see, sorry. Yes, definito."

Filcher grimaced. "For three please. And don't forget biscuits."

"Coffee for me," Luke said.

"Consider it done," Josh said. He didn't move.

"Now, Josh," Filcher said.

"Ah, right. On it."

Filcher turned to Luke. "He was imposed on me by the graduate scheme but he's ruddy useless," he said in a stage whisper as Josh clambered out from behind the desk. "I'd sack him if I could. We should only take Oxbridge if you ask me."

Luke followed Filcher into his office where he parked himself behind a large mahogany desk and gestured for Luke to sit in one of two armchairs opposite him, resulting in his eye level now being a few inches below Filcher's.

The office walls were panelled in wood to match the desk. There were several shelves of books behind Filcher and they were of two types: old leather-bound books with Latin titles embossed on their spines, probably never been read, and more modern works on managerial and executive techniques, probably never been opened.

The desk had the usual trappings. There was a laptop, a family photo showing a younger Edward with an older man, presumably his uncle, a phone, and several manilla files. In addition, and taking pride of place, was a large brass nameplate reading 'Edward Filcher, MA (Oxon)".

On the wall next to the window was a vomit-inducing poster bearing an image of two soldiers on a cliff edge, under which were emblazoned the words 'Loyalty is not a word it's a lifestyle'. Next to the poster was a photo of Filcher standing with a confused-looking Boris Johnson, each holding a champagne flute but only Filcher smiling at the camera while Boris stared at something out of picture, looking as though he was keen to make his getaway.

Luke gestured to the photo. "Were you at Eton together?"

"Why yes," Filcher said. "How did you know that?"

"Lucky guess."

"Mmm, yes, we're old buddies."

I'll take that with a pinch of salt, Luke thought but said, "Really? Much the same age then?"

"Well Johnno, we always called him Johnno, is 5 years older than me. We were both in Godolphin though. Jolly good laugh he was. I remember one time when…"

Luke neither knew nor cared what Godolphin was and was pleased when Filcher was interrupted by a knock at the door. Josh came in with a tray and placed it on the desk. He lifted the teapot. "Do you want me to be Mother?"

"Just go, Josh," Filcher said.

"Gucci."

"Gucci?"

"Yeh. Like the brand. You know, cool."

Filcher harrumphed and waved for him to leave.

Josh started to open the door, then turned back. "I forgot. Mr Baxter's here. Shall I tell him to come in?"

"Yes, Josh. And no interruptions."

"Sweet."

Filcher gave an exasperated sigh as Josh left the room. The door remained open and Luke heard him say "You can go in, Glen," and it dawned on him who Mr Baxter was.

One of the last people on the planet he had either expected or wanted to see.

Glen Baxter marched into the room, all bluster and action, his tight-fitting shirt struggling to contain his six-pack, and his hair in a buzz cut. It had to have been five years since their last meeting but aside from a slight greyness to his scalp fluff, he hadn't changed one bit.

He walked straight up to Luke and held out his hand, back held firm as he attempted unsuccessfully to match his height. Although built like the proverbial brick shithouse, with steroids and the gym playing equal roles in getting him to that state, at six feet two Glen was four inches shorter and that had always irked him.

"My, my, Luke," Glen said as he pumped his hand up and down. "This is a surprise. I was certain you and the force had an inseparable bond. Tell me, did you jump or were you pushed?"

"Always a pleasure to see you," Luke said, ignoring the question. He bent down and put his mouth to Glen's left ear. "I see you're still as much of an arsehole as ever."

Glen backed away. "And how's that stunner of a wife?" he said and then turned to Filcher and described a pear-shaped figure with his hands. "She's a ten." He turned back to Luke. "And friendly with it."

Luke's hands tensed into fists. Smashing one of them into the face opposite him was an awfully tempting idea. "So what's your role?" he said.

"Head of Security," Glen said.

"What?"

"That was the little job title thing I was talking about," Filcher said.

Luke felt his cheeks starting to redden. "You're not seriously saying I work for him?" he said, indicating Glen with his thumb. Glen, for his part, had taken a seat and was looking like the cat with the cream.

"No, no," Filcher said. "Definitely not. No, we had a bit of an incident and decided to restructure. We've promoted Glen and you'll be working alongside him, working closely with him I hope. The fact that you know each other will help I'm sure."

Like hell it will, thought Luke. "So what's my role if it's not heading up security?" he said.

"Congratulations, Luke," Filcher said, genuinely pleased with himself. "You are Filchers' Head of Ethics."

"I'm *what?*"

"You'll have a smaller team than we discussed at the interview."

"I've got forty staff," Glen said smugly. "Large department, Security. Lots of responsibilities."

"Indeed," Filcher said. "Ethics is very different though. Vital, absolutely vital, just as vital, probably more so, but focused, needs intensity."

"How many staff will I have?" Luke said.

"Two."

"Two?"

"To start with. Obviously, we'll increase your team if we need to, but yes, two. You'll have one of our most experienced staff working for you: Helen Hogg, excellent lawyer; and we also thought it would be good if you had a graduate under your wing. You've met him already."

"You mean Josh? But you said that he's, and I'm quoting here, 'ruddy useless'."

There was a snort from Glen.

"I'm sorry, Mr Filcher," Luke said, "but I accepted the job of Head of Security not Head of Ethics." He stood up.

"I'm sure you'll be able to find someone much more suitable."

"Ah, um…" Filcher's eyes widened in shock. "No, you can't. I need, ah, I mean…" He turned his attention to Glen and waved his hand dismissively. "Leave us."

Glen stood and turned to Luke. "Forty staff," he whispered.

"I said leave," Filcher said.

After he'd gone Filcher forced a smile. "Sit, Luke," he said.

"I really don't think there's any point."

"Please."

Luke could see that 'please' was a rarity in the other man's vocabulary. He decided to hear him out and sat down.

Filcher leant forward across the desk. "I need you to take this job, Luke," he said. "The government have insisted on a Head of Ethics."

"I'm sorry, Mr Filcher, but it's not what I signed up for."

"I know, I know." He swallowed. "The fact is I'm in a bind."

"Why not give Glen the job and make me Head of Security?"

Filcher snorted. "No, no. Wouldn't work. Glen's too much of a…"

"Twat?" Luke offered.

Filcher almost nodded before correcting himself. "He's got an abrasive personality and it wouldn't work."

"You could give him a try."

"The thing is…" Filcher swallowed. "Glen's been named as someone they won't accept."

"Really?" Luke smiled. "What did he do?"

"Had a run-in with one of their senior procurement consultants. Hit him actually." He paused. "You could give the job a month, see how it goes, and if you don't like it then you could leave. Please, Luke."

There was that word again.

"Okay, I'll give it a month," Luke said.

Before Filcher could reply the door flew open.

"I said not to interrupt me," Filcher said.

"Sorry, Mr Filcher," Josh said, "but Miss Klein's here and I thought you'd want…"

His demeanour changed in an instant. "Ah yes, please send her in."

Josh left and a statuesque blonde of about Luke's age came in. She was slim and smartly dressed, with a terrific figure for a woman in her early forties, but there her attractiveness stopped. Her face looked like she'd sucked lemons.

"Caroline, Caroline," Filcher said and smiled, the first time Luke had seen anything but a scowl on his face. He turned to Luke. "This is Caroline Klein from Human Resources. She'll complete your induction, get you to fill out all the necessary forms, and so on. She's one of our best. You're in good hands here." He looked at his watch. "You can use my office, Caroline. I've got a meeting." He pulled open the top drawer of his desk, slid a golf glove into his pocket and left without another word.

*

Admin had been the single worst part of Luke's last job. The constabulary was bureaucracy gone wild, but Filchers made Avon and Somerset Police look like amateurs when it came to paperwork. The first form was for next of kin and Luke found it painfully difficult to complete. Caroline queried his putting two names down but grudgingly nodded her understanding when he explained why. The second asked for his career history. He handed it over and she raised her eyebrows when she saw that he'd worked at Bath

Rugby before joining the police.

"You need to add your role when you were there," she said, indicating the final column with her pen.

He took the form back and wrote 'Winger'.

"Mmm," she said, and her eyes flicked to his shoulders.

Next was a form for payroll, followed by a form to confirm his understanding of the expense limits, then a form for his company car, and then a form for his ID pass.

"I'm surprised you haven't got a form to confirm my eating habits," he said.

"I'm coming to that," Caroline said, and passed him a form asking for any dietary restrictions and confirming that he would accept all risks if he ate in the staff canteen.

Oddly, the one piece of paper they hadn't got, and the only one he would have dearly liked to read, was a job description.

"Edward wants you to write it," she said, "but I suggest you meet your team first and get to grips with your immediate challenge. It's why your position was created after all. I'll take you down to the third floor. Helen Hogg is already there and she'll explain."

"Okay," he said, standing up.

She held her hand up. "Please sit down," she said. "I still need you to confirm any illnesses, hospital stays, prescriptions, phobias, etc." She passed him a form.

"And internal leg measurement?" he said.

She ignored him. "And this…" she passed another form over, "…covers your pension schemes and contributions. While this one…" she handed him another, "…confirms what we expect from you in terms of developing your staff."

'Both of them?" he said and smiled.

"Yes," she said, her lips pursed, a frown on her face. "Both of them."

Chapter 8

Luke looked around their office. It was about twenty feet square and painted that shade of off-white that seemed to be reserved for business spaces: white enough to keep workers awake but with a touch of cream to soften the blow. There were a couple of large framed photos of Bath on the walls, artful views of the Royal Crescent and Pulteney Bridge, but nothing personal anywhere. It was clear that it had been assigned to the new Ethics Team in haste.

The table he was seated at was in the centre of the room and would accommodate four comfortably, six at a push. Against two of the walls were six desks with laptops while the wall opposite the door was completely glass with a view over the car park.

Josh placed mugs down on the table. "One for you, Helen," he said, "white no sugar. Ditto for me and an extra strong black coffee for you guv'nor."

"No need to call me guv'nor," Luke said.

"Guv then? You know, because you were a Detective Chief Inspector. Only feels right."

The earnestness in Josh's eyes made him relent. "Okay," he said, "if it makes you happy."

"Cheers, guv." He was like a kid with candy now, smiling from ear to ear.

Luke turned to Helen. "You were saying."

She reminded him of his own mother in appearance: petite and with greying hair that met everyone's idea of a perfect granny. However, there the similarity ended. Helen was full of energy and totally down to earth, whereas his mother was as lazy as anyone he'd ever known and had her head very much in the clouds.

"Sauerkraut," she said in her soft Scottish accent. "That's what everyone calls Caroline Klein, though not to her face. I don't think she would appreciate the joke, and that's an understatement. Believe me, Luke, you'd better tread carefully where she's concerned. HR wields a lot of power in this place and she's close to Edward Filcher too so you need to watch out."

"Caroline said something about an immediate challenge, Helen," he said. "That it was the reason my role had been created."

"Yes, Project Iceberg. It's an outsourcing bid: taking on the finance and admin functions so that we can streamline processes and save them money. Standard stuff except it's for a major government department and very hush-hush. We're down to the final two and it's worth over fifty million so there's a lot resting on it."

"What's the problem?"

"Angie Johnson, one of the bid team, the number two in fact, has been taking money from our one remaining competitor, Bannerdown, in exchange for details of our solution and pricing. It all came to a head last Thursday when she walked out after the Iceberg Bid Director confronted her with it."

"Has she been sacked?"

"She's been suspended. We've had to crawl to the Home Office and assure them we're totally on top of everything. Our three existing government contracts account for nearly half of Filchers' revenue and they've threatened to pull them if we don't get our house in order. It was the Home Office that insisted we appoint a Head of Ethics to investigate what Angie's done, find out if anyone else was involved, and ensure she hasn't revealed government secrets."

"Government secrets?"

"Yes. Oh, I didn't say did I. Project Iceberg is for a contract with the Secret Intelligence Service."

"Right," Luke said. He'd had dealings with MI6 in the past and knew how difficult they were to deal with. "Helen, please can you look into the legal implications of what's happened, find out whether they can genuinely pull other contracts on the back of what's happened, that kind of thing."

"Will do."

"And I'll start with Angie - talk to her, find out what her story is and try to suss whether anyone else from Filchers has been involved."

"Here's her address, guv," Josh said, passing him a piece of paper. "What should I do?"

"Compile a list of contact details for the rest of the Iceberg team. I'll need to speak to all of them." Josh looked crestfallen. "What's wrong with that?"

"Nothing, guv. I can do that, no bother. But, well, I thought I might go on the shout with you."

"It's not a shout. I'm going to interview her, that's all." Josh still looked disappointed. "Okay then. Grab your coat."

"Sick," Josh said, jumping to his feet. "Thanks, guv. You go in the front and I'll cover the back in case she tries to get away."

"She's not…" Luke started to say but Josh was already at the office door.

Luke's last car, the one that he had sold after the hit-and-run, had been a Volvo estate, and a seven-year-old Volvo estate at that. It was cavernous inside and had happily travelled to Italy and back on several family vacations. He had loved it.

This company vehicle was brand new, smelt of cowhide and had about half the carrying capacity of the Volvo. And what on earth was the point of automatic gears? They certainly removed any residual pleasure in driving the damn thing.

"Nice Beemer," Josh said as he got into the passenger

seat. He was almost purring with pleasure. "Beats my car into submission that's for certain."

"What have you got?"

"A Renault Clio. So ancient I named it after an old war hero cos I reckon it dates from his era."

Luke gave him a sideways glance as he put the car into drive. "You've given your car a name?"

"Definito."

"Churchill?" Luke guessed.

"Why would I name it after an insurance company?"

Luke shook his head in exasperation and changed the subject. "Bathwick Terrace?" he said.

"Yes guv," Josh said. "2B."

They pulled up outside a large Georgian terraced house. The phone plate showed it had been split into four apartments.

"Any idea how I get around the back guv?" Josh said.

Luke let out a sigh. "You don't need to, Josh. You can come in with me."

"Cushty." He waved a notebook in the air. "I'll fill out an incident report."

"You can take notes if that's what you mean."

"Right guv, gotcha, take notes."

The buzzer for 2B had a sign next to it saying 'Talbot-Johnson'. Luke pressed it and after a few seconds a gruff male voice came through the intercom.

"Hello."

"Hi," Luke said. "Is Miss Johnson in?"

"No."

"Are you Mr Talbot?"

"Yes, I'm Rob Talbot. Who is this?"

"Luke Sackville. I'm from Filchers."

"Already told you. She's not here."

"Can I speak to you, Mr Talbot? I'll be brief I promise."

"I'll give you five minutes."

The door clicked open. One flight of stairs brought them to apartment 2B and the door was opened before Luke had a chance to knock. Rob Talbot was in his mid-thirties, of medium height, with black hair and a stubble beard. He sported blue denims and a short-sleeved white polo shirt. He gestured them into a large, elegantly decorated lounge.

"You might as well sit," he said, indicating the sofa. "But I haven't got long."

They sat down and Josh immediately pulled out his notebook and pen.

"Do you mind if my colleague takes notes?" Luke said.

"Yes, he can take notes. But why? Are you from the police? Has Angie done something?"

"Ex-police," Josh said, pride evident in his voice as he pointed his thumb at Luke. "Detective Chief Inspector."

"As I said earlier," Luke said, "we're from Filchers, not the police. I'm Luke Sackville and this is Josh Ogden. There's nothing to worry about but we do need to see Angie as soon as possible."

"Why? If this has got anything to do with Olivia…"

"Olivia who?"

"It doesn't matter. The fact is I can't help you. I haven't seen Angie since Wednesday evening."

"That's five days ago. Haven't you been worried about her?"

"Not really. We had a blazing row and she packed a suitcase and left. In Tuscany now for all I know."

"What did you argue about?"

Rob stood up angrily. "None of your fucking business," he said. "I've had enough of this." He gestured to the door.

As they left Luke passed Rob a business card. "Sorry to have intruded," he said. "If you do hear from Miss Johnson perhaps you could ask her to ring me?" Rob grunted but took the card before shutting the door behind them.

"Might be one of her team, guv," Josh said as they got

into the car.

"Who might be one of her team?" Luke said.

"That Olivia he mentioned. One of Angie Johnson's teammates is Olivia Nugent. Might be worth interrogating her first."

"We're going to interview people Josh, not interrogate them."

"Oh yeh, sorry guv." He paused for a second. "Uh, will we use one of those tape things, you know who's present, what the time is, and so on? Like in 'Line of Duty'?"

"No Josh. We'll be using your notebook."

"Oh." Josh looked momentarily disappointed then brightened again. "We'll have to read them their Madonna rights though won't we?"

"Did you see that in 'Line of Duty' as well?"

"No, it was 'Law and Order'. Oh hang on, I got it wrong. It's Miranda rights."

"Yes, it is. And I think you'll find 'Law and Order' is an American TV series. We don't have Miranda rights in the UK."

Josh got his notebook out. "Gucci. I'll make a note of that."

Luke raised an eyebrow. "How old are you, Josh?"

"Twenty-two, nearly twenty-three."

"And do all your friends use expressions like 'Gucci' and 'definito'?"

"Oh yes."

"Really?"

"Well no, actually. It's just me. Cool though, eh?"

"It certainly adds something to your personality."

"Thanks, guv."

On the way back to Filchers Josh booked a meeting room and rang each of the four remaining members of the Iceberg team. Eric Hughes, the Bid Director, had a meeting at the Home Office that he couldn't get out of so Josh arranged to meet him at ten the next morning. The other three were booked in for half an hour each from 3 pm, with Olivia Nugent in the first slot.

"Josh," Luke said as they pulled into Filchers' car park, "You can sit in on these interviews but only to take notes. I want you to let me ask the questions. Is that okay?"

"Roger," Josh said, drawing his index finger and thumb across his lips in a 'zipping it' gesture. "Over and understood."

As soon as Luke arrived in the Ethics office Helen collared him.

"Edward Filcher's secretary has been on the phone," she said. "He wants you to ring him straight away."

"Have you found that girl?" Filcher barked as soon as he was connected.

"Not yet," Luke said.

"Well get a move on, man. The Home Office has told me we have until the end of this week. That's only four days so pull your finger out." He hung up.

Luke stared at his phone, certain more than ever that Edward Filcher was going to be a considerable challenge and more of a hindrance than a help. His previous boss, Chief Superintendent Barrow, had been demanding, but it had been mostly legitimate and always with an understanding of what was possible and in what timescales. Barrow had had experience of detective work too and any contributions were usually helpful.

Filcher was in a different, and much more amateur, league.

For now, though, all he could do was concentrate on the problem at hand.

Chapter 9

Luke got to the meeting room at about ten to three to find Josh and a flask of coffee and three mugs awaiting his arrival. Josh was very pleased with himself.

"I ordered more coffee every half hour, guv," he said. "Thought we'd better make our suspects comfortable."

They're not suspects, Luke thought but decided not to correct him this time.

"If you're the only one doing the questioning…" Josh said.

"Yes, I am."

"…then will you be playing good cop as well as bad cop?"

Luke sighed. "Yes, I will."

"Copy." Josh tapped the side of his nose. "I'll watch and learn, guv. Oh, and I'll make notes of course."

At precisely 3 pm there was a knock at the door and a woman popped her head around the corner. A slim brunette in her late twenties, she introduced herself as Olivia Nugent and Luke invited her to take a seat while Josh poured coffees. She sat forward, rubbing her hands together nervously, then looked over at Josh.

"Are you the one who rang me?" she said.

Josh looked at Luke and drew his fingers and thumb across his lips in the same 'zipping it' gesture he'd made earlier. He then returned his attention to Olivia and nodded.

"Are you okay?" she said.

Josh nodded again.

"Don't worry about him," Luke said. He paused and looked over at Josh who was smiling, evidently pleased with himself. "He's got a few problems."

Luke cleared his throat. "Thanks for coming in, Miss Nugent," he said. "I'm Luke Sackville, Head of Ethics, and I've been asked to look into what's happened at Project Iceberg."

He heard a swallowed chuckle from his left then saw Josh scratching away at his notebook. He pushed the notebook in front of Luke and he saw that he had written *'Sorry - thought you said Head of Essex'*.

"So, Olivia," Luke went on, "Is it okay if I call you Olivia?"

"Yes, that's fine."

"I understand you work with Angie Johnson. You don't know where she is do you?"

"She's been suspended."

"Yes, but she's not at her home. Have you any idea where she may be staying?"

Olivia clasped her hands together again, then reached for the coffee and took a small sip.

"Do you take sugar?" he said.

"No, I'm fine. The coffee's fine."

She was worried about something, Luke could see that, and it was making her very ill at ease. He needed to get her to relax if he was going to get anything useful from her.

"Olivia, please be assured you're not in any trouble. I need to speak to Angie about Project Iceberg and can't locate her, so I'm hoping you can help. That's all."

"Have you asked Rob?" She paused before adding, "He's her, um, partner." He noticed her eyebrows twitch slightly. It was only for a microsecond but it was telling.

"Yes," he said. "We talked to him at lunchtime. He doesn't know where she is, but he did mention you might be able to help."

Olivia's cheeks reddened and out of the corner of his eye he saw Josh look up at him quizzically and then write *'No he didn't'* in the notebook.

"I can't help," she said. Her eyes moistened and she

moved her focus from her cup to the meeting room window. "I don't know why Rob would say that. I'm the last person she would tell anything to."

"Why?" Luke said, as gently as he could. "Aren't you friends?"

"We were." The tears were flowing now.

"What happened, Olivia?"

She looked up at Luke for the first time since she'd entered the room. "I…well Rob and I…we…" She hesitated then continued in a burst. "We'd been drinking and one thing led to another. It was stupid. I was stupid. And now she knows and I doubt she'll ever speak to me again."

"How did she find out?"

"He told her, the bastard. Apparently, he's done it before and she's always forgiven him but this time, it being me…" She put her head in her hands. "I'm supposed to be her best friend."

"Has this got anything to do with what she did on Project Iceberg?"

"God no. But she found out about… about Rob and me, on Wednesday so when the shit hit the fan on Thursday she must have felt her whole world had fallen apart."

"Do you think she might have done something stupid?"

Olivia opened her mouth in shock. "What?" she said. "You think she's killed herself?"

"We have to look at every possibility, but no, I don't think so." The relief was apparent on her face. "Rob suggested that Angie might have gone to Tuscany. Have you any idea why he would say that?"

"They were going away. She and Rob booked time off to decorate and she booked a week in Florence as a surprise. They were supposed to be flying out on Saturday. He could be right I guess. Maybe she went on her own."

"Is there anyone else she could be with?"

"Not that I can think of. Her mother's dead and her father remarried and moved to New York. She hasn't got any brothers or sisters. She must be in Florence. Right?"

"I'm sure she is." He paused. "Can you tell me why Angie was suspended?"

Olivia was on more comfortable ground now. "She sold secrets to our competition. Do you know anything about Project Iceberg?"

"The basics. I know it's an outsourcing bid for work at MI6."

"Yes, well there are some aspects of our bid that are crucial to our chances of winning. In particular, we have come up with an innovative way of cutting costs that we're convinced is original. Without it, Bannerdown's proposal is going to come in way more expensive than Filchers'."

"How do you know Angie sold secrets to them?"

"Someone found an email she'd sent to Bannerdown's bid director. In it, Angie asked if he'd received the information she'd sent and queried the payment she'd received. God knows why she did it though, it's not as if she's short of money."

"Who found the email?"

"That was June Jefferson."

"I see." Luke turned to Josh. "Are we seeing June this afternoon, Josh?"

Josh nodded and wrote '4 pm' on his notepad.

"Thanks for your time, Olivia," Luke said and stood up to shake her hand. "If you hear from Angie or think of anything else that might help us find her please give me a ring."

"I will do," she said, and couldn't leave the room quickly enough.

Luke sat down and turned to Josh. "Josh," he said. "When I said you weren't to speak I didn't mean you to take me literally. You don't have to stay completely silent but I want you to leave the questioning to me. Okay?"

"Oh right, guv. Gotcha."

"More importantly, what conclusions did you draw from our meeting with Olivia Nugent?"

Josh leafed through several pages of notes. "She was a good friend of Angie Johnson, she slept with Rob Talbot, she…"

"Not the obvious stuff, not the facts. I want you to develop your nose for things."

"Like a woman's instinct?"

Not for the first time that day Luke wondered if he was onto a loser with Josh but something made him want to persevere. "No," he said. "I was thinking of trying to tune your detecting skills. Actually, locating your detecting skills would be a good start. Did you think she was telling the truth about everything?"

"Oh I see, right, mmm…" Josh thought for a while, then tapped the side of his nose as if he had made the breakthrough they had both been waiting for. "She said she liked the coffee but I think she was lying."

"She was keeping something back," Luke said. "Whether it was about relationships or about Iceberg I'm not sure but there was definitely something."

"Oh yes, guv." Josh tapped his nose again. "That as well. Definito."

*

Luke's experience with accountants told him that they were often pedantic individuals who wore glasses and a three-piece pin-striped suit. This view was confirmed by their next interviewee whose first words were "Hi, I'm Tom Harris. I'm a chartered accountant, not a certified accountant."

Tom's two other notable attributes were elevator shoes, which brought his height to a sky-scraping five foot six, and an almost complete absence of personality. At one point in the interview, Luke had to kick Josh under the table to stop him yawning.

What was clear was that Tom was a loner who knew nothing about the alleged bribery and even less about what Angie or anyone else in the team got up to when they weren't in the office.

Third on the list was June Jefferson. She carried herself very upright and projected an aura of self-importance. Tom Harris had worn a suit, but as if born to it. It wouldn't have surprised Luke if his preferred loungewear when he got home in the evening was another suit, and he was sure it wouldn't be as daring as a suit without a pin-stripe.

June, on the other hand, wore her clothes like a weapon and they were, he was sure, only for the office. They were sharp: a black double-breasted jacket over a silk blouse and a tight leopard skin skirt. Her face was angular as well, neither attractive nor plain but most definitely severe, and her long blonde hair was scraped back into a ponytail. She was someone who sought power but was trying just a little too hard.

After a few introductory exchanges, Luke got to the point. "June," he said. "What do you know about the alleged bribery?"

"Not alleged," she snapped. "That memo proved what she did."

"Ah yes, I heard about the memo but I haven't seen it yet."

"I'll forward it to you."

"Thanks." He wrote down his email address and passed it to her. "How did you get a copy of the email?"

"How do you think? I was sent it."

"Who by?"

"The sender hid his email address. But what does it matter? It proves she's guilty, that's what's important."

"And you didn't think somebody who had it in for

Angie Johnson might have fabricated it?"

"Of course not."

"Who else got the email?"

"Just me."

"So how did your boss, ah…" he referred to his notes, "Eric Hughes get hold of it?"

"I sent it to him." She paused for a second then evidently felt a need to defend her actions. "It was my duty. What she did was unforgivable. That stupid woman has probably cost us the contract."

"And I understand that, with Angie's suspension, you have now stepped up to deputise for Eric."

"Yes."

"I see."

"What do you mean, 'I see'? Are you implying something?"

"Not at all, June, not at all." He paused. "Thanks for your time. If you think of anything else please get in touch."

"I will. I'm on annual leave tomorrow though. I'm going to a funeral."

"Okay. Thanks for letting me know."

Chapter 10

Angie returned to the beginning of the chapter for the second time. *Little Women* was one of her favourite books, but she couldn't concentrate. For all her efforts her attention kept wandering. She thought of Rob, of Olivia, of her father, but mostly of her captor, Mac, the man who had imprisoned her in this room.

He had told her it was a pigsty on her second evening there. A stone pigsty on farmland somewhere remote. It explained the lack of windows, the only light being a ceiling bulb that automatically turned on in the morning and off again in the evening. Or at least that was what she assumed; there was no clock and he had taken away her phone and watch. Her only luxury was a stack of paperbacks, piled up on the floor next to a carrier bag containing the previous 24 hours' rubbish. There was also a small suitcase which he'd brought the evening before containing clean underwear, sanitary towels and black bags. She'd thrown the wig and stilettos in there too.

It was only her sixth day but it seemed like she had been there for weeks. The books helped a little, but the loneliness was close to unbearable. Worst of all was the unknown, the fear of what he planned, of why he had brought her there in the first place.

He had not hurt her since he'd slapped her face that first morning and, thank goodness, there had been no sexual overtones to their encounters either. He had visited once each evening, around this time she thought, and brought food and drink for that evening and the next day, but he'd made little attempt to talk to her and had ignored her questions.

She looked back down at the book and tried yet again

to focus on the words.

With a start, she realised she could hear a noise that was new. Not the usual rhythmic rat-a-tat-tat on the vision panel that signalled Mac's arrival but a squealing. It was hard to make out against the low hum of the generator but she was certain it was there. It had a high pitch and sounded like an animal in pain.

She stood up, walked to the door and put her ear against the vision panel. She couldn't hear anything and thought she must have imagined it then suddenly there it was again, and she realised it wasn't an animal, it was a person, more specifically a woman. Her voice was weak but it didn't sound like she was far away. And she was repeating one word over and over again, and although Angie could only hear the words she could almost feel the woman shuddering and shaking between each utterance.

"Please."

"Please."

"Please."

After she had said this a dozen or so times there was a pause. Angie was about to call out when she heard footsteps and hastily retreated to the bed. A few seconds later there was a rat-tat-tat at the door. She sat back then remembered 'the rules' and retrieved the wig and stilettos from the suitcase and put them on. The vision panel opened and she saw Mac's eyes peering through at her. It made her feel like an animal in a zoo. He stared for a few seconds then pushed the door open and walked in.

"Good evening, Angie," he said, smiling. He looked her up and down. "As ever you look wonderful. And kind and gentle and soft and willing. I like that. I really like that. Now, please move back against the wall."

In one hand he held the butcher's knife and in the other a carrier bag which she knew would contain her supplies for the next day. He swapped the new carrier bag for the old one without taking his eyes off her. She thought, as she had each evening, of flying at him, of grabbing his hand, of gouging his eyes, but she knew it would be bound to fail. She had to think more cleverly, find a way of relating to him, of making him feel comfortable so that he might make a mistake.

"Did you have a good day?" she said.

"Terrific, thank you, darling."

She shuddered.

"I achieved a lot today," he said. "My job's very challenging."

"Oh really. How fascinating. What do you do?"

"I write erotic fiction." He paused then laughed. "I'm joking of course. I have a very important job. But actually, I'd like you to do some writing for me if you could."

"What?"

"Not erotic writing." He laughed again. "I'm not a pervert."

And yet you make me wear this wig and these heels, she thought.

He produced a pad and pen from the carrier bag and passed it to her. "I want you to write exactly what I tell you to. Are you ready?"

She nodded.

"Please begin by writing 'To whom it may concern'".

"But why…"

She stifled her question mid-sentence when she heard the woman's voice again. The door was open and it was much clearer. What she said was different this time but just as spine-chilling.

"Help me."

Mac looked at the door and then back at Angie. "Stay there," he said. He left the room, closing and bolting the door but leaving the vision panel open. Angie ran to the door and tried to put her head through the gap but it was too small. She heard the woman's voice again.

"No," she said.

There was a sound of skin smacking against skin.

"Mac don't," Angie screamed.

There was no reply then she heard his voice.

"I told you the rules." His voice became louder with each word. "Why can't you understand?"

For a moment Angie thought he was talking to her then realised he was speaking to the other woman.

"I told you," he went on.

She heard a whimper then a sharp inhalation of breath and a gurgling sound. There was silence for a few seconds then the sound of footsteps. She stepped back from the door. Mac's eyes appeared briefly at the vision panel then he closed it.

Angie didn't hear the woman's voice again.

Chapter 11

Luke held the wedding ring between his finger and thumb and turned it around. It was a simple gold band but brought strong memories of a very special day and of everything, good and bad, that had happened since.

The wedding itself had been simple but enjoyable, all the more so because his parents had refused to attend. He and they had had difficulties before he met Jess, but it all came to a head when he told them they were going to marry. His father, as ever, had been the mouthpiece for both of them and made it clear that they felt he was 'throwing his life away on that trollop' and that they were convinced she had deliberately got pregnant to marry above her standing. They had a stand-up row which ended with Luke storming out. He had only seen his mother and father twice in the two decades since.

"Are you okay, Luke?" Helen said as she put a mug down on the table in front of him.

"I'm fine," he said, sliding the ring back onto his finger. What am I like, he thought, second day in a new job and I'm already moping and maudlin.

She put a hand on his wrist. "If there's anything you want to talk about, anything at all, I'm here you know."

"Thank you, Helen, but no, everything's fine." He smiled and took a sip of his coffee. It was black and strong, exactly as he liked it. "Thanks for this. How did you get on yesterday?"

"I had a bit of luck, actually. I found something that may give us a clue as to where Angie's gone."

"Go on."

"I was looking at the draft contracts for Iceberg and I noticed a really odd clause which has been added by

Filchers. Here…" She opened a lever arch file and turned to roughly the midpoint in a document of sixty pages or so. "Read that," she said, pointing to a highlighted clause.

5.2.2 (iii) In the event of a losing bidder subsequently gaining intellectual rights over the process improvement innovations generating the economies in clause 4.3.1 then the agency shall transfer a sum (not exceeding the maximum amount specified in clause 7.6 adjusted to match inflation and interest as defined in the table in appendix 1 annexe IV) to the service provider's beneficiary as detailed in appendix 2 annexe III.

Luke read the clause, then read it again. He looked up at Helen and she smiled.

"See what I mean," she said, evidently pleased with herself.

He looked at her and read the clause again. Then for a fourth time.

"Morning, guv."

Luke turned to see Josh hanging his coat up and walking towards the table, a Starbucks coffee in his hand.

"What gives?" Josh said, looking first at Luke and then at Helen.

"Look at this," Helen said.

Josh read the highlighted text. "Gosh," he said, then leafed forward in the contract then back a few pages. "That explains it."

Luke turned to him in amazement. "Do you understand this gobbledygook?"

"Oh yes, guv," Josh said. "It's plain as day."

"But how?" Luke gestured to the page. "I mean that's just, well, nonsense." He shook his head. "Helen, can you explain it to me in plain English please?"

"It's really quite straightforward," Helen said. "If our

submission is successful and our remaining competitor then successfully challenges the innovative process streamlining approach within our solution then, subject to the economies table, funds will be transferred in accordance with…"

Luke held both hands up. "Whoah," he said. "That's still mumbo-jumbo."

"Let me explain, guv," Josh said. He collected his thoughts. "If we win and Bannerdown successfully challenges our approach then the Home Office has to give Filchers ten million pounds."

"Thank you, Josh, I understand now," Luke said. "Where's that memo June Jefferson forwarded?"

Helen pulled the email up on the laptop.

To: Danny Ogletree
From: Angie Johnson
*Subject: **Confidential***

Danny,

Thanks for confirming you received the details I sent of our innovative solution. However, please can you confirm the share would be as discussed? To date I have seen a sum that is far below what I had expected.

I await your response

Angie.

"So," Luke said, "it seems that Angie revealed details of Filcher's proposal to Bannerdown's sales lead in exchange for money."

"Yes," said Helen.

"Something still confuses me though." He turned to Josh. "How on earth did you understand that clause?"

"I went to Brighton Uni and my final dissertation was on contract law. Got a distinction for it."

"I see."

Josh looked at his watch. "It's almost ten, guv."

Luke grabbed his coffee and Josh led him to the Derwent Room. Eric Hughes stood and shook their hands when they entered, and Luke was immediately struck by the contrast between the man's size and his diffident manner. He struggled to look either of them in the eyes as they made their introductions, and even though at six foot three or so he was only a few inches shorter than Luke, and had six or seven inches on Josh, his shyness and lack of self-confidence were evident.

"Eric," Luke said, after they'd all taken their seats, "we've seen the memo that Angie Johnson sent to Bannerdown's Bid Director but there isn't a lot of detail in it. Have you seen anything else to support the bribery allegation?"

"Nothing else, no," Eric said. "As soon as I saw the email I passed it to HR. I did the right thing, didn't I? I mean it's up to them to investigate."

"Oh yes, that's fine, Eric. But tell me, how did the email come into your possession?"

"It was passed to me by June Jefferson, but she told you that yesterday didn't she?"

"Yes, she did. That's right isn't it, Josh?"

Josh looked back through his notebook. "Yes, that's right guv."

Luke turned back to Eric. "What about Angie Johnson herself? Is she a good team member?"

"Oh yes," Eric said. "Until this anyway." He laughed nervously. "She's normally very friendly and easy-going. She's a hard worker too."

"And how did she seem when she left on Thursday?"

"Pretty damn furious."

"And upset?"

"Very upset. She swore. Twice. And that's not like her. I don't think it was just her suspension either. She'd had some sort of argument with her boyfriend."

"Tell me, have you had any dealings with Danny Ogletree, Bannerdown's Bid Director?"

"I've met him once or twice at Home Office events, but I left Angie to deal with him for Project Iceberg. She's pretty good at that sort of thing, understands the sensitive nature of the bid and what she can and can't say." He paused. "Looks like she understood a bit too much as it happens."

"Perhaps," Luke said. "Have you got his contact details? Eric hesitated. "I have," he said, "but…"

"Don't worry, Eric, I won't mention anything I shouldn't."

Eric gave Luke the phone number but was clearly unenthusiastic about doing so.

"Thanks for your time," Luke said.

"No problem."

After he left Luke turned to Josh. "Well," he said. "Did you spot anything of interest in what he said?"

"I did actually, guv."

"I'm not interested in whether he liked the coffee or not?"

Josh laughed and tapped the side of his nose. "Spotted it guv. June Jefferson."

"What about her?"

"Eric said that he spoke to her since we saw her yesterday, despite being out of the office all afternoon and her being out of the office today."

"Well done." Josh visibly reddened. "He wasn't very keen to give me Danny Ogletree's number either," Luke went on. "Could be something and nothing but…" Luke got his phone out of his pocket to take it off silent and it immediately rang. "Sackville," he said.

"Luke, Gloria here, Edward Filcher's secretary. I've been trying to get hold of you."

"Sorry, I was in a meeting."

She lowered her voice to a whisper. "He's not very happy. Said you're to come to his office as soon as I get hold of you."

Chapter 12

"Please go in," Gloria said when Luke arrived at Filcher's office. "They're all waiting for you."

Luke opened the door to see Filcher at his desk and four other men seated around the meeting table.

"About ruddy time," Filcher said. "Sit down." He gestured to the space next to Glen Baxter.

"Luke," one of the men said, smiling as he stood up to shake his hand. "I didn't realise you worked here. I thought you were having a lengthy break."

"It's been six months, Pete," Luke said.

"Is it really that long? How are…"

"Can we get on?" Filcher snapped. "You two can reminisce later. You were saying, Detective Inspector Gilmore."

Before Pete Gilmore could say anything Luke gestured to the two men sitting between him and Filcher. "I'm sorry," he said. "We haven't been introduced. I'm Luke Sackville."

The man on the left held out his hand. He was the youngest person in the room, still in his thirties and with a confident air about him.

"Hi," he said. His grip was firm and his smile genuine. "I'm James McDonald, Head of HR. Pleased to meet you."

The other man stood next and held his hand out. He was much older, perhaps sixty, almost completely bald with round black-rimmed glasses.

"Arthur Bloomsbury," he said. "Marketing Director." He pointedly looked at his watch as soon as he let go of Luke's hand.

"DI Gilmore," Filcher said, his brows furrowed. "Continue."

"I was saying before you came in, Luke," Pete said, "that the body of a woman was found this morning in Moorham Woods. She left a note and in it she names a number of people at Filchers who she blames for her suicide. She said that she had been bullied by them."

"How did she kill herself?" Luke said.

"With a rope. A jogger found her hanging from a tree."

"Definitely suicide?"

"We're waiting for the post-mortem but yes, it looks that way."

"Do you know her name?" James said.

"The note was signed Marie Downing."

Arthur let out a small sigh. Luke turned to see he had put his hand to his mouth. "Did you know her, Arthur?" he asked.

"Marie was a member of my team," Arthur said. "She left suddenly a month or so ago."

"I've never met her," James said, "but I recognise the name. They were in the middle of a campaign and we had to find a replacement pretty damn quick."

"You mean she handed in her notice?" Luke said.

"No," Arthur said. "She left without telling anyone. Everything seemed normal, the campaign leader said she was happy in her work, then one day she didn't come in. Hasn't been heard of since."

"And neither of you looked into her disappearance?"

Filcher interrupted before Arthur or James could answer. "Luke," he said, "can I remind you that you work for Filchers now?" He gestured to DI Gilmore. "Leave questions like that to the real police."

"Perhaps I can talk to you about her disappearance when we've finished here," Pete said, addressing his comment to both Arthur and James.

"Yes, of course," James said.

Arthur nodded his assent.

"What were the names of the alleged bullies, Pete?"

Luke said.

"I can't let you have the note itself," Pete said, "but I have the names here." He produced an envelope and Filcher held his hand out for it then gave an audible *'huh'* when Pete handed it to Luke.

As they left the room Pete gestured to Luke to move where they couldn't be overheard. "There's something suspicious about this Luke," he whispered. "Do you fancy a drink after work?"

"Sure, Pete. 6 pm, Saracen's Head?'

"See you there."

Chapter 13

Luke had always liked the Saracen's Head. It had been brought up to date, but only with paint and newer lighting. The old wooden floors and overhead beams remained, as did the quirky layout and the many nooks and crannies which made it an ideal policeman's haunt. Easy to hide away and talk about the current case.

Today, though, walking into the pub felt surreal. His last visit there had been after the successful conviction of Oliver Penman, a man in his mid-fifties who had raped then killed a man he met through social media. The team hadn't celebrated exactly - you couldn't celebrate something like that - but they did have a collective sense of achievement from bringing the man to justice and providing the victim's family with some kind of closure.

Only two days after that his world had fallen apart.

"Drink, Luke?"

"Sorry, Pete, I was miles away. Butcombe would be great thanks."

They took their drinks to a hived-off area at the very back of the pub.

"Sorry I haven't been in touch," Pete said. "I thought it best to give you a bit of space."

"That's fine. I needed time to think about my future and also to focus on the twins."

"How are they faring?"

"Surprisingly well, on the surface at least. In the end, they elected to take up their places rather than defer for a year, which is probably the best thing."

"And you?"

Luke grunted and took a sip of his beer. "I'm pleased to be in a new job," he said, "though I was expecting to be

Head of Security not Head of Ethics."

"Is there much scope for Luke Sackville's famous truth wizardry?"

"Not sure really. I only started yesterday."

"Bugger me, and you work for that Edward Filcher guy. Good luck to you. There's a pompous ass if ever I saw one."

Luke smiled. "Pompous isn't the half of it," he said. "He's bigoted, racist, misogynistic, you name it."

"You've been dropped straight in it, especially with this…" he held his index fingers up and signed quotes in the air, "…suicide."

"You said earlier that it looks suspicious and yet the post-mortem results aren't even in. What's up?"

"In confidence, Luke?"

"Of course."

"Two things. First, the victim - she's been formally identified now so it's definitely Marie Downing - had bruises on her cheeks which don't seem to have happened as a result of the hanging. And second, her car's still parked outside her home, meaning she must have travelled to Moorham Woods with someone else, whether a friend, family member, taxi or bus."

"That's interesting. Those names you gave me earlier were intriguing too."

"Really. Why?"

Luke pulled the envelope from his pocket and unfolded the piece of paper. "Well," he said, "in my two days at Filchers it so happens that I've met two of these three so-called bullies and that accusation just doesn't sit pretty with what I know of them. Emily Parker I don't know, but Angelica is an unusual name so I'm pretty sure that this lady," he indicated the top name on the list, "works on reception. I've said hello a couple of times so obviously I don't know her well but Angelica Reid does not seem like bully material to me. And as for Helen Hogg," he indicated the name third on the list, "she works for me and is one of the nicest people I've ever met."

Pete paused for a moment. "Luke, can we work together on this?" Luke started to object but he held his hand up to stop him. "I don't want to wade into formal interviews with these three ladies when the accusations are in all likelihood baseless. Although it might not be completely ethical - ironic given your job title - I wonder if we might cooperate. You carry out the investigation within Filchers, essentially doing it on my behalf, and feed me what you find. Your unusual interviewing skills may well bring dividends. In exchange, I'll tell you anything we uncover."

Luke thought about it for a moment. "Okay," he said. "But you have to agree to share everything. I'd like to see the suicide note for starters, and the post-mortem report as soon as that's ready."

"Whoah, buddy." Pete smiled. "Good to see you haven't lost any of your old fire, but you have to remember it's my case."

"Sure thing."

"In that case, Luke, let's shake on it."

They shook hands and sat back. After a few seconds, Pete leant forward and clasped his hands together on the table. He looked down at them and shook his head slowly from side to side.

"What is it?" Luke said.

"They've set a date," Pete said. He paused then blurted the next few words out. "Thompson is being released on the sixth of July."

"He can't be." Luke sat back in his chair. He swallowed and added, almost under his breath, "Of course. God, it'll be nine months won't it."

"Yep. He spent three months on remand before the trial, which counts towards it."

Luke sighed and put his palm to his forehead. Julian

Thompson's half-smirk from the dock would never leave him. The primary school teacher, a married man with two small children, had been found guilty of possessing class A images, the very worst kind, along with what the prosecution described as a 'paedophile's manual'.

When he had seen a police car pull up outside his house, Thompson realised what they were there for and fled through the back of the house to his car. He was well away before they realised what he had done, and had driven less than two miles when he struck Jess on a zebra crossing before driving through the plate glass window of the cafe she had just visited. Thompson had to have three stitches in his arm. Jess had been killed instantly.

He had not been over the speed limit, and a witness had said Jess walked quickly onto the crossing without looking. This enabled the defence barrister to successfully argue that Thompson had caused death through careless, rather than dangerous, driving. Because he showed remorse, and had no previous, the judge had sentenced him to eighteen months for child pornography, and eleven months to run concurrently for causing death through careless driving. Release would be automatic after he had served half the sentence.

"I know it's no consolation," Pete said, "but he'll be on the sex offenders' register and banned from working with children. I can't imagine his wife taking him back either."

"I know, Pete," Luke said. "But we both know he'll do it again as soon as he's out. That bastard will be back in touch with his perverted mates and together they'll continue destroying children's lives."

"I'm with you. If I had it my way they'd lock him up and throw away the key."

"Amen to that."

Chapter 14

Luke was confident that managing Edward Filcher wouldn't be too much of a challenge. Yes, he was a pompous ass, but the very fact that he was full of his own importance could be used to gain an advantage over him. He didn't want to underestimate the man but he didn't seem like the sharpest tool in the box either. What was certain was that with two 'ethics incidents' on the go - Project Iceberg and now the bullying accusations - he was going to need more staff.

"Good morning, Gloria,' he said, as he emerged from the lift on the Executive Floor.

"Good morning, Luke," she said, returning his smile. "Are you settling in okay?"

"Fine thanks." He indicated Filcher's door with his thumb. "Is he in?"

"Not yet." She looked up at the clock. It was a quarter to ten. "He usually gets in between nine thirty and ten so should be here soon. Do you want to wait?"

"Wait for what?"

Luke turned to see Filcher wading towards his door. "Good morning, Mr Filcher," he said. "Have you got a moment?"

Filcher harrumphed. "Gloria," he said, "what's my day looking like?"

"You've got lunch with Percy Steadman from twelve to three. Nothing before that."

"Mmm." He turned to Luke. "I can spare a couple of minutes." He pushed the door to his office open and called back over his shoulder. "Tea, Gloria." He paused before adding, "…for one."

Luke followed him in. Filcher hung his coat on the stand and walked to his side of the desk.

"What is it?" he snapped as he sat down. "I'm a very busy man."

"I understand that, Mr Filcher, and I won't keep you long. I need two more staff."

"What!" A grunt issued from deep in Filcher's throat. "You've been here two days and you already want to double your team." He shook his head from side to side. "I cannot believe it."

Luke suspected that Victor Meldrew had never delivered those words with such magisterial arrogance. "I don't want to increase the team," he said.

"But you said you need two more people."

"I assure you I would rather not have more staff, Mr Filcher," Luke lied, "but it is clear from your appointment that the Board recognises that Internal Affairs is a vital directorate…"

"Indeed."

"…and Board Members doubtless recognise the importance of our government contracts and of close co-operation with the police…"

Filcher nodded sagely.

"…and of your critical role in maintaining those contracts and relationships."

"Critical role," Filcher repeated.

"So if by your actions we are able to solve the problems with Project Iceberg and enhance our relationships with the Home Office, which is of course responsible for UK policing, then I am sure the Board will be very pleased."

"I'm glad you see that, Luke. I was put in this role because I, and I alone if I may say so, possess the ability to coordinate the multiple strands of security, human resources and ethics. And, as you say, these incidents need to be dealt with effectively and efficiently." It was Luke's turn to nod sagely. "On your way out ask Gloria to tell James McDonald to come up and see me. I'll ask him to ensure you have two extra staff by the end of the day."

"One of them needs strong IT skills, while the other…"

Filcher waved his hand for Luke to stop. "Leave it to me," he said. "I'll ensure they're exactly what you need." He sat down and picked up a folder and Luke could see that he had been dismissed.

*

Caroline Klein rang Luke shortly after lunch, and she was as friendly on the phone as she had been in person.

"Hello, Luke," she said, the sourness in her voice already apparent.

"Hi, Caroline. How are you?"

She ignored the question. "As you're aware I look after human resources for Internal Affairs as well as Marketing and Finance."

He hadn't been but he let it ride. "Yes," he said.

"And James," she went on, "that's James McDonald the Head of HR…"

"I've met James."

She let out an audible sigh. Patience was evidently not one of her virtues. "As I was saying, James has told me to find you two extra staff, though why in your first week you need two more is beyond me."

"Good, good," Luke said. "I've prepared a short job description for each of them. Do you want me to email them over?"

"No need, I've found one of them already."

"But you don't know what I need."

"This is not the police force, Luke," she said in her most patronising tone. "You can't specify what you want at Filchers, not when you require someone urgently. We are a private company, answerable to our shareholders. We can't magic up exactly the right person for you."

"I understand that, and it's not easy in the police either, but it's important..."

"His name is Majid Osman," she said, "and he can start tomorrow."

"Thank you, but..."

"I will try and find you a second person this afternoon. Edward seems to consider this urgent for some reason."

"Shouldn't you at least look at my job descriptions?"

"You really don't understand how Filchers works do you, Luke?" she said. "If you want someone quickly then he or she will have to be available, which might mean they're not ideal for the role but you'll have to make do." She snorted. "We don't have people with policing skills sitting around waiting for a move to Ethics you know."

He could see he would get nowhere with this woman. "I understand that," he said.

"Good. Now if you'll let me get on I'll see what I can find."

"Okay. Thanks for your efforts, Caroline."

"Hmm, yes, well I'll speak to you later." She hung up.

Chapter 15

Sam liked Nick. He was slightly younger than her, not quite thirty, and easy to talk to. About five foot ten and slim, he had a long black beard which he tied together at the end with a white hairband. On anyone else she would have thought it over the top, but on Nick it worked.

"Water?" he said. They were at the water dispenser in the small kitchen shared by Finance and Marketing.

"No thanks," she said. "I'm going to have a cup of tea."

He filled his cup while she put the kettle on, then leaned back against the wall. "I had another run-in with Elizabeth yesterday," he said. Elizabeth Rogers, the widely disliked Head of Finance, was their boss. "I told Matt and he thought it was hilarious."

Matt was Nick's long-term partner. Sam had met him a couple of times and found him pleasant if on the quiet side.

"What did she do?" she said.

"I've always suspected that she didn't approve of me, because I'm open about being gay and she's such a batshit crazy Christian…"

"Nick, ssh."

He lowered his voice to a whisper. "…and yesterday she told me she didn't approve of the photo on my desk, you know the one of Matt and me with our arms over each other's shoulders."

Sam was appalled. "She can't say that!"

"She told me *she* didn't mind but quoted from the bible and told me there were others who might not approve."

"That's awful. Are you going to do anything?"

"I'm going to ignore her, that's what I'm going to do. The photo's staying. She's powerless to make me remove it and she knows it." He took another sip of water and watched her as she made her drink. "What about you? Has she said any more?"

Sam emptied her teabag into the bin. "Not since she confronted me last week. I'm with you though - there's nothing she can do so I'm going to ignore her and carry on as normal."

"She's got a point though, Sam darling." He smiled and looked her up and down. "Just looking at you makes me wish I was straight."

She laughed. "Shut up, Nick!"

*

Sam's lunch break had been brief but enjoyable. She had too much work to take a full hour so had enjoyed the pleasure of a hot but hasty baked potato with tuna in the staff canteen. She looked at her watch. It was half past one, time to be getting back. She took her tray to the stacking shelves and then walked back to the Finance department. As she was approaching her desk she heard rapid steps behind her and looked around to see Elizabeth walking towards her, eyebrows together and lips puckered. Elizabeth was only ten years older than Sam but she was dumpy and wore clothes to accentuate it. Today she was sporting an orange tent dress that did nothing for her figure.

"Sam," she said, "I need to talk to you. Could you come to my office please?"

"Now?" Sam said.

"Yes, now."

Sam followed her into her office. Elizabeth shut the door behind them but remained standing.

"What is it, Elizabeth?" Sam said.

"I'm sorry, Sam, but your skirt is too short."

"What?" She was taken aback. "What do you mean my skirt is too short? For heaven's sake, it's only just above my knees."

"It's too short and it's too tight," Elizabeth asserted. "And I don't appreciate your blasphemy."

Sam didn't know what to say.

"As for that blouse," Elizabeth pointed at Sam's top. "It's wholly inappropriate for a work environment."

Sam looked down at her blouse. It was cream and, she thought, rather elegant. It had certainly cost enough. You could see the faint outline of her bra beneath it but in no way was it transparent. She looked over her manager's shoulder to the photo on the wall. Three Filchers consultants, or at least actors pretending to be Filchers employees, were smiling as they cooperated on a report. No crazy manager for them to worry about.

"I've spoken to you before, yet you continue to wear…" Elizabeth gestured up and down again, "…this sort of thing."

"I, ah…" Sam was flummoxed. "What do you want me to do? Am I supposed to go home and change?"

"There is no room for you in our department, Sam. Your work is okay…"

"Gee, thanks." Sam couldn't keep the sarcasm from her voice.

"…but I've thought for a while now that the team might be better without you. I've seen the way some of the men look at you."

"What?"

"You're an attractive young woman. That should be enough. But no, you have to draw their attention to you with your flirtatiousness."

"I don't flirt," Sam said, but the other woman was on a roll.

"You're a distraction to the men in the team. Even the way you walk is suggestive, flaunting your figure." Elizabeth moved closer and almost hissed her next words. "To be honest, I've had enough."

Sam stepped back and tried to catch her breath. "So what now?"

"Expect a call from HR this afternoon to discuss your immediate transfer."

And with that, she opened the door and gestured for Sam to leave.

Sam walked back to the canteen and bought herself a cup of tea, then took it to a table by the window, cradled her mug in both hands and tried to calm herself down.

She looked around the canteen. There were a couple of people at the long trestle tables eating a late lunch alone, and a group of four having a meeting in the far corner. All happy little soldiers no doubt, with a boss who might mark them down for one or other aspect of their work, but not for their lack of godliness.

She was angry, but she couldn't let that anger eat her up. It wasn't the first time Elizabeth had told her off for her appearance, but before it had been delivered with a lighter touch and she'd dismissed it as a small eccentricity. This time, however, the woman had been more intense and had seemed to be serious about transferring her out of the department.

Elizabeth was bonkers of course, and HR would doubtless see that, but she still had to find herself a position somewhere else in the organisation. There was no way she could continue working for the woman after that little barrage of god-squad mumbo jumbo. She thought of ringing HR herself but the consultant who looked after Finance was Caroline Klein. She was snooty and overbearing and seemed to look down her nose at everyone, regardless of their grade or seniority. To her, staff were like cattle to be moved and corralled with no thought to their feelings or wishes.

No, she couldn't bring herself to contact Caroline. One

possibility would be to speak to James McDonald, the Head of HR. He seemed approachable, but she suspected he would only refer her to Caroline so there would be nothing to be gained.

Her mobile rang and she looked down to see Caroline's name on the display. Shit, she thought, it looked like the decision had been taken out of her hands. She hesitated for a moment, then clicked the green button.

"Hi Caroline," she said. "I thought you might ring. How are you?"

"Elizabeth Rogers rang me." That was typical of the woman. No time for pleasantries or small talk, just straight to it. "She tells me that you have not fitted in well and she has asked me to find you an alternative position."

"I think I've fitted in fine, but…"

Caroline gave her no time to answer. "I don't need to hear your apologies, Sam."

"Apologies. What do you mean apologies? I've got nothing to say sorry for. Elizabeth…"

"Sam, calm down. I think it would be better if we did this face-to-face. Are you in a union?"

"In a…" Sam was struggling to keep up.

"Where are you?"

"I'm in the canteen."

"Mmm. Elizabeth said you might be."

"What does that mean?"

"Wait there. I'll be down in a few minutes."

Five minutes later Caroline appeared at the end of the room, a document wallet under her arm and phone to her ear. As ever, her mouth was screwed up and the image she portrayed was one of 'I'm very important and no one else is worthy of my time'. She sat down opposite Sam and raised her hand to signal that she needed to wait for her to finish the call.

"We'll talk about this later," she said to the person on the other end. "Just do as I ask." She hung up and looked across at Sam. "Do you want to work for Filchers?"

Wow, thought Sam, talk about bedside manner.

"Because if you do," Caroline went on, "you're going to have to buck your ideas up."

"What do you mean?"

"Elizabeth told me about your timekeeping issues. You might have problems at home," she put the folder down on the table and pulled out the papers in it, "but that is no excuse."

"What do you mean timekeeping issues? And what problems at home for that matter?"

"I gather this canteen is no stranger to you."

"What?"

"And that you are frequently in late, often past 10 am, and usually disappear by 4."

"That's nonsense, I…" Sam paused and tried to collect herself. "Elizabeth doesn't like the way I look," she said. "She thinks I play on being attractive."

"Are you saying you're attractive?"

"No, I'm not saying that. But Elizabeth told me she doesn't like how the men in the office look at me, and I think she meant…"

"…because you're attractive."

"Because I flirt."

"You flirt with the men in the office?"

"No, of course not." My god, this woman was impossible. "But Elizabeth thinks I do."

Caroline held her hand up. Her face was sourer than ever now. "Listen to me, Miss Samantha Chambers." She wagged her finger in Sam's face. "It's women like you that give women like me a bad name. You waltz around, trying to grab men's attention…"

"I don't…"

"Let me finish," she said, and she almost shouted it, then lowered her voice so it was only just above a whisper. "You think you're the best, don't you? Because you're attractive and because you've got some skills, but in reality all you are is lazy."

"I'm not lazy."

"If I had my way you'd be kicked out of here."

"I'll take this to James, I…"

"You can't take this to anyone. Elizabeth has pointed out your lackadaisical attitude, your wantonness, your general uselessness. All I'm doing is trying to make the best of a bad situation." She pulled a piece of paper from the wallet. "I really do hope you leave our employment soon," she said, "but in the meantime, I have a position I want you to take up." She passed the paper over.

"Ethics team!" Sam exclaimed. "What the hell is an ethics team?"

"They're in room 3 on the second floor. I suggest you be there at 9 am tomorrow. In the meantime collect your things from Finance and go home." She looked pointedly at the canteen clock. It was half past two. "From what I hear, this is your normal home time anyway."

Chapter 16

Luke's phone rang and he was surprised to see Sally Croft's name on the screen. He had a lot of time for her. With over fifteen years experience she was regarded as one of the best forensic pathologists in the southwest of England. She also had a number of what could be generously called eccentricities, others might say madnesses, but he didn't blame her for that. If he had to spend his days dismembering dead bodies he'd need something to help him escape.

"Hi Sally," he said. "To what do I owe the honour?"

"I've had a body on my slab this morning and I believe you're involved in the investigation."

"Marie Downing?"

"Yes, and I've found a couple of anomalies." She paused. "I'd like to know what you think but rather than tell you over the phone is there any chance you could come in, say at 3 this afternoon?"

"I'd love to," he said, "but as you're aware I'm a civilian now."

"Poppycock. I'll sneak you in and no one need ever know."

"If you're sure?"

"Definitely."

"I'll be there."

Luke got to Flax Bourton at a quarter to three and true to her word Sally let him in at the back door.

"Luke, Luke," she said as she gave him a hug. She had so much energy it sometimes tired him just looking at her. "It's lovely to see you. We've missed you around here with your intuitive questions and complete lack of awareness as to what we actually do." He started to speak but she held both her hands up. "I'm messing with you." She smiled. "Your questions are rubbish. But anyway, how the hell are you? New woman yet?"

"No, I..."

"Well get a bloody move on then. What about me? Am I your type? Or am I too boring?"

"No one could ever describe you as boring Sally."

"Not your type then."

She led him through to her office and invited him to sit on the sofa before sitting down herself and putting her nike'd feet up on her desk. She was wearing bright pink slacks that matched the colour of her short curly hair. The ensemble was completed by a heavily patterned red and yellow waistcoat over a luminescent green top.

The sofa was the only nod to her personality in an otherwise bland office. True, there were a couple of abstract collage-type pieces of art on one wall, but otherwise it was only the bright pink Chesterfield that made the room different from any other pathologist's office. Her desk was covered in files, barring one small area which had been cleared to make room for a used plate and coffee mug.

The door opened and Pete Gilmore walked in. He spotted Luke but before he could say anything Sally said, "What about you DI Gilmore? Are you on the lookout for a vivacious sex kitten in her mid-forties?" She laughed when she saw the look of horror on his face. "It's okay," she said, raising her hands in the air, "you don't need to answer."

Pete looked at Luke. "What are you doing here?" he said.

"That's down to me," Sally said. "You can discuss it later. Please sit down."

Pete sat in the other armchair and Sally lifted her feet off the desk, leaned forward and clasped her hands together. "While I enjoy flirting with you two gentlemen," she said, her tone more serious now, "I need to bring you up to date on what I've found. Such a tragedy. That poor girl Marie Downing. Pretty young thing. Awful that she should be murdered in such a callous fashion."

"Murdered?" Luke said. "Definitely not suicide?"

"Oh no, Luke. She'd have to be superwoman to hold her own hands around her throat and squeeze hard enough." She put her hands around her own neck and started to squeeze. After a few seconds she began to go red in the face and let go. "Not possible you see. No, she was strangled, and it was someone with fairly large hands so probably a man."

"Time of death?" Pete asked.

"I'd say twelve to fourteen hours before she was found, so between 7 pm and 9 pm yesterday."

"You said you found something unusual?" Luke said.

"Yes. Hang on a minute." She turned around and rifled through a stack of photos on the shelf behind her, then placed one on the desk in front of them. Luke found himself looking at an open mouth, the teeth in good condition although there was one filling that he could see at the back left.

"What are we looking at?" he said.

"A mouth," Sally said before turning to Pete. "Didn't I say his incisive questions were amazing?" She pointed at the photo. "There, do you see that between the right cuspid and first molar?"

"It looks like a thin strand," Luke said. "Is it hair?"

"Bang on."

"And it's not Marie's?"

"No, she's a redhead. It's a single strand of blonde hair. It's not dyed so from someone who's in their mid-forties tops, probably in their thirties or younger."

"Most likely from our killer then?" Pete said.

"It's a possibility." She paused. "Before you ask, I can't be certain whether the hair is from a man or a woman. I've sent it off to the lab but they'll only be able to tell the sex if there's some of the root attached."

"You said you can't be certain. What's your opinion?" Luke said.

"The hair is a lot longer than it looks in that photo. It was coiled under her tongue and measures 52 centimetres. Not many men have hair that long. I think it's from a woman."

Before they could comment further Sally reached behind her and pulled out another photo. This time it was a close-up of the side of Marie Downing's face. "There's also this," she said, pointing to a red welt on the right cheek. "She had been slapped more than once, and whoever hit her used their left hand so I think it's safe to assume he or she is left-handed. There's also a clear mark here." She pointed to a purple patch in the middle of the red welt in the skin. "I think that's from a ring on her attacker's left hand."

"What type of ring?" Luke said.

"There's more intense bruising but no indentation," Sally said. "I'd say it's unlikely to be an engagement ring, or any ring with a stone."

*

"We now know for certain it was murder," Pete said as they walked back to the car park, "but we had an expert check the so-called suicide note against samples of Marie's handwriting and she definitely wrote it. The callous bastard must have forced her to do it." He paused. "You realise we're going to have to take this forward on our own from here on. You're a civilian now and I can't share details of an ongoing case with you, especially one that involves murder."

"I appreciate that," Luke said.

"Thanks for being so understanding."

"But I won't be putting a complete halt to our investigations. Marie Downing was a Filchers' employee, she accused other Filchers' staff of bullying her and she disappeared on our watch. I have to ensure there's nothing that links her disappearance and murder to the company."

"You're a bugger, you know that don't you?"

Luke smiled. "I'll keep you up to date with what I find," he said. "If you wouldn't mind…"

Pete held his hands up. "Okay, okay. I'm not going to be able to share everything but I'll do what I can."

"Thanks, Pete, and give my love to Janice and the girls."

"Will do," Pete said, but he was shaking his head as he walked back to his car. Before he got in he turned and shouted "You owe me one."

Traffic was light on the trip home. Luke took the southerly route via Chew Magna rather than going through Bristol. It took slightly longer but he found the rolling hills and soft landscape helped him to wind down after what was always a stressful visit to Flax Bourton. The journey also gave him time to reflect on what he had found out.

It was now beyond doubt that Marie Downing had been murdered, but he needed to keep an open mind about the sex of her killer. Sally Croft had been fairly certain it was a man, but the blonde hair found in the victim's mouth was a curve ball. Its presence could be unconnected, or it could be that the murderer was carrying out some kind of fantasy. He needed to find out more about Marie's circumstances and relationships.

He also needed to find time to look into where Angie Johnson had gone, and whether she was genuinely taking bribes. At the moment it all seemed to rest on a single email which could easily have been faked, but if so by whom and why?

The more he thought about it, the more he realised it was vital he get more team members as quickly as possible. He hoped that HR would come up trumps.

As he drove into Norton St Philip he was struck by a memory of coming home on the twins' 18th birthday. Jess had been at the top of the drive tying balloons to the two cypress trees on either side of the entrance. It was a tradition she had started when the children were one and had done every year since. A tradition she wouldn't be able to continue this year. A feeling of emptiness overwhelmed him as he drove up to the old farmhouse. A house once filled with family but now devoid of sound.

Or at least it was until Wilkins heard the car and started barking. Luke opened the front door to find him rocketing left then right in the dog crate, desperate to see him. He bent down and opened the crate door. The spaniel immediately leapt at him, ears flopping and tongue hanging out.

"C'mon, you old bugger," Luke said. "Let's go for a walk."

Chapter 17

Sam got off the bus in Widcombe and started the walk up the hill. She was mentally exhausted after the arguments with first her manager and then Caroline from HR. Everything had turned topsy turvy at work, and she savoured the idea of stretching out on the sofa in her onesie, glass of bubbly in one hand and an open paperback in the other. Then she wanted an early night so that she could be in first thing the next morning and give this peculiar 'Ethics Team' assignment her best shot.

But there was always the chance that Tony would be there, and that was most definitely not what she wanted. He had a habit of turning up unannounced and she knew he wouldn't be interested in anything she had to say. His focus would as ever be on all the people he loved, which was to say himself.

Initially she'd fancied him. And why not. He was a good laugh, great to look at, and had a lovely smile. He was terrific in bed too. But to give him a key after only two months together. She must have been mad. Now, another month on, she could see him for what he was.

His car wasn't outside the building. That was a good sign. She turned the key in the lock and pushed the door open. There was music playing. If you could call it that. Billy-Z-no-mates or some such. She hated rap but it was Tony's favourite. His head appeared at the end of the hall.

"Hi, Sammy baby," he said. "I've bought us a Chinese. Thought we could celebrate together."

She hated Chinese food. She also hated being called Sammy. "Great," she said as she hung her coat up. "What are we celebrating?"

"Me," he said.

There's a surprise, she thought but said "Really. What's happened?"

He moved towards her and gave her a kiss on the lips. He was clearly feeling amorous but she moved back.

"I need the loo," she said, forcing a smile. "When I'm back you can tell me what's happened."

When she returned Tony called her into the lounge. He was sitting on the sofa looking self-satisfied and holding two glasses of prosecco. As ever his appearance was immaculate, short brown beard freshly trimmed and short-sleeved white polo shirt showing off his chiselled pecs and taut biceps. The appeal was gone though. It was his personality, or rather the lack of any, that now shone through. He patted the sofa, inviting her to sit down. She took the glass offered to her but remained standing.

"Guess what I've done?" he said.

"I don't know."

"Go on, guess."

She wasn't in the mood for games but knew he'd pull his petulant face if she didn't go along with him. "Had a promotion?" she said.

"No. Try again."

"Tony, I…"

"Go on. Try again."

"You've won the lottery?"

He paused, then made a drum roll sound which was largely ineffective since Billy-Z-no-mates was still busting his guts in the background. "I went to the jewellers today," he said, and Sam had a sudden fear that he might do something utterly dreadful. And then he did. He knelt in front of her and pulled a small box from his pocket.

"You're not…" she said.

"Sammy darling," he said. "Will you marry me?"

She stood open-mouthed, unable to speak.

"You're the girl of my dreams."

"But you've never even told me you love me."

"Oh I do, Sammy, I do. And you love me. I can see that. We're so good in bed together. You're so passionate, and we gel."

"Gel? What do you mean we gel? Marriage is more than sex you know."

"And we're suited. Look at the interests we share."

"Like listening to you talking about yourself?" He looked so shocked and upset she almost felt sorry for him. "Sorry," she said. "But I have to say no."

"I'll give you time, Sammy," he said. "Think about it and let me know tomorrow."

"I don't need time."

He smiled. "Come on, Sammy baby." He patted the sofa again. "Let's share this bubbly and have a great evening…" he pointed his thumb at the ceiling and winked, "…and night. Then tomorrow we can plan the rest of our life together."

Sam tried to calm herself down. "Tony," she said. "It's a 'no' and that's not going to change."

"I think you need some space. Time to think about me and what we could be together."

"I…"

He held his hand up. "No, Sammy," he said. "I understand this is a big decision and you want to make sure it's the right one. I'll leave you alone this evening and come around again tomorrow. You can give me your decision then. I know you love me."

"Tony, I don't. I…"

He stood up. "I'll be back tomorrow." He bent forward to give her a kiss but she pulled away from him. He smiled then grabbed his coat and left before she could say another word.

*

"Did he give you back his key to your apartment?" Hannah said, in between bites of a spring roll..

"No," Sam said. "I didn't get a chance to ask. It all happened so quickly."

"Then you need to change the locks."

Hannah had been her closest friend since sixth form and had come over as soon as she'd called. She was spread across the length of the sofa, curly black hair down over her shoulders and a serious look on her face. Sam was perched on the edge of the armchair, still feeling shaken.

"I've always thought he's a creep," Hannah said.

"He's not a creep," Sam said, but why she was defending him she wasn't sure.

"He's been married before, hasn't he?"

"Yes, but you can't hold that against him."

Hannah's left eyebrow went up. "Bit odd that he still wears the wedding ring."

"Not really. It was his late father's."

"Still seems odd to me. And you agreed to him coming around again tomorrow?"

"I didn't agree. He just said he would."

"You need to ring him then. Tell him not to. Do you want to finish with him?"

"Oh yes," Sam said without hesitation. "I'd been thinking I would anyway and with this, yes, definitely."

"Then ring him and tell him." Hannah stood up and picked Sam's phone up from the coffee table "Here," she said. "Do it now."

Sam looked at the phone for a second then up at Hannah.

"Go on," Hannah said.

Sam clicked on Tony's number. He picked up after only one ring.

"Sammy," he said, "that was quick." She could hear the excitement in his voice. "Best decision of your life, baby," he went on. "You won't regret it."

"Tony…"

"You want me to come over. Sure thing."

"No, Tony, listen to me for once. I don't want to marry you, in fact I think we should stop seeing each other."

"You mean take a break?"

"No, Tony, I don't mean that. I don't want to see you again. We're finished."

"No."

"What do you mean 'no'?"

"You need time, Sammy baby, that's all."

She was shaking now. "Listen, Tony, it's over. You can post my key back to me."

There was a few seconds silence then his voice came back on the phone. "You cow," he said, and there was real malice in his voice. "You're nothing but a prick-tease."

"Tony, I know you're upset, but…"

"I'll give you fucking upset…"

She hung up before he could finish and looked over at her friend who had heard every word.

"That went well," Hannah said.

Chapter 18

Sam thought long and hard before deciding to call her Mum. She wanted to confide in her, needed to confide in her, but wasn't sure how she'd take the news that she had ended the relationship. She had really taken to Tony and Sam knew that in part this was because he was attractive and muscular. It made Sam feel a little queasy but it was the truth. Her Mum became quite girly and flirty when she was with him, laughing at all his one-liners, funny or not. She had even gone so far as to praise Sam on finding someone like him, implying in her tone that she was punching well above her weight.

Thursday was her bridge night, but it was ten o'clock so she'd be home by now. Hopefully, she had had a good evening. Sam metaphorically crossed her fingers and picked up her phone.

"Kate Chambers."

The tone of those two words told Sam immediately that her Mum was in a good mood. Thank goodness for that, she thought. "Hi Mum," she said.

"Hi, Darling. How are you, and how's that lovely boyfriend of yours?"

"Tony proposed,"

"That's great news."

"No, Mum, it's not."

"But he's…"

"He's not right for me, Mum. We're worlds apart. There was a physical attraction but we haven't got the same interests. I like mixing with my friends, karate, reading, the theatre. Tony only has one major passion - himself. It took me a while to realise it but we have nothing in common. And besides I don't even think I like him."

Kate surprised Sam with her next comment. "I think you've done the right thing."

"You do?" Sam breathed a sigh of relief. She had been anticipating resistance, but her Mum clearly was in a great mood.

"Yes," Kate said. "I was talking to Lizzie this evening and her daughter Ellie is a spinster like you…"

"Mum!"

"You know what I mean, darling. Her daughter is single, hasn't found anyone and is about your age. She's signed up to a dating site and has been inundated. Mind you, Ellie is a very pretty girl, so I'm not surprised. But you're good-looking so I'm sure you'll get some interest."

Damned with faint praise, Sam thought.

"It's called 'Plenty of Fish'," Kate went on. "There's another one too, I think it was 'Cinder'."

"It's 'Tinder', Mum."

"That's it. You swipe up and down, find the fit ones, click and set up a date. Ellie's had great success apparently."

"Online dating is not my thing."

"You should think about it, darling. You're not getting any younger and I'd love another grandchild. Talking of which, your sister's coming for a meal on Saturday. Can you join us?"

"I'd love to, Mum, but I'm going to Hannah's."

Sam was sorry she couldn't go. She and her sister got on brilliantly and her nephew was an absolute delight. He was almost two and at that perfect innocent age. "Give them all my love please."

"I will, darling. And don't forget: 'Plenty of Fish' or 'Tinder'."

"I won't, Mum. Love you."

"Love you, darling."

Sam hung up. No way was she using an online dating site. She would meet someone through normal channels, the same way she'd met Tony.

*

Sam had changed her mind as soon as she'd put the phone down. She clicked on the button to review her profile. She'd used a photo from the previous summer's holiday in Lanzarote. Hannah had taken the photo and she felt she looked reasonably good in the light pink and white summer dress she was wearing.

Next, she had to select a phrase to specify what she was looking for. The site had suggestions but they all seemed too cheesy or cliched. She didn't want to specify she was looking for a long-term relationship, but neither did she want to meet a man who was only after a one-night stand. She settled on 'interested in meeting up but most important is a good sense of humour'. The site then told her to specify age range, height, all sorts of things, but she kept it simple and hit the 'commit' button.

She sat back. That was interesting but probably fruitless. She would leave it twenty-four hours, then see if there had been any interest.

Her laptop beeped. Then it beeped again. She clicked on the screen to see she had already received two invitations to chat. The first was a very overweight man claiming to be 'just over forty' but looking like he was sixty. The second was a woman with a skinhead haircut and a face covered in tattoos.

Clearly, she did need to be more specific about what she was looking for. She clicked on 'edit my profile' and worked her way through the options.

Chapter 19

Angie was ravenous. Mac had left a two-litre bottle of water two nights earlier, and she still had about a third of it, but the food was long gone. No one else knew where she was and she believed what Mac had said about the remote location. Which meant that, much as she dreaded it, she needed him to return. If he didn't she could die of starvation or lack of water. She was sure it wouldn't be long before the light clicked off for the night. That was the worst time, stuck with her thoughts, unable to read to take her mind away, however fleetingly. She dreaded that light going out.

She had inspected every part of the pigsty looking for a way out, but she'd had no luck. He had been right about the door. It was rock solid and securely attached. The roof had seemed promising. It was corrugated iron bent in a low curve and supported by three metal joists. At first sight it appeared flimsy, but it was so strongly bound to the joists and to the tops of the stone walls that there was no way she could either move it or break it.

For the umpteenth time she recalled the noises she had heard a few days earlier. It sounded as if Mac had hurt that other woman badly, if not killed her. Was he going to return and kill her too? Or with the other woman dead had he fled and left her to die?

Her thoughts were interrupted by his knocking, the casual nature of it at odds with the tension she felt in every bone of her body. She reached for the carrier bag, her hands shaking. Quickly she retrieved the wig and put it on before sliding first the left shoe and then the right one onto her feet. As she finished she heard the bolt slide back then the door was pushed open and Mac walked in. Again he had the knife in one hand and a carrier bag in the other but the first thing she noticed was his face. He had bruising around his left eye and his smile, such a permanent fixture previously, was replaced by a scowl. No, not a scowl. More a pout, like a little boy who had been told off.

"Sit at the head of the bed," he said, and even his voice sounded younger now, more high-pitched than it had been. "I've brought you food and water." He put the carrier bag on the table and began pacing up and down. After a moment he paused and turned to face her. "I've done a very bad thing," he said and raised his hand to his black eye. "I deserved this."

"What happened?" she said.

He ignored her question and began pacing again.

"Did that other woman give you that?" she said. "What did you do to her?"

Again he ignored her. "I should have listened and been more understanding," he said, and she realised he was talking to himself. "But I failed. I let her down. She put her trust in me and I disappointed her. Weeks she was in there and I looked after her, cared for her, brought her food, drinks. I even brought her a couple of presents." He looked at Angie, the little boy's pout gone, replaced by a grin that showed teeth but wasn't a smile. "But it was the wrong thing to do. She was a bad person, Angie, and I should have understood that and acted more quickly. But I'm too nice, that's the problem. Too easy-going, too welcoming, too trusting."

He paused, the toothy non-smile still there and his eyes piercing into hers. "Do you think I'm a nice person Angie?"

She swallowed. "I… ah… well…"

Before she could say more he climbed onto the mattress on his knees. Instinctively, she pressed her head back against the cold stone as he started to move towards her. He grabbed her throat with his left hand, knife still held high in his right. "I want us to be together for a long time," he said, "and I want you to enjoy our time together. But you mustn't make it difficult, otherwise…" He started to squeeze her throat and she found it difficult to breathe. She felt helpless and looked into his eyes, wanting to plead for her life but unable to speak.

He removed his hand from her throat and started stroking her face, his eyes now only a few inches above her. "I like you," he said, and his all-too-genuine smile was back now. "Do you like me?"

She swallowed, not sure what to say.

He slapped her across the face. "I said, do you like me?"

"Yes," she said, her voice quivering.

"Good, good." He rubbed his index finger gently down her right cheek. "If you do as I say, I will look after you and we can be happy together. I want to save you, to let you live. The last thing I want to do is hurt you."

He clambered off the bed and she decided she had to ask, had to find out. "Is that other woman…" She couldn't bring herself to complete the sentence.

"Dead, Angie?" He bent his head to one side. "Yes, she's dead."

She shuddered.

"I should have done it sooner, but killing someone is not easy. I failed to act early enough because I was weak. I need to be stronger." He stared at her face for a moment before continuing. "You look scared Angie but please don't be. I know there are some aspects of your stay here that are a touch uncomfortable but let's make the most of it shall we."

The man was stark raving bonkers.

"In the next few days," he went on, "I'll be bringing you something special."

"What do you mean? Is it…"

He put his hand to her lips.

"Shush, shush. No guesses, darling. Let it be a surprise."

Chapter 20

Luke could not believe what he had just heard. If he requested a member of staff in the police he was always given the option to review the experience and skills of the officers put forward to ensure they were a good match for what he needed. He would be sent their CV and talk to officers they'd worked for or alongside. They might have worked in a different department, but always in the police. Even if they worked in a supporting role they would understand what it meant to keep the law and to always serve in the best interests of the public. He thought back to Tom Harris, to his introverted nature, his thick glasses and his charisma by-pass.

"Are you serious, Josh?" he said. "They're giving us an accountant."

"I'm serious." Josh read from his post-it. "Sam Chambers, thirty-two years old." He looked up. "Suddenly became available yesterday."

Luke felt his hackles rise. This was too much. "We've got two investigations on the go," he said. "The last thing I need is a bloody bean counter."

"Guv, ah…"

"And why has this Sam Chambers become available? Is he useless, lazy or both?"

"I really think…"

"I mean, what bloody use to me is a vacuous number-crunching four-eyes with the personality of an empty ledger."

"Guv!"

Luke realised that Josh was gesturing behind him and turned to see an attractive blonde clutching a notebook and smiling nervously. He held out his hand. "Sorry," he said.

"We've got a bit of a problem." He realised he recognised her. "We met on Monday morning, didn't we? I'm Luke Sackville. How can I help?"

She shook his hand. "Pleased to meet you, Luke."

He could see now that, while attractive, and of much the same height and build, this woman bore only a superficial resemblance to his wife. Jess had had a refined, rather narrow nose, while this woman had a petite button nose, either side of which were a few freckles. Her cheeks were rosier too.

She held up her notebook. "My personality is in here."

"What?"

"It's an empty ledger."

Luke's face looked blank, and then it dawned on him what she meant. "You mean, you're Sam Chambers. But you're not..."

She completed the sentence for him "...a man. No, I'm not a man. Nor do I wear glasses. I can number crunch though."

"Oh, ah, I'm sorry about that."

She looked down at his shoes. "Nice pair of shoes," she said. "Did you buy them at Marks and Spencer?"

"Funnily enough, I did," he said.

He turned to see Josh gawping at each of them in turn. "Cool detective work," he said to Sam. "You'll have to tell me how you did that."

There was a knock at the door and they turned to see a tall, lean, clean-shaven and completely bald black man standing at the office entrance. He wore a white shirt and grey tie under a grey suit with the words 'Filchers Security' stitched onto the jacket.

Josh walked towards him. "Hi, can I help you?" he said.

The man looked at Josh and then at the door. "Is this room three?" he said with a strong Bristol twang.

"That's right. Are you looking for someone?"

"I've been told to come here for my detail this

morning."

"I'm sorry, this is the Ethics Team."

"No, that's right. I was told it was the Ethics Team. I had a phone call from HR yesterday."

Luke stepped forward. "Are you Majid Osman?" he said.

"Yes, that's me. But please call me Maj. Only my mother calls me Majid."

"In that case, you're in the right place, but we…" He paused. The man had something of a spark about him and surely his security experience would be of some value to their work. Besides, did he have any choice? "Come on in, Maj. Welcome to the team." He gestured to the table. "Sam, Maj, please take a seat. We, and when I say we I mean Josh, will get the drinks in and I'll explain what we're up to. We can then decide what our next steps are."

*

Once he'd brought Sam and Maj up to speed, and found out a little about their backgrounds, Luke invited Helen and Josh to join them at the table.

"It's pretty clear," he said, "that on the surface we have a peculiar set of skills and abilities. However, I'm confident we can be a highly effective team and I've got some ideas on how we share the work between us."

He looked first at Helen. She had the most experience of all of them, both in terms of her length of time as a legal advisor and her service at Filchers. She seemed to know everyone in the company and was honest, if sometimes a bit too honest, in her appraisal of them.

"Helen," he said, "I need your input when it comes to contracts and other legal documentation." She nodded. "In addition, I'd like you to be our team co-ordinator, make sure we're working well together and don't miss anything.

In the first instance, I want you to create an evidence board."

"Cool," Josh said. "A crazy wall."

"You're thinking 'Law and Order' again," Luke said before turning his attention back to Helen. "Use those two whiteboards to pull together what we know about Marie Downing and Angie Johnson. It'll help us to visualise who's who apart from anything else."

"Will do," Helen said.

He turned his attention to Maj.

"Maj, can you look into security logs, CCTV, and so on and see what we can piece together about Marie's and Angie's movements?"

"Should be easy enough."

"And Josh..." Josh looked up eagerly. "...I want you to get our drinks and biscuits for meetings, sort out lunches, ensure our expenses are up to date. I'll prepare you a full list."

Josh gawped. "I...ah...what...ah..."

Luke had never seen anyone's expression move as quickly from utter excitement to immense disappointment. "I'm joking," he said. "I want you to log and track every bit of information and evidence we get hold of. And I also want you to continue in your role of documenting our interviews. I've been impressed by your thoroughness."

Josh's cheeks went a slight shade of pink. "Thanks, guv," he said.

"And last, but not least, Sam..." Luke said.

"You want me to crunch numbers?" she said.

He ignored this but the corners of his mouth turned up slightly. "There are a bunch of people we need to speak to," he said. "Too many for me to deal with on my own. I need someone to share that work with and I think you could be ideal."

"Well if you're sure?"

He smiled. "Let's give it a shot shall we," he said then

turned to the others. "Right, team, let's get to it."

"Gucci, guv," Josh said. "After all, you know what they say?"

"What's that?"

"The only way is ethics."

*

By the end of the afternoon, Helen had, with Luke's help, marked up what they knew on the two whiteboards. He'd fed in what they'd learned from the pathologist, but both boards looked painfully bereft of anything resembling a solid lead on either case.

When it came to Marie Downing, his paymaster was Filchers and they wanted him to focus on the three alleged bullies. However, his policing instincts told him he needed to look wider than that and try to find out why she disappeared and who killed her. After all, it was only if he found those things out that he could be certain the bullying was genuine.

As for Angie Johnson, the company was concerned about the alleged bribery and nothing more. However, the girl had vanished and it seemed to be impossible to find out what she had and hadn't done without talking to her. It was vital she was tracked down quickly.

He called Maj over and pointed up at the boards where Helen had added the dates Marie and Angie had last been seen. "Maj," he said. "I want you to look at the CCTV footage for the few days running up to Marie's and Angie's disappearances."

"No problem." He noted down the dates.

"And can you also get hold of their email accounts, have a look through them and see if there's anything relevant there?"

"Can do."

"Great. Also," he gestured to Maj's clothes, "you don't need to wear that tomorrow."

"If you don't mind, I think I will. There are parts of Filchers I can access more easily if I wear this uniform."

Chapter 21

Luke was in the office early. He knew that it was essential that he and his team had job descriptions, if for no other reason than to keep Human Resources off his back. He wasn't going to spend long on them though: half an hour tops.

After twenty minutes he was still defining his own role and responsibilities and fast giving up the will to live. It came as a relief when his phone rang. He looked down to see his daughter's name on the screen.

"Chloe," he said. "A bit early for you isn't it? Are you okay?"

"It's Granddad," Chloe said.

Luke's heart sank. "What's he done now?"

"He's written an article for Tatler."

"Let me guess. He wants photos of us all lounging around the house."

"No." Chloe paused for a second. "You're not going to like this. It's about Mum."

"What!"

"He's written about how he and Grandma welcomed her into the family and made her feel at home." She paused again and Luke could sense the worst was yet to come. "Also about what a tragedy her death had been for them, and how hurt they had been by your refusal to let them go to the funeral."

Luke took a deep breath. "Has it been published yet?"

"No, the editor at the magazine rang me yesterday to see if I would supply a comment to add in from me or Ben or you."

"What did you tell him?"

"It was a her. Fiona Pembridge-Cook. I told her to

email me the draft article and I'd speak to you and then give her a call." Another pause. "I've just received it and you're not going to like it. I'll forward it to you but please, Dad, can you talk to me before you get back to her?"

Luke gave his assurances and promised to ring her later in the morning.

His email pinged a few seconds later and he was about to click on the attachment when Sam came into the office. She nodded hello and he was struck by how tired she looked. She had dark circles under her eyes too. Must be the new job, he thought, and hoped she would be able to cope with the complete change of direction.

"I'm pleased you're here," he said, deciding he would give his father's article the attention it deserved later. "It'll give us a chance to plan our approach before the others get in." He pulled up a chair next to hers and was instantly struck by how nice her perfume was. It was more floral than the Chanel No.5 Jess had been fond of, and had a hint of orange blossom.

He smiled at her and was pleased to see it returned, albeit weakly.

"I want to have a team meeting twice a day," he said, "so that we're all up to speed with progress. It'll be good if you and I get our plans straight beforehand."

"And you're okay with me interviewing people?" she said. "I'm an accountant, not a police officer, so it's not exactly what I'm used to."

"You'll be fine." He smiled again in what he hoped was a reassuring way. She looked on edge and needed to relax if she was going to be effective. "I suggest you have Josh along with you," he said. "He can take notes while you concentrate on finding the right questions to ask. And try not to worry. You'll soon get the hang of it."

"All right, I'll give it a go. Where do I start?"

"I'd like you to focus on Marie Downing. She may or may not have been forced to write that note about bullying.

Either way, you need to talk to the three people she named and see what they know. I also want you to find out more about Marie herself, where she lives, who last saw her, any strong relationships, and so on."

"Won't the police be doing that?"

"You're right, but they'll be doing it from a different angle. Our investigations can complement theirs if we approach it from the Filchers perspective. Pete Gilmore is the DI on the case and he's promised to keep me in the loop so as soon as I hear anything I'll pass it on to you."

"Great."

"For my part, I'm going to get to the bottom of Angie Johnson's disappearance. I've got a couple of ideas that I want to work on." He heard a noise and turned to see Helen and Maj. They were laughing.

"Hey Luke," Maj said, "are you a City fan?"

"Rugby's more my game," Luke said.

"Your mistake. Just found out we both support the Cider Army."

Josh appeared behind them. "I'm with you, guv," he said. "I try to go to the Rec at least once a month. Bath are playing Exeter on Sunday." He hesitated. "Uh… I've got a spare ticket. I don't suppose you fancy going?"

He looked so excited that Luke thought why not. He hadn't been since his playing days and it might do him some good. "What time's the game?" he said.

Josh's smile stretched from ear to ear. "Three."

"Okay then."

"Gucci. South Gate, say quarter to?"

"I'll see you there." He returned his attention to the other team members. "I think we need to have twice daily catch-ups. It's eight-thirty now. I want us to meet at this time every day and then again at four-thirty. Is that okay with all of you?" They nodded. He looked up at the whiteboard and they followed his gaze. "Not much up there at the moment," he said. "Two cases; unconnected other than the fact that both women worked for Filchers."

"And both were whispers," Josh said.

He was off on one again, Luke thought. "You mean they were quiet talkers?"

"No, not that. But they both went AWOL didn't they?"

"Marie did. Angie was suspended. But what does whispering have to do with it?"

"Well, they both went missing, didn't they?" Josh looked around at the others but no one seemed to be following his train of thought. "So that means they're…" He hesitated, then realisation dawned and his cheeks went the shade of pale beetroot.

"You mean mispers," Luke said.

Helen let out an involuntary snort.

"He's right though," Maj said, coming to his rescue. "They both went missing so they have got that in common."

"Yes, you're right, Josh," Luke said and Josh's smile reappeared. "Add that to the board please, Helen." He paused for a second. "It may be relevant, but for the moment we should treat these as separate investigations. However, it's important we keep our eyes and ears open for anything that might link them."

"Can I suggest codenames for the investigations?" Josh said, and this time they all gave him a questioning look. "Okay, okay," he said, raising both hands in mock surrender.

"Sam and Josh are going to focus on Marie," Luke said. "They're going to start by interviewing the people she supposedly accused of bullying her."

"Sorry, Helen," Sam said.

"No problem," Helen said.

"Helen," Luke said, "I want you to keep the whiteboard updated as and when we get extra information in, but can you also continue looking at the documents associated with Project Iceberg?" She nodded her agreement and he turned to Maj. "Maj, can you find out if any security records shine a light on what happened to either Marie or Angie when they left Filchers on the day they became…" He looked directly at Josh and lowered his voice. "…whispers?" Josh's cheeks went red again. "Focus particularly on CCTV."

"Right, Luke," Maj said.

"We'll get together again at half four, but if you find out anything significant in the meantime please let Helen know and she'll add it to the whiteboard." He looked around the team and could see they were all eager to get started.

"Be safe everyone," Josh said, and there was a collective groan around the table.

Chapter 22

As soon as the meeting was over, Sam, Josh and Helen left to discuss the bullying accusation, while Maj stayed behind to ask Luke a couple of questions. He wanted to clarify his boundaries, reasonable given the newness of his job.

Luke was beginning to believe the five of them could be a highly effective team. They certainly had more get-up-and-go than many of the trained officers Luke had had working for him at Avon and Somerset. He had no problem leaving them to get on with their tasks while he concentrated on trying to locate Angie Johnson.

First though…

He opened the top drawer of his desk, shuffled around for a moment or so and sighed when he realised he was bang out of snacks. Not to worry. The M&S on Brookbank Avenue had a small food section.

He grabbed his coat and made his way out of the building, nodding hello to a couple of people as he went. It was a chilly day, not unusual for April, and he walked briskly. Once there he perused the aisles, paid for a 5-pack of Twix and almost collided with a bulging slab of biceps and testosterone as he turned away from the till.

"Ah," Glen said. "So pleased I bumped into you."

"I wish I could say the same," Luke said, then paused before asking, "Have you still got forty staff?"

Glen's eyebrows furrowed in confusion. "Yes. Why?"

"It doesn't matter." Luke moved to walk away but Glen held out his hand to stop him. "I wanted a word actually," he said.

"What is it?"

"A couple of things. A favour for you and a favour for me. You scratch my back, I scratch…"

"I get the picture."

"I want to give you some advice."

"I always value your advice," Luke said, not bothering to hide the sarcasm in his tone.

"Good, good," Glen went on, as ever oblivious to anything that even bordered on the subtle. "That man Majid Osman. You need to watch him."

"And why is that, Glen?"

"He's trouble, that's why."

Luke suspected he knew what was coming. "Please explain."

"He's too clever for his own good."

"I thought as much," Luke said, half to himself.

"He tried to mess with my rotas by suggesting changes."

"Improvements?"

Glen ignored the question. "It's not his place to change what I've set up. He was out of line. I suggest you keep a close eye on him."

"And that's your favour to me?"

Glen nodded. "A friendly warning, that's all."

Luke shook his head. "Warning noted. And you have a favour to ask of me?"

"Yes. It's personal actually."

This was intriguing. Luke had never thought of Glen as having a personal side.

"You've run out of steroids?"

Glen grunted. "I have a hobby."

"The gym?"

"A second hobby." He paused. "I'm an actor."

Luke swallowed a laugh. "An actor? Really? Stage or film?"

"On stage."

"I see. Is it a big part?"

"Um, ah, fairly."

Luke had never seen Glen blush before, but there was a

definite rosy tinge to his cheeks now.

"And how can I help?"

"I've got a performance on Friday week and it clashes with the Annual Security Awards and Filchers has to be represented."

"Can't one of your team stand in for you?"

"No. It's a rank thing. Has to be a 'Head of'."

Luke sighed. "Okay, I'll do it."

"Thanks."

"So what's your role?"

Glen looked at his watch. "Oh, look at the time," he said. "I have to go."

He marched towards the food aisle leaving Luke perplexed. Glen's nature was to boast about everything so why was he suddenly so shy about his acting? He decided he would ask around and see if he could find out more.

Once back at the office, one Twix already consumed en route, he put the remaining bars in the top drawer of his desk before pulling out his phone and ringing the number Eric Hughes had given him. It was answered immediately, and the accent took Luke by surprise.

"Danny Ogletree."

Deep South definitely. Alabama maybe. "Hi," Luke said. "I'm Luke Sackville from Filchers. I wonder if…"

"Woah, Mr Sackville. You stop right there ya hear."

"Please don't worry, Mr Ogletree. This isn't about the MI6 bid, well not directly anyway."

"It isn't? What's it about then?"

"It's about a missing woman."

"Who?"

"Angie Johnson."

"Angie's missing?" He sounded genuinely concerned. "Well look, if Angie's missing then that sure is deeply worrying but I don't know how I can help y'all."

"I've got a copy of her email to you, Mr Ogletree. And I think she may have gone missing because of the deal you and she had."

"Which email is that?"

"Were there many between you?"

"Not many, but a few. She was the main, in fact the only, point of contact with Bannermans for the bid. Those were confidential exchanges though. How did you get copies?"

Luke ignored the question and looked down at the printout in front of him. "In one email," he said, "she says to you, and I quote, 'Thanks for confirming you received the details I sent of our innovative solution. However, please can you confirm the share would be as discussed? To date I have seen a sum that is far below what I had expected.' Do you recall that?"

"Yes, I remember it. But as I said it's highly confidential and I'm not willing to discuss it."

"Please can I remind you that a woman has disappeared, Mr Ogletree. I'm concerned for her welfare."

"I understand that but what's the email got to do with her being missing?"

"She was suspended because of the email."

"You gotta be kidding me." He sounded genuinely shocked. "Why would she be suspended because of that?"

"Isn't it obvious? If she sent you the most valuable elements of Filchers' solution in exchange for money, then that is very much a sackable offence."

"But she didn't."

It was Luke's turn to be surprised.

"Please explain," he said.

*

Luke rang Eric Hughes as soon as he hung up. Luckily he was in and agreed to come straight over.

"What is it?" he said as he sat down. "Have you found

Angie?"

"Unfortunately not," Luke said. "However, I managed to get hold of Danny Ogletree."

"Really?" Eric said. He looked down at his hands and started to twiddle with his wedding ring.

"He told me something very interesting."

Eric mumbled something.

"What was that?" Luke said.

"Sorry. I, ah…" He looked up. "Did he confirm what had happened?"

"He did."

Luke looked into the man's eyes. "Eric, tell me the truth about the email."

"June gave it to me. But I told you that yesterday."

"What about the content?"

"What do you mean?" He returned to fiddling with his wedding ring. "It seemed pretty clear what Angie was up to so I passed it to HR."

"You asked her to write it didn't you?"

"What? No."

"That's what Angie told Danny."

"But why would I? You've read it. She was taking money in exchange for information."

It could be that Eric was a very good actor but Luke was inclined to believe he was genuinely confused. He needed to probe more to be certain. "But that's it Eric," he said. "She wasn't taking money was she?"

"I don't understand."

"You wanted a joint proposition to MI6, didn't you? Filchers and Bannerdown working together, using the best elements of your solution alongside the best of theirs and sharing the revenue."

"That's rubbish!"

"And you used Angie as the front person to negotiate. She was sharing parts of your solution to impress them. But it was all at your behest. And when she referred to the share not being as discussed she meant the share of revenues between the two companies, not money she had been given."

"Nonsense."

"It wasn't going to plan though, was it? Danny Ogletree wanted Bannerdown to be the lead partner, and was insisting they take three-quarters of the revenue, so you decided to back out."

Eric was staring open-mouthed at him now.

"So you…" Luke pointed his finger at Eric, "…decided to throw Angie to the wolves. That's why you and June put this plan together."

"June? What's she got to do with it?"

"You thought you'd kill two birds with one stone, didn't you? Blame Angie for your cocked-up attempt at partnership and at the same time get a promotion for your lover."

"I've never heard anything so ridiculous."

Luke had been watching the other man carefully but there were no unusual twitches or glances. Eric was wringing his hands together but that was the pressure of the situation.

"You and June are in a relationship aren't you?" he said.

"That's none of your business."

"I think you need to come clean, Eric. Angie has disappeared remember? You don't have anything to do with that do you?"

Eric stood up. "You're so wrong about this."

"About your relationship with June Jefferson?"

"Well no, but…" He sat down again and took a deep breath. Again there were no micro-expressions that told of a falsehood. "I know how this must look, but it wasn't me."

"What do you mean?"

"If Danny says that was what Angie said then I believe him. No reason for him to lie after all. But I didn't put her up to it."

"Who was it then?"

"I don't know, but it must have been someone higher up than me."

"Any idea who?"

"I don't think it would have been anyone directly above me. The Government Sector Head left everything to me so I'd be very surprised if it was her. I was surprised that Marketing and HR were both very interested though. The Heads of both those departments asked a few questions that I found a little odd but I just put it down to idle interest because the contract had such big potential."

Chapter 23

The meeting room was in the Executive Suite, a favour to Josh from Gloria, Edward Filcher's PA, which meant it was more stylish, and definitely more comfortable, than any of the rooms on the other floors would have been.

Sam admired the photos on two of the walls. They showed the early days, back in the eighties when Ambrose Filcher's new company had taken on the more peripheral processes from first Unilever and then other large manufacturing conglomerates. There were also a couple of photos of Filchers staff in the finance department at the Foreign Office in the early 1990s. It had been the company's first government contract.

She sat down on one of two red leather armchairs in front of a low coffee table. Josh sat next to her on the other one while Helen was opposite on a matching Chesterfield.

"I'm sorry, Helen," Sam said. "I'm sure the bullying accusations are nonsense, but I need you to tell me anything you know about Marie Downing, and why she might think such a thing."

Helen took a deep breath. "I'll help as much as I can," she said, "but I'm a wee bit baffled by it to be honest."

"Why don't you start by telling us what you know about her?"

"Okay." Helen paused for a second. "I first met Marie nearly four years ago. She was new to Filchers and came along to a meeting as Marketing's representative, then joined the team for three or four months until our bid was submitted. I remember being struck by how good her ideas were. I think she'd come from a management consultancy."

"Accenture," Josh said, referring to his notes. "She

joined us exactly four years ago."

"That makes sense," Helen said, then turned back to Sam. "What was immediately apparent was her assertiveness. She was never aggressive, but she was very good at getting her own way."

"Manipulative?" Sam prompted.

"I wouldn't go that far. But she could be very persuasive."

"A strong character then?"

"Definitely, but we always got on really well and I'm baffled by her saying I bullied her."

"Did you ever argue?"

"We had one or two differences of opinion, but they were always resolved amicably and they were only about business."

"Did she argue with other people?"

"A fair bit, yes. She was like a dog with a bone when she got an idea in her head, and that sometimes caused friction."

"Any specifics?"

Helen sat back in the chair and thought for a few seconds. "I can think of three significant disagreements," she said. "First off, she took issue with our Bid Director Harry Beckett over the perceived lack of priority he was giving to Marketing." She waited for Josh to write this down before continuing. "She also got very annoyed when HR refused to give her a Marketing Assistant. That one went all the way to James McDonald, and I heard she had a run-in with him. Lastly, she had an argument with the team's accountant over budgets."

"Do you know the accountant's name?" Josh asked.

Helen gave them the name and Josh jotted it down.

"I know him," Sam said. "He's another very strong character."

Helen smiled. "It's funny," she said.

"What?"

"My next job after this meeting is to put myself up."

Sam frowned. "Put yourself up?" she said.

"Of course," Josh said, and he was smiling too now. "Helen's going to get her own entry on the crazy wall."

"Did you work with Marie again?" Sam said.

"No," Helen said. "And we didn't socialise together either. We nodded hello and exchanged pleasantries if we saw each other after that bid, which we won by the way, but I wouldn't say we were friends. We were colleagues who got on reasonably well."

"I see." Sam thought for a moment. "When did you last see her?"

"A couple of months ago. She was rushing somewhere and nodded hello as we passed."

"And there's no other information you can give us that might be useful?"

"Not really, no."

*

Interviewing Angelica Reid was not as straightforward. The girl at reception had told them she worked part-time and had gone home at eleven. However, Sam was keen to make a good first impression with her new boss, especially after she had been accused of being lazy in her previous position, and decided they should call on Angelica at her house.

"I want to see her today," she whispered to Josh as they stood by the entrance door. "But I don't want to ask HR for her address."

"No probs," he said. "Wait here."

He turned and walked back to the reception desk, and it was as if a beam of light had hit the girl who had taken over Angelica's duties. She smiled at him as he bent over the counter, and after a few seconds he opened his notebook and began jotting something down.

As Josh walked back to Sam she could see the beam of light had hit him too.

"Did you get the address?" she said.

"Definito," he said. "I'm picking Leanne up at seven. But don't worry," he added quickly, holding his hand up, "I got Angelica's address as well. She's in Walcot. We can get the number 19 bus."

Half an hour later they arrived at Walcot Yard, where Angelica's was the end house in a small development of modern terraced properties. Sam rang the bell and they heard voices inside then a boy of no more than ten or eleven opened the door. He looked at Sam, then at Josh, then back at Sam.

"Are you Plymouth Brethren?" he said.

Before Sam could answer a woman rushed through from the back room. Sam recognised her immediately.

"Daniel," Angelica said, looking down at the boy. "The Brethren won't be coming again." She shooed him away, then looked up at Sam. "Sorry about that. He gets a bit carried away sometimes. How can I help you?" She hesitated and looked from Sam to Josh then back again. Her eyebrows went up. "You're from Filchers aren't you?"

"Yes," Sam said. "Sorry to disturb you at home. Would you mind if we asked you a few questions?"

"How intriguing. Of course not, no. Please come in."

She showed them into a lounge that was immaculately clean. It was stylish too, with a Rossiters cream sofa and chair backing onto walls that were decorated with four matching pieces of abstract art. There was the obligatory TV but it was flat against the wall and had minimal impact. No books were in evidence but on either side of the modern electric fire were a variety of ornaments on glass shelving.

They introduced themselves and Sam declined the offer of a cup of tea, much to Josh's evident disappointment.

"We won't keep you long," she said. "It's a little sensitive. Do you mind if Josh takes notes?"

"Not at all," Angelica said.

"We're here about Marie Downing. Do you know her?"

"I certainly do. Is she okay?"

"I'm afraid not." Sam hesitated, seeing the concern on Angelica's face. "I'm sorry to tell you she's dead."

Angelica's lips opened and she turned her head to stare out of the window. After a few seconds she looked back at them, and Sam could see moistness in the corners of her eyes.

"That poor girl," Angelica said. "She can only have been in her twenties. Was she in a car accident?"

Sam hesitated, unsure how much to reveal. She could see that the other woman was fighting back tears. "I'm really sorry to have to give you this awful news," she said. "Were you close?"

"I wouldn't say we were close, but we certainly got on well. A few months ago I had a problem at work and she helped me to fight my corner." She smiled. "She can be a real terrier when she gets going, and her support helped me no end." She paused, and the smile vanished. "Sweet Jesus," she said. "I can't believe she's dead."

Sam could see her mind switch gears as she moved from the image of her friend being dead to the two of them being there in the room.

"But why are you here to ask me questions?" Angelica said. "We weren't that close."

Sam swallowed. "Angelica," she said, "a note was found next to Marie and your name was on it."

Angelica's eyes furrowed. "How odd."

"The note says that you and two others bullied Marie."

"Bullied Marie!" Angelica shook her head. "But that's nonsense. I don't think we've ever even argued. She very kindly helped me out and after that we got together for lunch fairly regularly. We were friends, that's all."

"It may be that it's connected to that problem she helped you out with," Sam said.

"I don't see how."

"Perhaps you could tell us what it was though, in case it's relevant?"

"There's no harm I suppose." Angelica thought for a minute before continuing. "When I joined Filchers I was clear on how important my family were, and they promised I could change my shift to cope with any change in the children's school hours. So when Daniel moved up to big school I asked to be moved to morning duties so that I could drop him off for breakfast club and then pick him up at three in the afternoon. All I got was a point-blank refusal, but Marie took it upon herself to make sure they lived up to their promise. She went directly to the Head of HR for me and they agreed to the change after all."

"That would be James McDonald?" Sam said.

"Yes."

"And who was your manager at the time?"

"Roger Ackerman was the guy who first offered me the job, but he retired two years ago. My boss now is Sharon Hislop."

Sam was pleased to see Josh was jotting all this down. "Was it Sharon who refused the change?" she said.

"Not really. I'm pretty sure she passed it straight up the line and just relayed the reply back to me. I remember she was embarrassed about the whole thing."

*

"A couple of things for the crazy wall there," Josh said as they walked into the Ethics office.

"Yes," Sam said. "There's clearly a link between Marie and both Helen and Angelica, but I don't believe it's anything to do with bullying. So the big question is why their names were on that note." She turned to see Josh bent forward over his lap, trying to conceal a smile.

"It's hardly a laughing matter," she said.

"It's not that," he said looking up at her. "It's you."

"What about me?"

"You were really good in there. You were asking questions like, well, like a real detective."

Sam smiled inwardly. Sacked accountant to sounding like a detective, all within a couple of days. Things might be looking up after all. "Anyway," she said, determined to stop any blushes before they began. "Next on the list is Emily Parker. Do we know anything about her?"

"Just a sec." He sat down at one of the desks, logged onto the system, and tapped away at the keys for a few seconds. "Found her," he said. "She's a looker."

Sam looked over his shoulder to see a girl's photo on the screen. Emily Parker probably was attractive, certainly to a testosterone-fuelled post-adolescent like Josh, but hers was a brash and obvious beauty. She was blonde, almost certainly dyed blonde, with big blue mascara-laden eyes and perfectly sculpted eyebrows. Not much out of her teens, the caked-on foundation and heavy eye makeup and lip gloss made her all but indistinguishable from a billion other girls.

"Maybe you could fit her in tonight after you see Leanne?" she said.

Sam was pleased to see him squirm slightly at this.

"I meant…" he said then paused as he realised she was teasing him. "I'll see if she's available."

"What's her job?" Sam said.

He clicked a few buttons. "Works in the call centre. Joined two years ago. She's only twenty-one but is one of the supervisors so doing all right for herself." He paused. "Ah, here's her extension." He picked up the office phone and dialled a number. It was answered immediately, and Sam could hear a man's voice at the other end but couldn't make out the words.

"Hi," Josh said. "I'm Josh Ogden. I was wondering if I could speak to Emily Parker... No, this is about work... I see... When will that be?... Right, thanks." He hung up.

"Well?" Sam prompted.

"She's not in today. Called in sick, but expected back on Monday. Do you think we should contact her at home?"

"We'll check with Luke when he comes in," Sam said, "but it doesn't seem fair, not if she's ill. I suggest we wait until after the weekend."

Chapter 24

No one challenged him when he waltzed into the security team's office, his uniform giving him access privileges that a suited Maj could only have dreamed of. He hoped he didn't run into Glen Baxter or one of the Shift Supervisors. They knew he'd been transferred to Ethics and would chuck him out in the blink of an eye. So far, though, he'd been lucky. Mind you, Glen was known to hang out on the Executive Floor whenever he could, so the chance of seeing him in the bowels of the building was minimal.

The office was in the basement, although 'office' was over-stating it. It was tiny. In the corner opposite the door was a kettle, coffee and mug area, for those caffeine-fuelled drinks that kept you alive when you'd been wandering the corridors doing nothing all night, and in the middle of the room there was a small formica table with four plastic chairs around it. But that was about it if you discounted the tyre company calendars of topless women on the walls.

All the security guards were men and had been for all the time Maj had worked at Filchers. There was nothing formally set down to stop women from being recruited, but everyone knew that Glen Baxter, and his predecessor before him, would never let someone of the fair sex into their holy empire.

Maj walked over to the kettle and flicked it on. There was a noise behind him and he turned to see Abdi Godane, decked up in identical gear and looking absolutely shattered. He was also tall and lean but sported an expansive mop of curly black hair and was a few years younger.

"Hey, Abdi," he said, and they fist-pumped. "How are you doing?"

"Knackered, my friend," Abdi said, fighting a yawn. He

had an even deeper voice than Maj and there was still a trace of his Somalian accent.

"It's Omar," he went on. "He's not sleeping. Which means I'm not sleeping. What a pair of lungs that boy has." He paused and rubbed his eyes. "And I'm on monitor duty until six then on patrol. Honestly, Maj, I don't know if I can manage three hours in there today."

Manning the monitor room was mind-blowingly boring. Everyone hated it and Abdi was no exception.

"Tell you what," Maj said. "I'm helping out with a security investigation today and my boss is right chilled. Why don't you do the first hour then I'll cover three 'til four, give you a chance to catch forty winks?"

"What about Jimmy?" Abdi said. Jimmy Kenny was one of the shift supervisors.

"You know him," Maj said. "Lazy sod probably won't even check on you. And if he does I'll just say you've popped to the loo and text you to come straight back."

"If you're sure man, that would be ace."

"No problem. I'll see you at three."

*

At five to three, Maj popped his head around the door of the monitor room and was pleased to see that Abdi was still awake and, even better, was alone.

Abdi stood up immediately. "Thanks again," he said.

Maj waved away his apologies. "Just grab some sleep, Abdi," he said. "And don't worry if it's a few minutes past four. I'll be fine here. Anything I should know?"

"No, been as boring as ever. Usual stuff, no incursions. All barriers and entries working. Cameras too." He yawned. "Okay if I go."

"Sure thing."

"I owe you, man."

"No problem." Maj closed the door after his friend and leaned back against it. He knew this room oh so well, had spent hundreds of mind-numbingly boring hours staring at screens in it but now, well now he felt like a man with a mission.

The room was about ten feet by eight feet, and half of it was taken up by a metal desk stretching across the entire width. There were no windows and the overhead lights were dim. The main source of light came from twelve monitors mounted to the wall behind the desk in three rows of four. They were set as default to monitor the main external entrances, but there was a multitude of additional internal cameras covering all shared areas and corridors.

The system was only two years old and had a bunch of clever features. Footage was stored in the cloud, so there was no need to change storage media or perform backups, and there were clever triggers built in to, for example, warn if there was an unexpected incursion. And it could all be accessed from your own laptop, but not if you'd been transferred and had your access rights taken away. No, if you didn't have access rights then the only way to view footage was to be on monitor room duty.

Maj had an hour, which wasn't really enough so he needed to be smart. He took out his pad and checked on the dates. The first thing was to use 'Otto', the system which logged when individuals entered and left the building, to check when Angie Johnson had been at Filchers in the week leading up to her disappearance. Then he would look at CCTV footage for those days, starting with the day she went AWOL and working backwards. This should enable him to piece together what she'd done and who she'd been with. He'd give it half an hour then do the same for Marie Downing.

*

Maj was shocked when he looked at his watch and saw that forty minutes had passed. He needed to move on to Marie Downing before he ran out of time.

He'd made several pages of notes for Angie Johnson but there was nothing that stood out, no unusual encounters or angry corridor meetings. He'd seen her leave after being suspended and had forwarded the footage to his own email address, but the meeting room itself had no CCTV so all it showed was her storming down a couple of corridors before exiting the building.

He checked on the date for Marie's disappearance and looked her up on 'Otto'. She'd left Filchers by the main entrance at five thirty-three and it didn't take him long to find the camera footage. There was no sound, but it looked like the lady on reception smiled and said goodbye but only got a cursory wave of the hand. Marie kept her head down and something in the way she held herself made her look like she was upset or possibly angry. He made a note to check who was on reception so that he could talk to them about it.

Maj traced Marie's progress back to the time she left Marketing to go home. The Marketing department was an open-plan office and had a couple of cameras focused on it, one of which covered her cubicle. He went rapidly backwards through the footage, at a rate that meant each minute was passing by in two seconds, keeping his eyes peeled for anything out of the ordinary. Marie had her back to the camera but she was slightly side-on. He could see the laptop open in front of her and she seemed focused on the screen, her head moving slightly but not jerkily even on fast rewind. He continued backwards for a minute, half an hour in real-time. Nothing out of the ordinary, he was getting nowhere with this.

With a start, he paused the footage. There was something odd but he couldn't put his finger on it. He looked at his watch again. Only fifteen minutes until Abdi was due to return. He needed to press on. He clicked on fast rewind again. A few more seconds passed, several minutes for Marie. Then it hit him. He pressed play.

Marie wasn't doing anything. That's what was wrong. She wasn't pressing keys, wasn't on the phone, wasn't talking to anyone. All she seemed to be doing was staring at the laptop's screen and occasionally reaching for a tissue. She had been upset by something. That explained the tissues and the cursory wave when she left to go home. With a growing sense of excitement, Maj pressed rewind again. He needed to find out what had upset her.

It didn't take long to find the cause of her distress. It had happened about ten minutes after she'd had lunch, and what he saw shocked him to the core. He closed the laptop and took a deep intake of breath. He needed to think for a moment, plan his next steps. Had what he had seen been enough, or did he need to go further back, look at what happened in the morning? He looked at his watch. Shit, it was five to.

There was a creak behind him.

"Abdi, you're early," he said, his mind a million miles away, but it wasn't Abdi who walked through the door.

"What the fuck," said Glen Baxter, "are you doing in here?"

Chapter 25

"I think we had better begin," Luke said, and looked at his watch again. Twenty-to-five and still no Maj. It didn't bode well for his first full day in the team. "I'll start."

"Sorry, Luke," came a voice behind him.

He turned to see Maj striding into the room, but rather than looking apologetic, he was smiling. "I've made some progress," he said, looking straight at Luke. He pulled up a chair next to Josh and nodded hello to him then to Sam and Helen who sat opposite.

Luke turned his attention to Sam. "Sam, how did you get on in your interviews with Helen and her fellow bullies?"

"Hey," Helen said.

Sam shared what she'd found out. "So in conclusion," she said, "I don't think the accusations are genuine but I still need to talk to Emily Parker and she was off sick today so that will have to wait until Monday."

"Any thoughts on why that letter named those three as bullies?"

"Not really."

"Anyone else?" Luke said looking at the others.

"No," Josh said, "but there's got to be a connection hasn't there? I mean between Marie's death and those three people being named."

"Very good, Josh," Luke said. "And I want each of you to think on that over the weekend. Why would someone fake a suicide and include a note that named those particular individuals as bullies?" He turned to Maj. "Last but not least, Maj," he said, "it seems like you've made some sort of breakthrough. What have you got to tell us?"

"I found out why Marie Downing may have gone

AWOL," he said. "Here, let me show you." He went over to his desk and signed into the laptop. The others stood behind him as he went into his emails and clicked on an attachment. A video started and showed three women and one man sitting at desks in separate cubicles in an open-plan office. Maj pointed to the girl on the left. "That's Marie," he said. "Watch carefully."

She was tapping away at a keyboard, and although the screen wasn't visible and there was no audio everything seemed normal. After twenty seconds or so she turned towards someone invisible to the camera, probably standing below and to the left of it Luke thought, and said a few words then smiled before turning back to the laptop.

"Here it comes," Maj said a few seconds later.

A figure appeared from out of sight and then walked away from the camera towards Marie. It was clearly a man, and he was wearing a dark suit, but he was only visible from the rear and his head was out of view. She turned, smiling, but her smile disappeared when she saw who it was. The man bent over to whisper something in her ear. They could see his head now, his hair short, brown and very neat. A few seconds passed then the man stood up again and walked away from Marie and the camera, his face still not visible. Marie put her face in her hands then grabbed a tissue and turned back to the screen.

"What do you think?" Maj said.

"It's interesting," Luke said.

"I think she was upset about it for the rest of the day," Maj went on. "I watched the next couple of hours before she left and she didn't touch the keyboard once."

"And?"

"Watch," Maj said.

He tapped away on the keyboard, rewinding the tape to just before the man arrived and zooming in on the bottom half of Marie's body.

They all watched closely. The man walked towards

Marie and then stopped. After a few seconds, a hand appeared and he pushed it under Marie's skirt and up the inside of her thigh.

"My god," Helen exclaimed.

"No wonder she was upset," Sam said. "That poor girl."

"Well done," Luke said. "The trick now is finding out who that man is." He looked at Maj, who was still smiling. "You know who he is don't you?"

"Oh yes, Luke. I know him very well." He pointed to the screen. "That man…"

He was interrupted by a pounding at the Ethics Room door, followed by a dramatic entry as a red-faced Glen Baxter marched in.

"What do you want?" Luke said.

Glen marched up to him. "I want you to sort out your bloody team, Luke, that's what I want." He gestured over Luke's shoulder at Maj before continuing. "Your new recruit broke into our security office. He acted illegally, conned one of my team, used false credentials to… to…." He spluttered to a halt. "This is not good enough. A week on the job and you're already crossing lines. I might have known it. You wait until Filcher hears about this."

"Glen," Luke said, "why don't you sit down a moment."

"No, I…" He sat as a chair was pushed up against the back of his knees.

"Thanks, Josh," Luke said.

"No problems, guv," Josh said. "Shall we, uh…" he gestured to the door.

"Good idea." He turned back to Glen as the others filed out of the room. "Was Maj a good security officer, Glen?"

"That's not the point."

"I believe it's very much the point," Luke paused for a second before continuing. "Maj has initiative, and he used it to find information that is going to be crucial in finding out what happened to Marie Downing."

"What did he find?"

"We were just getting to that when you stormed in, Glen, but to be honest it's not relevant. What I'm saying is that Maj is a bright cookie. So what I'm wondering is why you released him. Don't get me wrong, I'm pleased to have him on my team, but I'm intrigued. Why would you let someone as capable as him go to another team? It can't just be because he suggested rota changes."

"There were reasons," he said.

"What reasons?"

"I can't, I mean I shouldn't..." Glen stood up and Luke could see the cogs turning as he realised he had lost the high ground and needed to do something to regain it. "That's not the point," he blustered. "I don't want you and your team, ah..."

"Doing their jobs," Luke offered.

"Stepping outside their boundaries," Glen said.

"Or you'll tell Filcher?"

"That was just, I mean." He raised his hand and wagged his finger up into Luke's face. "I've got power here, Luke, so watch your step."

"And you've got a bigger team."

"Yes, I've got a bigger team," Glen said, the sarcasm lost on him. "So, ah, watch your step."

"You already said that."

"Exactly." Glen waved his finger once more then turned and marched to the door. He wrenched the door open and marched through, attempting to slam it on his way out but defeated by the strongly sprung hinges.

Luke shook his head. Amazing he thought, how little the guy had changed. He rang Josh and told him they could return to the office. As soon as they re-entered Maj started apologising and Josh asked what had happened.

"It was something and nothing," Luke said. "Maj, who was it you saw with Marie?"

"Dale Cartwright," Maj said. "He's one of the shift

supervisors in Security. Been here a couple of years and a bit of a loner. Friendly though and to be honest seeing that," he gestured to the screen, "surprises me. He always seems a pretty decent guy. Stood up for me once with Baxter too."

"Well done, Maj," Luke said.

"Want me to get hold of Dale Cartwright?" Josh said. "Set up an interro… ah, interview?"

Luke thought for a moment. "Good idea, Josh, but no," he said. "I want to take this more informally, find a way of doing it without Glen knowing." He addressed his next comment to Maj. "Are you on well enough terms to arrange to meet him for a coffee?"

"Yes, sure," Maj said.

"Then do that." He turned to Sam. "And Sam," he said, "I'd like you to accidentally come across them in the canteen and ask if you can join them. After what we've seen on screen I'd like to know how he reacts."

"Okay," she said.

He addressed his next comments to all of them. "I think it would be good to have an out-of-office get-together. I don't suppose any of you are free to come around to mine for a few drinks and nibbles this Sunday, early evening? No bother if you can't."

"That would be great, guv," Josh said.

"Count me in," Helen said.

"Me too," added Sam.

"I'll have a word with the Mrs," Maj said, "but I'm pretty sure I can make it too."

"Great."

*

It was only when the team had left that Luke remembered his father's Tatler article, although to be fair the thought of it had been niggling away at him ever since Chloe's phone call. He didn't know what was worse, his father's claim to have welcomed Jess into their home or the lie that he and his mother had been mortally upset by her death.

He clicked on the attachment in his daughter's email and was surprised to see a fully formatted and illustrated article pop up on his screen. He had expected a words-only document but this had a heading, sub-heading and photos. It looked ready to go. The title was *'Upstairs Downstairs in Real Life'* beneath which in slightly smaller script were the words *'The Duke and Duchess of Dorset embraced a servant but found joy and tragedy'*. Underneath was a photo of his mother and father sitting in armchairs on the croquet lawn at Borrowham Hall, the curving drive and Elizabethan stately pile behind them. Standing next to them was Jess, elegant as ever in a simple green summer dress. All three were smiling but the strain on his wife's face was evident. It was the first and only time he had taken her to meet his parents, and it was after this meeting that they had made it clear to him what they thought of her.

He started to read and couldn't believe the sheer hypocrisy and lies. How could his father bring himself to do this? The answer came to him. It was simple. Kudos. His father had always sought the admiration of his peers, in both senses of the word. He loved nothing more than to host a grand house party and boast about the size of his estate or his meetings with minor royalty. Luke could all too easily picture him in the Peers' Dining Room at the House of Lords talking about the Tatler article and expounding on his ability to mix with 'the common people'.

But this time he had gone too far. He rang Chloe. "I've read it," he said as soon as she answered.

"I can tell you're angry, Dad," she said, then paused before adding, "What are you going to do? Are you going to ring the editor?"

"I haven't decided," Luke lied. He knew very well what

he was going to do and his parents were not going to like it one bit. "Leave it with me, and I'll let you know after the weekend."

Chapter 26

Dale Cartwright was a scumbag, there was no doubt about it. Sam wondered how men like that could live with themselves. Clearly, he got some kind of kick from assaulting women, but did he think about the impact it would have on them, that they would feel dirty and abused, that it would keep them awake at night? No, of course he didn't.

Tosser.

She took another sip of her prosecco and decided to forget about Dale Cartwright until Monday. It was Friday night and she was alone and she needed to relax and unwind. The absence of Tony was a bonus and she wished she had ended it sooner. He hadn't tried to ring her since she'd dumped him, which meant the message must have finally got through his thick skull, thank goodness.

She idly clicked on her dating app and saw that she had 3 new messages, from men called Doug, Paul and Jeremy. She had had a couple the day before after she'd revised her profile and they'd been interesting but not worth pursuing. Perhaps one of these three would be her type and looking for the same kind of relationship she was, not just for a quick lay.

She clicked on Doug's profile. He was certainly fit, in both senses of the word, but not modest. His photo showed a bronzed torso over tight denim jeans, and he described himself as 'a builder with aspirations to be a writer'. Intriguing, she thought with a smile. She clicked on his message. '*Hi Sam,*' it said. '*Want to get together for a good time? I bet you look good naked!*'

Bugger! She hit the delete button, then blocked him from further contact. A relationship, if you could call it that, with a man like him was definitely not what she was looking for.

She breathed in. Perhaps Paul would be more up her street. She clicked and his photo came up. He was also handsome, but slimmer and less muscular. He was fully dressed, she was pleased to see, and said that he was a dentist. She opened his message. '*Hi Sam,*' she read. '*Want to get together for a good time? I bet you look good naked!*'

Sam sat up in her chair. "What the fuck?"

She hit delete and block, then hesitated before taking the plunge.

Jeremy was older than the first two men, perhaps late forties and with long curly hair. He had a nice smile though and was an art dealer. She held her finger over the button, wary of what his message might be, hoping it would be different, then clicked.

'*Hi Sam,*' she read. '*Want to get together for a good time? I bet you look good naked!*'

*

Hannah stared at Jeremy's photo, a quizzical look on her face.

"I recognise him," she said. "Not sure where from, but I've definitely seen him somewhere."

"Has this ever happened to you?" Sam asked. She was feeling a little better now that Hannah was there, but those three messages had really shaken her up.

"Never. You deleted and blocked those first 2 accounts so…" She went quiet for a minute. "Tell you what. I'll set a profile up for me and see if I can find them. Pour me another glass would you?"

Sam filled Hannah's glass while she downloaded the app and entered her details, then passed it to her and stood behind her chair while she searched.

"Doug was it? Builder?"

"Yes, he was the first."

Hannah hit a couple of buttons and a photo came up. "Him?"

Sam shook her head and Hannah swiped. Sam shook her head again. Hannah kept swiping until Sam said 'Stop, that's him."

"Mmm," Hannah said. She took a screenshot. "And the second one called himself?"

"Paul. He said he was a dentist."

Hannah pressed a couple of buttons and started swiping through photos without checking with Sam, finally stopping and holding the phone up. "This is him, isn't it?"

"Yes, that's him. But how did you know?"

"I recognise all three of them. You've never heard of Linkin Park then?"

"Isn't that in Chicago?"

"Link-in Park," Hannah said, emphasising the last syllable, "not Linc-on Park. They're a rap metal band. These are three of the founding members and they're certainly not called Greg, Paul and Jeremy."

"So someone's used their photos to set up false accounts?"

"Exactly."

"But who would... Hang on, did you say rap?"

"Rap metal, yes. It's kind of a fusion between rap music and heavy metal."

"It's Tony," Sam said. "The bastard." She grabbed her phone.

"Are you going to ring him?" Hannah asked.

"In a minute, but I've got another call to make first."

The phone was picked up after a couple of rings.

"Kate Chambers."

"Mum," Sam said. "Have you been talking to Tony?"

"He's very upset darling. Rang me a couple of times. He said you haven't been returning his messages."

"He hasn't left me any messages."

"That's not what he told me." She paused for a second. "Have you thought of giving him a second chance?"

Sam ignored the question. "Did you tell him I was on a dating app?"

There was no response.

"Mum?"

"I might have mentioned it."

"Oh Mum!"

"What's wrong with that? He was asking if you were coping without him and I told him you seemed to be, and then he asked how and, well, yes I told him about Plenty of Fish and Tinder."

Sam's shoulders dropped. "He's using it to stalk me, Mum."

"What do you mean 'stalk you'?"

"He's set up 3 false accounts, perhaps more for all I know, and sent me messages from them."

"It's only because he loves you, darling, and can't bear to lose you."

"The messages suggested I look good naked."

"What?"

"They weren't messages of undying love, they were crude and they were intended to hurt."

"That doesn't sound like Tony, Sam. He's a lovely, considerate boy. Are you sure you read them correctly?"

"Mum, if he rings again please don't talk to him."

"He's…"

"Mum!"

"Okay, darling."

"Promise?"

"Yes, I promise."

Sam hung up and turned to Hannah.

"Did you change the locks?" Hannah said.

Sam shook her head. "I'll get it sorted on Monday."

She keyed Tony's number into her phone, hesitated for

a second, then hit the button.

"Hello Sammy,' he said, a cheery note to his voice. "Ready to say 'yes' now?"

"You've been stalking me, Tony,' she said.

"Don't be silly, darling, I haven't been near you. Thought I'd give you some space."

"Did you set false profiles up on Plenty of Fish and send me messages?"

"Oh that," he said and laughed. "Yeah, that was me. Did it for a laugh."

"That's your idea of funny is it?"

"Yeah, it is. Anyway, darling, are you ready to get back together?"

Sam shook her head in exasperation and looked over at Hannah who whispered 'Tell him to fuck off'.

"The relationship is over, Tony," she said. "You need to return my keys and stay away. And don't contact my Mum."

"I'll contact her if I want to."

"Don't!"

"You can't stop me."

This was descending into a pointless and futile argument.

"Tony," she said, trying to speak calmly, "if you contact my Mum, or me, or try any of your online tricks, I'll report you to the police for stalking."

"You had better watch out," he said.

"Are you threatening me?"

"Be careful, is what I'm saying. You never know what might happen." He hung up.

Sam stared at the phone. She was shaking more than ever now.

"Try not to worry," Hannah said. "Tony's weak. He'd never do anything to hurt you."

Sam hoped her best friend was right, she really did.

Chapter 27

Josh pedalled hard up the hill past the Weston pub, now sadly closed, and wished he'd taken his car to work. It had been nearly six when he left the office and he needed time to get ready before meeting Leanne. It was important he made a good first impression and his hair was a mess.

He turned up Combe Park and then into the drive of his parents' house opposite the cricket club. It was a large semi-detached, probably a hundred years old but Josh had never really thought about its age. It had been his home all twenty-two years of his life and he knew he took it for granted.

He leaned the bike against the side of the house and went around to the kitchen at the rear of the house. His Mum was at the island chopping vegetables.

"Hi Josh," she said. "Good day?"

"Fine Mum," he said. "Gotta dash though. Going out."

He was through the kitchen and at the bottom of the stairs when she called out. "Dinner will be about half an hour. Is that okay?'

Buggery buggery. He should have rung and told her. "Sorry, Mum, I have to be out by then." He turned to see her appear in the hall.

She smiled. "Is it a girl Josh?'

"Yes." He felt his cheeks flushing.

"She can come for dinner if you want."

"No Mum. This is our first date. I can hardly bring her to meet my parents."

"You can bring her back for a drink afterwards. We'd love to meet her. What's her name?"

"I'll tell you later." He bounded up the stairs towards the bathroom.

"Joshy's got a girlfriend, Joshy's got a girlfriend." His thirteen-year-old brother stood outside the bathroom, grinning from ear to ear and singing his words.

"Let me through," Josh said.

"What's she like? Are you going to put your tongue down her throat?"

"Shut up, Noah, and get out of my way."

Noah stood to one side and Josh jumped into the bathroom.

"Joshy's on a snogfest, Joshy's on a snogfest," were the last words he heard before he locked the door.

*

It was just gone seven when Josh got to Las Iguanas and he immediately spotted Leanne through the window. She was facing him at a table set for two, fiddling with her phone and doubtless wondering if he'd turn up. She looked gorgeous, with her long curly blonde hair and immaculate makeup. Younger than him perhaps but not by much. He felt a frisson of nerves, hoping she would like him and also that he didn't do or say anything embarrassing.

He took a last look at himself in the reflection. His hair looked okay he thought, and rubbed his fingers across the sides above his ears. Not so sure about his eyebrows he slid his index finger across the top of his left eyebrow and then his right eyebrow. He stood back a pace and realised that Leanne was looking straight at him, the corners of her mouth turned up.

He pretended not to see her and walked to the entrance and then over to her table.

"You're worse than me," she said as he sat down. She was still smiling.

"What do you mean?" She pointed to the window. "Oh." He decided to change the subject. "That's a lovely outfit. Is it your mother's?"

"What?"

"Sorry, I meant uh, did she buy it for you, ah, no, whoops, oh buggery buggery, I mean, was it a present?"

"It was a present actually. From my husband."

"Your husband!"

"I'm joking, Josh." She gave a little snort and put a hand to her mouth. "Excuse me, bit of a habit I'm afraid."

"No problemo."

"You're very funny, do you know that?"

"Funny laugh with me or funny laugh at me."

She thought about this. "A bit of both I think. Whatever, you make me laugh."

A young female waitress appeared beside them. "Can I get you two young lovers a drink?" she said, and winked at Leanne.

"We're not," Josh stumbled. "I mean we haven't, we've only just, she's…"

Leanne came to his rescue. "I'll have a Thatchers Haze please," she said.

Josh hesitated, looked across at Leanne then at the waitress who was staring at him, a quizzical look on her face. "Me too," he said after a moment's hesitation. "Thatchers Haze for me as well."

*

After four Hazes Josh was feeling a lot more relaxed. It wasn't just the drink either. He found Leanne easy to talk to and her gentle teasing and his reaction to it made them both laugh. He put his hand over hers.

"I'd like to do this again," he said.

"Me too, Joshy." She had been calling him this ever since he had told her what his little brother had said earlier in the evening. Her face took on a serious tone. "As long as we don't tell my husband."

He laughed. "But still your heart fair maiden," he said in his best imitation of a Shakespearian actor. "The evening is set fair, and there is not one but two dancey bars around yonder corner."

She snorted. "Two what did you call them?"

He returned to his normal voice. "Dancey bars, you know, bars with, well, with dancing."

"I guessed that, but I've never heard them called dancey bars before."

"Stay with me, honeydew, and you'll hear a lot more nonsense."

"Of that," she said, shaking her head, "I'm quite certain. I also have a suspicion your dancing is going to be somewhat entertaining."

"This man can boogy," Josh said, only realising he'd said it loudly when the couple at the next table turned their faces his way. He dropped his voice to a whisper. "Believe me baby, I can cantaloupe with the best of them."

"Cantaloupe?"

"Not cantaloupe. Sounds like cantaloupe though. A type of dancing."

"Can can?"

"No, wait a minute. Tip of my tongue." After a few seconds he yelped and the neighbouring couple turned their heads again. "Sorry," he said to them then turned back to Leanne. "Hip hop, that's what I was thinking of."

"That doesn't sound in the slightest like cantaloupe. You seem to have melons on the brain." She gestured down to her breasts. "I hope it's nothing to do with these."

He fought to keep his eyes from following hers. "I, ah…"

She stood up and held out her hand for his. "Come on, Joshy," she said, "Let's pay the bill and go to one of these dancey bars you like so much. Seeing you strut your stuff is going to make my evening."

Chapter 28

It was the first time Luke had been to watch Bath since he'd left the club and boy had it changed. The ground had been redeveloped and it was no longer as intimate. It was more professional, he guessed, but somehow the magic was gone. Probably him. After all, he had been with Jess when he'd been at the club and for most of his time there, brief as it was, he'd had a blast. Any visit back there was bound to be an anti-climax.

"Wowzer isn't it," said a voice behind him.

Luke turned to see Josh, his suit replaced by smart chinos and an oversized Bath rugby shirt. The ensemble served to make him seem even younger.

"Guess you've never been to a rugby match, eh guv?" Josh said.

Luke started to speak but Josh held a hand up to stop him.

"I know what you're going to say," he said.

"You do?"

"Don't call you 'guv' off-duty." He raised his hand again. "Not sure I can cope with Luke though, guv, and Mr Sackville sounds all wrong." He pointed a finger in the air and clicked his fingers. "I know, I know…"

"What Josh?"

"I won't call you anything. Easier for both of us." He clicked his fingers again. "Ace-ee-oh."

"Good idea, Josh,"

"Thanks, guv. Oh blast. I mean thanks, uh…"

"Just thanks."

"Oh yeah, thanks." He pulled two tickets out of his pocket. "We're in the Dyson Stand. Superbo seats between the halfway line and the twenty-two." He paused and held his hand up in a gesture of apology.

"What is it, Josh?' Luke said.

"I'm using jargon. Sorry. The twenty-two is a line that's near the try line but closer to it than it is to the halfway line."

"Twenty-two yards from the try line?"

"Yes, guv, I mean yes… uh, yes. That's why it's called the twenty-two."

"Thanks, Josh."

"No problem gu…uh…no problem. There's a five-yard line too but it's not called the five because, well…"

"Don't worry I'll catch on."

"Great. Any other questions uh," he dropped his voice to a whisper, said "guv" then raised his voice again, "Just ask away."

"Right, Josh, thanks."

"No problemo uh…" he drew his fingers across his lips, "…uh… no problemo."

*

Luke was surprised at how much he enjoyed the game. Bath lost, but it was end-to-end stuff and there was plenty of action. After a while he tired of Josh's continual explanations of what was going on and told him he'd once played rugby. He didn't reveal that he had been a professional, but it was enough to stop the continual, often incorrect, narrative about rucks, mauls, offside and so on.

They stood as soon as the full-time bell rang, and waited for others in the aisle to move along. They in turn were waiting for others and it was slow progress.

"It's always like this," Josh said, then blurted out, "So where did you play rugby then, guv?"

Luke started to answer but Josh interrupted him.

"Hey look," he said, gesturing over the others in the

aisle towards a young blonde woman who had already reached the central aisle and was making her way slowly up the steps. He turned back to Luke. "That's Emily Parker, the other one on the bullies list."

Luke glanced over to see an attractive, if in his eyes somewhat over made-up, woman of twenty or so. She was holding the hand of a man ahead of her, and having to continually apologise to others as she was semi-pulled through the crowd. Luke tried to see the man's face but he was wearing a baseball cap and his face was hidden by the people around him.

"She's supposed to be ill," Josh said. "Although the man I spoke to did say she'd be back to work on Monday, so I guess it could be one of those twenty-four-hour bug things."

"Was it her boyfriend you spoke to?" Luke said.

"Not sure, could be but he sounded well older than her." Josh paused for a minute before continuing. "Tell you what, guv. Why don't I take advantage of this and have a word with her now?"

Luke started to reply but Josh was already making his way towards her, muttering 'excuse me' and 'sorry, emergency' to ensure people gave way. Luke decided not to follow him and called "Meet you at Gate 3" to which he got an over-the-head thumbs up before Josh was lost in the crowd.

He had to admire Josh's enthusiasm. The lad was bright too, although he often did everything in his power to conceal the fact. And speaking to Emily today was probably a good idea, if nothing else than to ensure she came in on Monday when they could conduct a proper interview.

The route to the exit was at a snail's pace, everyone being slowed up by the narrow gap at the top of the stairs. It was several minutes before Luke reached the top after which progress became easier. He turned right as he emerged and headed towards gate 3. As he did so his eyes were drawn to a crowd of people standing by the wall to his left.

"Is he okay?" someone said.

"Head wound," came the reply. "Seems to be unconscious. Must have fallen against the wall.'

"Drunk, probably," said a third.

As he said this two St John Ambulance medics arrived, a painfully thin man of thirty or so and a woman who was slightly older and looked twice his weight and waist size. It was the woman who took control, spreading her arms wide to clear their route.

"Please move away," she boomed, and as the onlookers made way Luke saw first the trainers, then the chinos, then the quaffed hair and realised that the man on the ground was Josh. He moved forwards but the female medic, who seemed to have adopted the secondary role of bouncer, held her arm across in front of him.

"Sorry sir," she said. "Please leave us to treat this man."

"He's a friend," Luke said, and gave the medic a look that made her immediately pull her arm away. He bent down next to the male medic. Josh appeared to be unconscious but as he lifted his head his eyes opened and he stared up at Luke.

"Guv," he said.

The medic looked first at Luke, then at Josh, and then back to Luke. "Are you a policeman?" he said.

"No," Luke replied.

He nodded his head. "Concussion then."

"What happened, Josh?" Luke said.

"It was him," Josh said. "I was talking to her, but it was him."

"She was a him?" the medic said.

"No, with him," Josh said. "She was with him and I was with her and she said 'it's him' and it was him and…"

The medic turned back to Luke. "Definitely concussion," he said. "Why don't you step back over there, sir, and my colleague and I will treat your friend and then he can tell you about the hims and the hers."

Luke waited while the female medic bent down to check Josh's wound, after which she wiped it with antiseptic and wrapped a bandage around his head. She and her fellow medic helped Josh stand up and guided him over to Luke before saying their goodbyes and leaving.

"How are you feeling?" Luke said.

"A little bit sick guv to be honest," Josh replied before a big smile spread across his face. "Exciting though, isn't it?"

"What happened?"

"I caught up with Emily, told her who I was, said I'd like to speak to her on Monday then, well then I was waking up with that medic leaning over me."

"Did she hit you?"

"No, she was treating me."

"Not the medic." Luke sighed. "Was Emily the one who hit you?"

"No, definitely not. I was hit from behind. I saw her eyes open and was starting to turn when, bang, I felt a crack on my head. It must have been that man she was with."

"And you didn't see him?"

"No guv, sorry." He brightened. "But someone else must have seen it. There were loads of people around. There will be CCTV too. Shall we check?"

"What we should do now, Josh," Luke said, "is take you to the hospital to get your head seen to. On Monday morning we'll talk to Emily to find out what happened."

"Right guv, got you guv, Gucci."

Chapter 29

To her surprise, Emily really enjoyed the rugby. Okay, she didn't know what was going on half the time, but the men were fit, in both senses of the word, and it was fast-moving. The atmosphere was lively too, a full house of partisan supporters cheering on every move. And as ever Mac had been lovely. This was their third date. The first two times they had had dinner then moved on to a club. They had kissed but nothing more. She wasn't that kind of girl. But she could feel herself becoming more and more attracted to him.

Then as they were leaving everything had changed. A young man had approached her and when Mac saw him he flew into a jealous rage. He reacted violently, knocking the man to the ground with his thermos. Emily had wanted to help, but Mac grabbed her arm and shepherded her away, all the while mumbling under his breath. She asked him what he was doing and he grabbed her arm tighter, ignoring the glances of those around them.

"I have to do it," he said. "Now is the time." They returned to the car, his hand still tight around her wrist.

"Stop it, Mac," she said. "You're hurting me."

And then he hit her, a full-blown slap across the face. She stared at him, shocked and stunned. "Get in!" he said.

Meekly she obeyed, fearful of what he might do if she didn't.

And now they were driving out of Bath, had left Combe Down and headed towards Paulton, then taken a series of left and right turns. She had lost all sense of the direction they were heading in. She tried once more to talk to him but the look he gave her was so vicious, so evil that she looked away, tears coming to her eyes.

Eventually, they turned into a narrow road and then onto a lane towards two low stone buildings standing sentinel against the sky. They were dark and foreboding and she felt herself shiver. What was he going to do to her? She tried to block the thoughts from her head, and risked a glance over to him but he was concentrating hard, trying to avoid the many holes in the little-used track. They stopped about forty yards short of the nearest building. Mac sat back and unleashed a deep sigh.

"Where are we?" Emily almost screamed. "What are you going to do to me?"

He turned to her, and his smile was back. "This is for your safety," he said. He reached over her and she flinched automatically. He opened the glove compartment and pulled out a small bag.

"What's that?" she said, but he ignored her. She watched him open the bag and remove a syringe and a small vial of liquid. She turned to grab the door handle but he was too quick. A fist connected with her jaw and her head fell back, her top lip now cut and bleeding. She felt as if she was going to faint and could only watch as he filled the syringe from the jar and stabbed the needle into her upper arm.

He looked into her eyes as they slowly closed and her head fell forward.

Chapter 30

Angie woke with a start. The lights were off but something seemed wrong and she was shivering. It was probably nothing, a nightmare that had shocked her awake. She was alone, as always. Being stupid, that was all. She sat up and rubbed her eyes. It was pitch black and she was breathing deeply, on the verge of having a panic attack. This was no good. She had to control herself, go back to sleep.

Then her nose caught something in the air. It was a new smell, faintly antiseptic. "Mac," she said, and was startled at the sound of her own voice. "Is that you?" Tentatively, she turned and put her feet on the floor beside the bed. She tried to control her breathing and took a deep intake of air.

Then she heard it. It was a soft, smooth sound and it was coming from the base of the wall in front of her. Then the sound was gone. Then back. Angie tried to relax her body but she was taking huge gulps of air again, the panic starting to rise. She raised her legs back off the floor, turned to lie on her back, pulled the duvet over her body, then over her face.

She could no longer hear anything. Her breathing was calming again and there was no other noise. Had she imagined the sound? Was she going crazy?

There was a movement against the duvet, down by her left leg. It was gentle, no weight behind it, almost unnoticeable. Then it became firmer, pressing down.

Angie screamed.

Chapter 31

Luke spent the ninety-minute drive trying to decide how best to tackle his mother and father, but knew his biggest challenge was going to be controlling his temper. After everything they had said and done over the years, the Tatler article felt like the last straw.

He had had an enjoyable childhood, down in large part to his nanny and the friends he made while boarding at prep school and Brighton College. After A levels he had started a law degree at Bristol Law School but was soon courted by Bath Rugby and his parents had been proud of his joining them as a professional rugby player. In hindsight, it was clear this had been because it gave them something to show off about.

They had been certain he would complete his law degree after toying with professional sport, and were appalled when he joined the police after he tore a ligament during a game. The fact that he started as a bobby on the beat was, for them, the lowest of lows. And when a few months later he announced he intended to marry Jess, who was then a struggling artist making ends meet by working for a cleaning company, they had to all intents and purposes disowned him.

That had been twenty years ago and he had only seen them on two occasions since, once at the twins' christening, when they made a brief appearance at the village hall, and once eight years ago when his maternal grandmother had died a month short of her one-hundredth birthday.

He pulled up at the entrance gates and was pleasantly surprised to see they were open. The last thing he wanted was to be turned away at the first hurdle. The drive curved through the trees for several hundred yards before

Borrowham Hall was revealed in all its glory, looking exactly the same as it had when he had last visited and his father had shouted at him never to return. It was nearly five hundred years old and had been in his father's family since it was built. The central section was three stories while the east and west wings stretching to either side had two. There were twenty-three bedrooms, three kitchens, two libraries, a billiard room, a ballroom and countless other memories of a bygone age including a Duke and a Duchess.

He rang the bell and it was answered a few seconds later by a young woman of twenty-five or so. She wore a classic black and white housekeeping dress and smiled up at Luke.

"Good morning," she said, her accent showing her to be a Dorset native. "I'm Amy. Please come in, Doctor Phillips. The Duchess is in the salon."

"I'm not…"

Luke was interrupted by the sound of a car braking to a halt on the gravel drive. A middle-aged and significantly overweight man wearing a three-piece suit clambered out with some difficulty. He was almost completely bald, with a puggish face not helped by a snub of a nose, and carried a briefcase. He seemed not to notice the other man at the door, somewhat of a rarity given Luke's towering presence.

"I'm - Doctor - Phillips," he said, his delivery sharp, almost staccato. "Where - is - her - grace?"

"She's in the salon, Doctor."

"Good - good," he said and brushed past her.

"I'm Luke Sackville," Luke said. "Can you tell Hugo I'm here please Amy?"

"Sackville?" she said. "Are you a relation?"

"I was once."

She raised her left eyebrow at this.

"Long story," he said.

"He's in the conservatory. If you'd like to wait in the hall I'll tell him you're here."

"It's okay, I can find the conservatory myself."

"He likes…"

Luke was gone before she could finish. He headed to the library, then from there through the billiard room to the conservatory. His father had his back to him, staring out at the terraced garden to the rear of the hall, his tall frame slightly stooped and with a walking stick in his right hand. He turned when he heard the door closing and Luke was struck by how much he had aged. He should have expected it at seventy-six, but it was a shock nonetheless.

"I thought you'd come," Hugo said, his tone flat.

"Why have you written it? " Luke said, fighting hard to control his temper. "You didn't take Jess in. You and Mother did the opposite - you rejected her and practically threw us out."

"She wasn't good enough for you. We could see that, but you couldn't."

"The article is full of lies, Father."

"It's my understanding - our understanding - of the truth. I want to get it out there before it's too late."

Luke felt the muscles in his neck tensing up. "Too late for what?" he said.

"Never you mind." Hugo sighed.

Luke was exasperated. Getting his father to open up was like getting blood from a stone. He chose his next words carefully and spoke them as calmly as he could.

"Your memory of what happened is clearly different to mine. Tell me, Father, what was it about Jess that you disliked so much?"

Hugo turned and looked at his son, and it was his turn to deliver his words in a measured tone.

"She wasn't right for you."

"Because she wasn't from a wealthy background?"

"No, because of what she was up to behind your back."

"What nonsense!" Luke tried to catch his breath. "Tell me then. What was she up to?"

Hugo looked away and stared out of the window. "It's best you don't know."

"This is ridiculous!"

"Excuse me, your grace."

Luke turned to see Amy standing nervously at the door.

"What is it, Amy?" Hugo said.

"Doctor Phillips would like a word," she said.

"I'll come through in a second. Please show my son out."

Luke stared at his father open-mouthed as he brushed past him and followed Amy down the corridor.

Chapter 32

Luke was shocked by the confrontation with his father but keen to make the most of the evening ahead. He rang Josh on his drive home from Dorset.

"How are you feeling?" he asked.

"Okay thanks, guv. My headache's gone and I feel right as rain now."

"Are you okay for this evening then?"

"Sure thing. Helen's giving Sam and me a lift and she's picking me up at seven."

"Great. I'll see you later."

Luke diverted to the M&S Food Hall in Trowbridge to pick up some nibbles and canapes. He'd warned the team he wouldn't be giving them a full meal, but he wanted to offer them something. He threw Prosecco and lemonade into the basket, then went back for a bottle of Merlot. It dawned on him that he knew next to nothing about any of them, not even what their favourite tipple was. What if one of them was a vegetarian, or worse still a vegan? He checked the canapes and felt reassured when he saw he'd thrown in some vegetable spring rolls.

Of course one of them could be glucose-intolerant or allergic to nuts or...

He realised he was being stupid and it was because he was nervous. Nonsense really but inevitable. He was in a new job with new people around him and he had a responsibility to make things work for himself and them. Well tonight would help settle them all. A bit of bonding over a drink or two never went amiss.

"In your crate, Wilkins," he said and the spaniel obediently went in. "Can't have you leaping up for all these tasty nibbly things, can we?"

Maj was the first to arrive. He looked smart in grey chinos and a flowery Bermuda shirt.

"Nice house," he said as he walked into the open-plan kitchen-diner. "Is it old?"

"Early 1700s," Luke said. "It used to be a farmhouse." He gestured to the container resting on the table. "Cider?"

"I won't thanks. I don't drink alcohol. Got any lemonade or coke?"

"Sure."

The doorbell rang as Luke was passing Maj a glass of lemonade, and when he opened the door it was to three smiling faces.

"This wee man has had us in fits," Helen said, indicating Josh with her thumb.

Sam was chuckling to herself. "His little brother sounds like a nightmare."

They followed Luke in and exchanged hellos with Maj. Josh's hair was for the most part back to its polished shiny best, with only a small strip of bandage interrupting the sleekness at the top of his scalp.

"Prosecco, ladies?" Luke said.

"Now you're talking," Helen said. "I love a bit of the sparkly stuff."

"Me too," Sam said.

Luke poured them each a flute-full and saw Josh eyeing up the cider container.

"What's that, guv?" he said.

"That, my boy, is proper Somerset cider."

"Thatchers or Bulmers?"

"Neither. It's from Wilkins Cider Farm."

"Never heard of them. Can I give it a try?"

"Of course you can." Luke opened a wall cupboard and pulled out a half-pint glass.

"Haven't you got any pint glasses, guv?"

"Are you sure?"

"Definito."

Luke put the smaller glass back and pulled out a dimpled pint glass. He filled it up and passed it over. Josh took a sip. "Very, uh, appley," he said.

"It's cider," Helen said. "What did you expect?"

"Tastes like apple juice." He knocked some more back. "I can see how it might grow on you. Not like Thatchers Haze, that stuff can be lethal, but nice if you're a lightweight."

"It's quite alcoholic," Luke said, but Josh had spotted the canapes and wasn't listening.

"Are those tempura prawns?" he asked. He leaned over and nabbed one without waiting for an answer, then knocked back more of his cider. "Okay if I top myself up?

"Of course, but be careful."

"Don't worry, I won't spill any," Josh said, completely missing the point.

The next hour went by in a flash and Luke found he was enjoying the others' company. Helen had displayed a wicked sense of humour, while Maj shared fascinating stories about his upbringing in Somalia and his thoughts when he arrived in the UK. Sam was the least gregarious, not a wallflower by any means but less open about herself than the others.

Josh, meanwhile, had become progressively quieter. He was leaning back against the table now, slightly away from the rest of the group, and almost fell as he turned to top his glass up.

"Oopsy," he said, before taking a sip of his drink.

"Are you okay?" Luke said.

Josh looked up at him and Luke could see he was having trouble focusing. "Fine," he said. He opened his mouth to add something else then decided against it and bent his head to his glass instead.

"What strength is that stuff?" Helen asked.

"Nearly 7%," Luke said.

"I thought it might be something like that." She

downed her glass. "This has been lovely but I think we ought to leave," she nodded her head in Josh's direction, "before he does something he regrets."

"I'm fine," Josh said, picking up on this. "Just need the toilet."

"It's through that door on the right," Luke said, gesturing to the door that led to the cloakroom and boot room.

"Okay." Josh headed for the door, concentrating hard on doing so in a straight line. He shut the door behind him harder than he had intended.

"How much has he had?" Sam said.

"Three or four pints I reckon," Maj said.

There was a loud crash and they heard a yelp and then laughter. Luke raced to the door and opened it to reveal Josh on his back chortling while Wilkins stood over him licking his face.

"What's his name?" Josh asked as he turned his head from side to side in a vain attempt to avoid the spaniel's tongue.

"Wilkins."

Josh looked blankly up at him. "That's the cider."

"It is."

"Uh?"

"I named my dog after the cider."

"Because he's brown?"

"No. Because he's strong."

Chapter 33

"Thanks, Josh," Luke said as he was passed his coffee.

"Double espresso with 2 extra shots?"

"As you requested, guv."

"Terrific."

Josh handed the other drinks around and sat at the table opposite Maj. Helen sat next to Josh and looked her usual invigorated self.

Sam too looked much happier than she had the previous week and had clearly enjoyed her weekend. Something had lifted her spirits and Luke wondered if it was a man. Hell, he didn't even know if she was in a relationship. She was side-on to him as she listened intently to something Helen was saying and he was struck again by how striking her profile was. It was the petite button nose, he supposed, but also her smile which felt very genuine.

He shook himself and cleared his throat.

"Thanks for updating the board, Helen," he said.

"Nay problem."

"I'm sure Josh has told you what happened at the rugby," he went on.

"Oh yes," Maj, Helen and Sam replied in unison.

"Three times at yours yesterday and once already this morning," Maj added.

"Seeing Emily Parker is even more important now," Luke said. "Maj, did you manage to get hold of Dale Cartwright?"

"Yes," Maj replied. "I'm meeting him when he comes off shift in…" He looked at his watch. "…about fifteen minutes. At nine-thirty."

"Great. Sam, are you okay to wander in on them?"

"Sure," she said.

The CCTV footage Maj had found showing Dale Cartwright assaulting Marie Downing was one of their best leads and Luke was keen to make the most of it. What they had seen on camera might be as far as Cartwright had gone but he needed to be sure. Even if that was the case, he intended to ensure proper action was taken against the man.

He supposed all companies had people like him in their employ. Hell, the police force had its fair share. And all too often those individuals were able to get away with it, leading to more innocent victims down the line. But that wouldn't be happening on his watch. They were the scum of the earth and needed to be dealt with.

"Try to arrange a follow-up meeting, Maj," he said. "I'd like to ask Cartwright a few questions myself, but don't tell him I'll be there."

He turned to Josh.

"Josh, you and I will talk to Emily and try to get to the bottom of what went on on Saturday."

He was interested in Emily for two reasons now: the fact she was accused by Marie of being a bully, and the assault on Josh by her companion at the rugby. He hoped something would turn up from talking to her or to Cartwright, but there was one other less promising lead that still needed to be worked through.

"Helen," he said, "can you speak to Angelica again and line up a meeting with her boss?" He turned to Josh and raised an eyebrow. Josh stared blankly for a few seconds then the penny dropped and he leafed back a couple of pages in his notebook.

"Sharon Hislop," he said to Helen. He was smiling now like the proverbial cat with the cream.

"And her boss? Luke said.

"Oh yes, uh…" Josh looked down again. "Roger Ackerman," he said. "He's retired."

"I'll track him down," Helen said.

"Thanks," Luke said. "Hopefully we can get to the bottom of this today."

They all stood up.

Josh cleared his throat and they all looked at him. "Be safe," he said, "And remember, the only way is…"

Luke stilled him with a glance.

*

"She's not at work," Josh said. "Shall I try her at home?"

"I'll do it," Luke said. Josh passed him the number. He rang and it was answered after only one ring.

"Emily?" said a male voice.

"No, this is Luke Sackville from Filchers."

"Sorry, I thought it would be my daughter. Is there a problem?"

"Not at all, Mr, ah…"

"Parker, Andy Parker. Emily's not at work yet then? I bet she's overslept. That girl. Sorry about that Mr Sackville. Are you her boss?"

"No. I'm ringing about something else. It's nothing to worry about."

This wasn't true. After what had happened at the rugby there was every reason to be worried. Nothing to be gained by sharing his concerns with her father though. There was still a fair chance that she was safe and well somewhere.

"You don't know where she was staying last night do you?" he asked.

"She was meeting one of her friends on Saturday. Anne or Roanne or something. Must have decided to stay for the weekend."

"And you don't have this other girl's number?"

"Sorry no." He paused before continuing, almost talking to himself. "And Emily's mobile is switched off. I despair sometimes. If I've told her once I've told her a thousand times: she's an adult now and needs to act like one. Timekeeping has never been one of her strong suits."

"If you hear from her, do you think you could let me know?"

"Of course."

Luke gave him his number, hung up and told Josh what Emily's father had said.

"I'm worried about her, Josh."

"Who did he say she was meeting?"

"A friend, but he wasn't sure of her name. Thought it might be Anne or Roanne."

Josh smiled, clicked the fingers of his left hand and held his mobile phone up with his right. "Or Leanne, perhaps," he said.

"What?"

"I had a date on Friday night, guv."

"You said."

"I did? Oh yeah, at the rugby. Anyway, her name is Leanne, and she said she was meeting a friend on Saturday. And putting two and two together…"

"Could be," Luke mused. "We're due a bit of luck."

"You've met Leanne," Josh continued. "She was on reception this morning."

Luke cast his mind back to just before eight, when he'd exchanged a couple of words with the girl at the front desk.

"You're punching above your weight there, Josh," he said.

"Yeah, I… What?" Josh's hand instinctively went to his hair.

"Come on," Luke said. "We're paying a visit to see your girlfriend."

"She's not, I mean we're not. We haven't, well we have, but we're not, you know…"

"What?"

"We're not…" Josh's voice dropped to a whisper even though there was no one else in the room. "We're not boyfriend and girlfriend."

"So you don't want me referring to you as her boyfriend."

Josh held his hand up. "Defo-notski."

"Defo what?"

"Please, guv."

"We'll see, Josh, we'll see. Come on."

Leanne smiled when she saw Luke, and her smile broadened still further when she spotted Josh just behind him.

"Hello Mr Sackville," she said.

"Hi Leanne," Luke said. "Please call me Luke."

She looked over at Josh. "Hi Joshy," she said.

Luke turned to see Josh squirming slightly.

"Hi Leanne," he said, his voice an octave deeper than normal.

"We were wondering if you might be able to help us," Luke said. "Do you know Emily Parker?"

"Oh yes, she's one of my best friends."

"And did she spend the weekend at yours?"

Leanne's cheeks started to redden. "Um…ah…no," she said.

"Her father told us she had."

"The truth is she's got a boyfriend and she stayed at his. But she knows her father wouldn't approve."

"Why not?"

"Because he's old."

"Really?" Luke said. "How old?"

"Mid to late thirties," Leanne said and misread the look on Luke's face. "Yeah, you'd think he'd be past it, but Emily says he's lovely. Wouldn't tell me his name but said I know him."

Chapter 34

Sam hit send on the WhatsApp message. It was the third time she had thanked Hannah for their time together on Saturday. They had had a blast but it had been an odd combination, an afternoon's senshi karate class at the University followed by an evening at Hannah's karaoke-ing to Bowie.

Sam found karate oddly relaxing. It was intense while sparring and left her physically exhausted, but it was also like having the best massage of your life. After a vigorous encounter with a worthy opponent she felt she could take on the world. She and Hannah had taken it up when they were both eighteen, but her friend had dropped it after only a year while Sam had progressed quickly, eventually gaining her second Dan. It was a more occasional hobby now, but her fellow Senseis always welcomed her back with open arms.

One of the best things about the weekend had been the absence of Tony, either in person or on the phone. Her last conversation with him on Friday evening had shaken her up and she dreaded the thought of speaking to him again. He was the stalker type, the type of man who was convinced you loved him regardless of what you said and did. And he had ended their last phone call with what seemed to be a threat, but surely he wouldn't...

She was so deep in thought she didn't see Maj and knocked into him as they joined the canteen queue at the same time.

"Hi Sam," Maj said.

"Hi Maj, how's everything?"

"Great thanks. This is Dale."

He gestured to the man standing next to him. He was

slightly taller than Sam, clean-shaven and, she had to admit, attractive.

"Hi Dale," she said smiling.

"Hi," he said, smiling back, before moving his eyes down to her chest and lingering there for a few seconds. "Nice to meet you, Sam."

With some effort, he lifted his eyes back to hers and held out his hand. She shook it and was struck by how weak his grip was. His fingers also felt ever so slightly moist and she felt the urge to wipe her hand clean.

"Do you want to join us?" Maj said.

"Yes, that would be lovely," Sam said, though her instincts told her the opposite.

They sat at a table and almost immediately Maj stood up again. "I forgot the sugar," he said. "Back in a moment."

Without hesitation, Dale held his hand forward over the table and whispered, "Take this, Sam."

She looked down to see a note in his hand.

"My number," he said.

"Why would I want your number?'

He put the note next to her coffee cup and smiled. Then she felt his foot nudge hers under the table. She moved her leg away and was about to say something when Maj reappeared.

"All right, guys?" he said, aware that Sam was sitting stiff-backed in her chair.

"Fine," Dale said, still smiling. "Just getting to know each other aren't we, Sam?" He winked and Sam's stomach twisted again. She stood up.

"Sorry Maj, I can't stay. I've got to meet Helen. I completely forgot." She picked up her coffee.

"Don't forget …" Dale said, gesturing to the piece of paper she had left on the table.

"Believe me," she said. "I haven't forgotten anything."

"Nice meeting you," he said, oblivious to her discomfort, his eyes now focused back on her breasts. He watched her turn and walk away. "How do you know that piece of delight?" he said, all his attention now on her rear.

It was Maj's turn to feel a little sick. He picked up the piece of paper Sam had left behind, unfolded it then shook his head. "Two minutes you've known her," he said, "and you're already trying to give her your phone number."

"You know me, Maj. I'm fond of the girls, especially blondes. And she's got a tremendous…"

Maj had heard enough. "Like Marie Downing?"

"Who?" Dale said.

"Is Marie Downing one of the girls you're fond of?" He held out his phone in front of Dale. On it was an image from the security system with a hand placed against a woman's thigh. Maj swiped to the next photo, which showed a man walking away from the camera. "That's you, isn't it?" he said.

'Is that Marie Downing? I don't know her name but I'll believe it if you say so. Fit she is. Likes me too." He paused for a second. "What's it got to do with you though?" He gestured to Maj's phone. "And why have you got those photos?"

"I'm not in Security any more, Dale. I'm in the Ethics Team."

"The Ethics Team. What's one of those? Political correctness gone wrong, that's what it is. I like girls and girls like me. End of."

"She's dead, Dale."

"Who's dead?"

"Marie Downing."

"What's that got to do with me? I hardly knew her."

"Would you mind answering a few questions?"

Dale bent forward so his nose was almost touching Maj's and whispered "Yes, I fucking would." He stood up.

"Sit down," Maj said, then lowered his voice to a whisper. "It's better you talk to me than to the police."

Dale grunted, then sat down again. "This is rubbish,

Maj. You know I wouldn't hurt anyone. Least of all Marie."

"So you did know her name?"

Dale squirmed in his chair. "We went out once, then she kept finding reasons not to see me. I know she liked me though. I could tell."

"So why lie? Why pretend you didn't know her name?"

"You said she's been murdered. Just wanted to avoid, you know…"

"I didn't say she's been murdered." Dale sat back in his chair and grunted again. "And you said you didn't know her before I even said she was dead."

"Yeah, well. My love life is nothing to do with you is it."

"Feeling girls up is not what I'd call your love life, Dale." Dale started to speak but Maj held his hand up to stop him. "Rather than involve the police," he said, "I think the best way for you to clear your name is to answer a few questions so that we can establish your alibi and prove you had nothing to do with Marie's death."

"I suppose so," Dale said. "Go ahead."

Maj gestured to the others in the canteen.

"Not here," he said. "I suggest we meet in our office. When does your shift finish?"

"At one."

"Okay, I'll see you then."

*

Luke had a difficult choice and reflected on his options. He looked first to the one on the left and then to the other. They were both inviting but it couldn't be both. One today, one tomorrow. That was reasonable and fair. He reached for the one on the left. The Bounty could wait, though perhaps not until Tuesday. Later today perhaps. A bit of a gap, a light lunch then a mid-afternoon treat.

He recalled Jess scolding him, a half-smile on her face,

telling him to look after his weight, be careful. What had it been about? Then he remembered. Lemon drizzle cake, made by her. The last piece. She'd relented of course, and he'd eaten it, relishing every bite down to the last crumb on the plate.

The Double Decker wasn't the same. Mass-produced in a factory, but tasty nonetheless. He tore into the top of the wrapper and peeled it back.

"Mind if I have it?"

He looked up to see Maj pointing down at the Bounty.

"I love coconut," Maj continued. "So if you're having that…" He indicated the chocolate bar now inches from Luke's mouth. Maj picked the Bounty up, taking the lack of an answer as approval. "Thanks, Luke," he said, already tearing into the wrapper. "I owe you one. Don't you just love the milk chocolate version, much sweeter than the dark, goes better with the coconut too?"

"Mmm," Luke said, taking a bite from the Double Decker in case he lost that too.

"I've just been with Dale Cartwright," Maj said. "I didn't have long but he admitted it was him in that video with Marie Downing and agreed to come here when he finishes his shift at one. Does that time work for you?"

"Definitely," Luke said, deciding that in future he would keep his sweet treats out of sight until he was ready to devour them.

Chapter 35

Mac smiled to himself, reflecting on what he had achieved. If he hadn't been there for them then who knows what would have happened. His care and support had ensured their survival. Without him they stood no chance.

God worked in mysterious ways.

They were his darlings and everything he did was for their benefit. He had no doubt that over time they would realise this, grow to admire him, recognise him as their saviour. Perhaps one day they would even love him.

What happened with Marie had been unfortunate. He hadn't killed her of course. Well not intentionally. But she had fought him, hadn't realised that he was helping, had gone too far, tried to hurt him. It had been self-defence. A shame but her death had also been a blessing. It opened up opportunities, made keeping the others alive easier.

He hoped for their own sakes that the others would be more compliant, more accepting of him. Angie had been well-behaved so far and was kind and gentle. Everything he looked for in a woman. She seemed to like and admire him too.

As for Emily, only time would tell. She was young, little more than a child. But he would look after her, care for her and protect her. He was sure that over time she too would grow fond of him.

It was unfortunate that they had to share a room but he had no option. Hopefully, they would get on and he would make them as comfortable as possible.

He needed Marie's room for someone else.

Chapter 36

Sam's phone pinged. She smiled in anticipation of a WhatsApp from Hannah, perhaps suggesting another get-together. What she saw was more than a disappointment.

"Ready to say yes?"

It was Tony. The man was so obtuse he still hadn't got the message. Should she reply? Or was it better to ignore him? Before she could decide another message came through.

"We're good together, Sammy."

She stared at the screen, debating what to do. Deep in thought, she jumped when there was a tap on her shoulder. She turned to see Caroline Klein who pointed at her watch.

"You haven't learnt your lesson have you?" she said.

"What do you mean?"

"Your timekeeping has been a serious problem, and now I find you exchanging personal messages with someone at half past ten in the morning when you should be working."

"How do you know these are personal messages?"

"You admit it then?"

There was no answer to that. "I don't have to listen to this," Sam said.

Caroline moved towards her so that their faces were only inches apart. "Oh, but you do, Miss Samantha Chambers. I have had my eyes on you and I was right when we met last week."

"Right about what?"

"You are a lazy bitch, full of yourself and intent on causing problems for everyone around you." She lowered her voice to a whisper, and there was real menace in her voice. "I hope your new boss realises what you're about, sees through your flirting and recognises you for the trollop that you are."

"You can't talk to me like that."

Caroline moved back a pace. "You had better watch your step," she said, "or your position here might be permanently terminated." She gave Sam one final withering look then pushed past her and headed down the corridor.

Sam gulped, trying to take in what she'd just heard. It was all ridiculous but what could she do? Caroline Klein was not that senior but as HR Manager she wielded considerable power. She was being totally unreasonable but this was rapidly escalating into a vendetta. Should she talk to Luke? He would listen to her but he was new to the organisation and it would be unfair to land him with her problems. James McDonald, the Head of HR, was another option but that meant going over Caroline's head. If she found out she could be in even more trouble.

But then again, how much worse could it get? She could explain what had happened and he would surely see sense. She was neither lazy nor was she a flirt. He would understand this when he met her and he must know what Caroline was like. Yes, seeing James was her best bet.

Caroline had headed off in the opposite direction to the HR department so now was her best chance to catch him without her knowing.

James's secretary was sixty or so, diminutive with a broad smile and a Brummie accent. "Hello my dear," she said when Sam walked up to her. "How can I help?"

"Is James here?" Sam said.

"He is but I'm afraid he's awfully busy."

"Oh, ah…"

She was interrupted by a man's voice behind her. "I've got a moment if it's urgent."

She turned to see a man younger than she had been expecting. He was smiling at her and beckoned for her to go into his office. "Please come in," he said. "I'll always make time available if I possibly can." He addressed his next words to his secretary. "Doris," he said, "no interruptions for the next fifteen minutes please."

"Right you are, Mr McDonald," she said.

He followed Sam into his office and gestured for her to sit down before moving around the desk to his own chair. "How can I help, ah…"

"Sam," she said.

"Pleased to meet you, Sam. If I may say so you look a little wound up. Is everything okay?"

"Ah no, not really. James, is it okay if I call you James?" He nodded. "James, can I tell you something in confidence?"

"Of course you can," he said, and smiled again. He really did have the most attractive smile and she felt herself relax. She explained everything that had happened first with her old boss and then in the two encounters with Caroline.

"And Caroline called you a lazy bitch?"

Sam nodded. "And a trollop," she said. "She also said it would be my word against hers, which is why I didn't come to you the first time."

James shook his head. "This really is shocking, Sam, but I must admit I'm not totally surprised she called you a lazy bitch."

Sam couldn't stop the tears from coming to her eyes. "You mean you…" She started sobbing and stood up. "I thought you would help. I didn't think you would agree."

"No, no, Sam." He stood and walked around the desk. "I meant it's in her character. I have heard other stories about her behaviour."

"Oh I see," she said, but the sobs were full and furious now. He passed her a tissue and she wiped her eyes and gave a deep sigh. "Sorry," she said. "It got to me then. I'll be all right in a second."

"No need to apologise, Sam," he said. "It's totally understandable. Take a few moments to get yourself together and don't worry. I'll sort everything out so that you're not bothered by Caroline any more."

"Thank you," she said, then forced a smile. "Honestly, I'm okay now."

She turned to leave but he put his hand on her shoulder. "If there's anything else, please don't hesitate to come to me. Okay, Sam?"

"Thanks, James," she said. "I will."

Chapter 37

Dale Cartwright was not what Luke had been expecting. It was hard to believe he was the womaniser Maj had described him as. By all accounts, his behaviour was that of the proverbial dirty old man, but he was young, clean cut and seemed very relaxed and self-confident.

"Thanks for coming in, Dale," Luke said, once Maj had made the introductions. "I'm sorry this is necessary but we have to make sure you're in the clear."

"I didn't do anything wrong," Dale said.

"I'm sure you didn't," Luke lied. "Can we start with what you were doing on the day Marie Downing disappeared?"

"When was that?"

"It was the day of the camera footage."

"The photos I showed you," Maj clarified. "Thursday 23rd March."

Dale hesitated for a second. "I was working that day," he said.

"We know you were working," Luke said. "But what happened immediately after your encounter with Marie? Did you go straight back to work?"

"That was my work. I was doing the rounds, checking fire exits and secure entry doors were working, that kind of thing. Marie was on my route."

"And what time did you finish that day?"

"Six in the evening. It was a day shift."

Luke noted this down on his pad then sat back and watched Dale closely. His earlier self-confidence was beginning to evaporate under the questioning. Time to poke even harder. "What did you do after your shift, Dale?" he said. "Immediately after. Did you walk home, drive, meet a colleague…?"

"I ah…" Dale looked across at the window before continuing. "I got a bus home straight away." He half laughed. "Played Grand Theft Auto on my Xbox all evening if you must know."

"I see," Luke said. "So you didn't see Marie again after that?"

"No, no, not at all."

"Good. And did you see anyone else that evening, anyone who can corroborate your story?"

"No, I, ah, wait. Yes, I popped to the shop for a ready meal. About eight it was. The corner shop on Laughton Avenue. Mr Singh was there, he can confirm it."

"That's great, Dale." There had been no tiny twitches and no hesitation in his response. Luke was confident he had been telling the truth and made another note. "Can we go back a bit now? When did you first meet Marie?"

"Oh, now you're asking," Dale said. "I mean she's one of many, you know." He smiled, but it vanished when he saw the hard look on Luke's face. "A couple of months before that I guess. January probably."

"What happened?"

"A friend introduced us. We went out for a meal, then onto a club, then back to her place."

"Did you spend the night at hers?"

"Nah, shame but she wasn't having it. Said she wasn't the sort to do it on the first date. I could tell she liked me though."

"And what happened on your second date?"

Dale squirmed slightly. "We didn't have a second date. I, ah, I decided she wasn't right for me."

"And yet…" Luke indicated Maj's phone.

"Yeah, well…"

Luke had heard enough. He closed his notebook. "Thanks, Dale," he said. "If we need anything else we'll be in touch."

Dale stood, clearly relieved his ordeal was over. "Right, okay. See you."

Maj showed him out.

"Mmm," Luke said. "That was interesting."

"In what way?" Maj said.

"He fancies himself as a womaniser, but it's also clear that Marie Downing rejected him after one date. Comes on very heavy by the sound of things."

"Do you think he's our man?"

"Doubtful, I'd say. He was lying a fair bit, but only to avoid being, in his eyes, a failure with women. His answers to where he was on the night of her murder were honest, I'm sure of it. That, though," he indicated Maj's phone again, "is totally out of order. I think I ought to speak to HR about him. Who looks after HR for the security team?"

"Caroline Klein," Maj said.

"Wonderful," Luke said, recalling their encounter the previous week. "I can't wait. I'll call her now." He picked up his phone and then paused, thinking back to his meeting with Glen.

"What is it, Luke?" Maj said.

"I had a really odd meeting with Glen Baxter and I wondered if you could shine a light on it."

"Was he complaining about me?"

"He did some of that, yes, but it was more what he said about a hobby he's got. He told me he was an actor."

"An actor?" Maj was equally mystified. "Glen couldn't act his way out of a paper bag."

"It does seem way out of character. He asked me to stand in for him at the Annual Security Awards because he has a performance that night and there's no way Glen would miss a shindig like that if he didn't have to."

"I can ask around the guys in Security if you like. See if any of them knows anything about it."

"Thanks Maj."

Luke's phone rang.

"Luke Sackville."

"Luke, it's Rob Talbot here." His voice was still gruff but there was an edginess to it as well.

"Good afternoon, Mr Talbot. Have you heard from Angie?"

"No, but I've found something. It's a bit odd but it might explain her disappearance."

"What is it?"

"Best if I show you. Could you meet me?"

"Yes, sure. Shall I come to your apartment?"

"Okay,"

"This afternoon?"

"No, I'm ah, I'm busy this afternoon. Could we meet tomorrow morning, say at ten?

"That'll be fine, Mr Talbot. I'll see you then."

Luke hung up and looked at his watch. It was gone six and about time he headed off. But first, he had to make a phone call.

"Chloe," he said when his daughter answered. "Could you do me a favour?"

"Of course," she said. "What is it?"

"I read the draft article, and I spoke to your grandfather about it, and I got nowhere."

"You want me to try?"

"Please. Turn on the charm offensive. Tell him how wonderfully eloquent he is in the House of Lords."

"Butter him up?"

"Exactly. Then tell him you've heard from the editor at Tatler and you've thought of a few small improvements to the article, and would he mind if you changed it."

"That's sly, Dad!"

"You'll do it though?"

"Definitely."

"And can you ask about your grandmother too? There was a doctor there when I visited and I'd like to know why."

Chapter 38

Sam was in two minds. On the one hand, her conversation with James had gone really well and she was convinced he would try to help her. He seemed a lovely man and genuinely sympathetic to her problems. A complete contrast to Caroline Klein.

On the other hand, she had stirred the hornets' nest. How was he going to tell Caroline, and what would her reaction be? Damn, she should have asked him not to mention her name, make it a general complaint. Should she ring him, voice her concerns? No, he was sensible enough to tread lightly. She had to trust him, but it didn't stop her from being on edge as she made her way back to the Ethics Room, nervous that she might run into the HR Manager again.

Luke and Maj were deep in conversation when she returned. Helen and Josh were at the whiteboard so she joined them. It was looking quite busy now, and there was a new dotted line between Angie and Marie's photos. She was about to ask why when she spotted a post-it with Dale Cartwright's name. It was connected to Marie's photo and there were also lines connecting him to Emily and Angie, though there were question marks above the lines. Interesting, she thought, and her stomach turned over as she considered what those links might mean.

"Helen," Luke called over. "Can you add a post-it next to Rob Talbot? He's found something of interest and I've arranged to meet him tomorrow. Josh, any luck finding Emily?"

"Nothing guv," Josh said. "I tried her phone again and there's still no connection. Think she's still with this mysterious boyfriend?"

"She could be," Luke said, "but I'm getting concerned. She was on the same list as Angie and now both have gone AWOL."

"Should I be worried?" Helen said, half-jokingly. "I was on the same list."

"Yes," Luke said, and he was deeply serious. He stood up and joined them at the whiteboard. He pointed at the photos of the two women still missing. "Until we've found one or both of Emily and Angie I think you should stay with a friend."

"You can stay with me,' Sam said. "I've got a sofa bed in the lounge. And it would be great to have the company."

"Thanks, Sam," Helen said, then turned back to Luke, "but are you sure this is necessary?"

"Yes," Luke said, his voice firm. "I'm becoming increasingly convinced that Marie's and Angie's disappearances are linked and now we have Emily missing. We know what happened to Marie so there's no sense taking any risks." He paused for a second before continuing. "Sam, I want you to go back to Helen's with her to collect some things then head straight to yours. We can't be too careful. I want you two to stay together for the time being. Okay?"

They both nodded their agreement.

*

Helen's house was large, much bigger than Sam had expected given she lived on her own. It looked to date from between the wars, with large windows to the main rooms at the front and a drive that swept around the side to what she guessed was a decent-sized back garden. Entry Hill had a number of large houses but she'd expected Helen to live in one that had been sub-divided, not have a whole detached villa to herself.

"This is nice," she said.

"Aye, it's my wee hideaway. Bought it when my hubby was alive. House of our dreams." She smiled at the memories and gestured to a photo of a young man on a table in the hall. "That's him."

"He looks lovely," Sam said.

"Oh yes," Helen replied. "He was adorable." She nudged Sam. "He was an accountant, mind you, but still fun."

She smiled wistfully at the photo for a few seconds. "He was the love of my life," she said, "but been gone near thirty years now. Boating accident on Loch Fyne." She took a deep intake of breath before continuing. "Now come upstairs while I pull some things together."

Sam followed Helen to a large bow-fronted bedroom and took a seat on a chintzy pink and red armchair. Helen pulled out a bag from the bottom of a wardrobe and started stuffing it with clothes, hairbrushes and other ephemera.

"Fancy a haggis pizza?' she said, looking back at Sam. Sam raised an eyebrow and Helen grinned. "Only kidding. But what about a pizza this evening? My treat."

"If you're sure."

"Very much so." She opened a bedside drawer and pulled out a menu. "Here ya go," she said, passing the menu over. "Bath Pizza and Deliveroo combo. Always works for me. I'll have an American Hot, choose one for yourself and what do you think, shall we say an hour and a half?"

Sam nodded. "That should be plenty of time."

She looked through the menu, deciding on a BBQ chicken pizza for herself, then ordered through the app, asking that they deliver as near to eight-thirty as they could manage.

*

It was ten past eight when they got to Sam's. She felt almost embarrassed by the size of her small upstairs apartment after the relative grandeur of Helen's house, but Helen was wildly enthusiastic about it.

"You've got great taste, Sam," she said, as she admired a bright watercolour that had been a present from her Dad. "These tulips are so realistic you want to touch them."

"I'll take the sofa bed," Sam said.

"Nonsense. One wee question though."

"Yes"

"Are you a morning shower person or an evening shower person?"

"Morning."

"Great, great. Me, I've always been an evening shower person. Mind if I jump in now?"

"Not at all, Helen. Please treat the place as your own. While you're in there can I get you a drink? No Irn Bru I'm afraid but would a Sauvignon Blanc be of interest?"

"Now you're talking my language. I would love a glass of wine." She gestured to the doors out of the lounge. "Which one's the bathroom?"

Sam pointed to the door on the left.

"Great," Helen said and picked up her bag. "I'll see you in a few minutes."

Sam went into the kitchen and got the white wine out of the fridge. She filled a glass for Helen and was pouring one for herself when the intercom buzzed. She looked at her watch. It was only ten past eight so too early for the pizzas. She pressed the button. "Hello."

"Pizza," came a crackly male voice through the intercom.

She gave a sigh, said "Coming down," and turned the oven on so that she could keep the pizzas warm until Helen was done.

When she reached the front door all she could see through the smoked window was a figure, slightly taller than herself and looking like he or she was sporting a hoodie. Her mouth went dry as she recalled Luke's warning, but she could hardly ask the Deliveroo driver to wait while she waited for Helen to emerge from her shower. She put the door chain on and opened the door as far as it would go, which was only a few inches. Hearing it, the figure slowly turned. It was a young man, no more than twenty she guessed.

"Miss Chambers?" he said.

"Yes,"

"You'll have to open the door properly."

"Why?"

He gestured down to the boxes of twelve-inch pizzas he was carrying.

"Ah," she said. "Sorry. Just a second." She closed the door and unclipped the chain before re-opening it again.

The delivery guy handed the pizzas over, said "Enjoy" without really meaning it and left. He was back on his bike before the door was shut.

Sam looked down at the boxes and took in the aroma. They smelt delicious. She turned to go back upstairs, then looked down again. She was holding four pizza boxes when it should have been only two. Quickly she pulled the door open and ran down the drive, hoping to catch the delivery boy's attention before he disappeared around the corner. Turning left at the gate she saw his rear lights for a second or so then he was gone. Too late. The poor kid wasn't going to realise his mistake until he got to his next delivery stop.

She became aware of something moving behind her.

"Is that you, Helen?" she said.

She started to turn but as she did so felt something, someone, press against her back. A hand came from behind and clamped itself over her face before she could scream. She tried to react, to wrestle back control, but there was a sharp jab in her arm and her body immediately went limp and refused to do as she wanted. She had the sense of floating outside of herself as her resistance ebbed away.

The pizza boxes crashed to the floor and Sam followed a millisecond later.

Chapter 39

Luke poured himself a mug of cider and leaned back in his favourite armchair. Wilkins had followed him into the lounge and sat curled at his feet.

It had been an interesting day. They had moved forward a step or two and Rob's phone call was intriguing. It could be that the document he had found proved Angie's disappearance to be innocent and that there was no connection with Marie Downing. They would still need to locate her of course, so that they could talk to her about Project Iceberg and find out whether she had been unethical in her dealings with Danny Olgletree at Bannermans. However, it would free time up so that their main focus could be on the more serious case: Marie's disappearance and murder. They would need to establish once and for all if there was a link to her being a Filchers employee or whether it was a coincidence.

He realised that he was thinking like a policeman. In Luke's head what mattered most was Marie's murder. Edward Filcher, on the other hand, would doubtless tell him that his priority should be whichever affected the company's bank balance more. He took a sip of his cider. Sod Edward Filcher.

The only person who had come to light so far as a suspect in Marie Downing's killing was Dale Cartwright, the security team leader, but while he was slimy, and certainly a nasty piece of work, Luke didn't think he was capable of murder. He had lied about a couple of things in their meeting but seemed genuinely surprised to find Marie was dead. Cartwright was either telling the truth or was a brilliant actor. Luke leant towards the former.

He needed to know what had happened between

Marie's departure from Filchers that day, upset by what Cartwright had done, and her arriving at Moorham Woods. In particular, how did she get there? Did she go by taxi or did her killer drive her? If the latter, did he force her into his vehicle, or was he known to her, a friend or colleague or even a member of her family?

They still had a few avenues to explore. Nothing useful had come from Angelica and Helen, but Emily Parker, the third person named on the note next to Marie's body, might know something useful. First, they had to track her down though. Her father and Josh's girlfriend Leanne hadn't seemed too bothered about her being uncontactable. In all probability they were right and she was staying with the 'really old' man in his thirties that Leanne had talked about. However, there was that connection with Marie through the note and the fact that someone, probably the boyfriend, had hit Josh. There was a definite chance that her disappearance was more sinister.

Worst case was that the man who had killed Marie had now abducted both Angie and Emily. If that was what had happened they had to find them and find them quickly.

He had so little to go on. And such limited resources - a hotchpotch of a team who were trying their best but were limited in what they could do. Not so much by their experience, hell he'd known police officers whose experience had upped their skills by jack shit. No, one of the big problems was that his team lacked the power to arrest, formally interview and charge people. And if they did want to follow up a lead it was made more difficult by their inability to access police systems and databases.

They couldn't access systems themselves but…

He took his mobile phone out. It rang a few times and he was preparing to leave a message when a female voice came on the line.

"You do know it's nearly eight thirty, Luke," she said, disapproval evident in her tone.

"Hi, Janice."

"Just a second." There were muffled voices and the phone was handed over.

"Evening, Luke," Pete said.

"Sorry about that, Pete."

"No problem. I was going to ring you anyway. We tracked CCTV footage from the day of Marie Downing's disappearance and spotted her getting into a white Hyundai i20 about half a mile from Filchers on her walk home. Unfortunately, we couldn't see the number plate, and our view of the driver was too fuzzy to even make out if it was a man or a woman."

"Did she get in voluntarily?"

"She appeared to, yes."

"Any idea where the car went?"

"Another camera caught it heading south on Wellsway, a good mile or so beyond her house. Again no number plate but it suggests the car was heading towards the Combe Down or Odd Down area of Bath or perhaps further out to Radstock or one of the surrounding villages."

While of interest, Hyundai i20s were hardly a rare sight on the roads and Luke wasn't sure this moved the investigation forward very much.

"There's something else, Luke," Pete said.

"Don't keep me in suspense."

"We conducted a search of the woods. As ever there was loads of stuff, and a few red herrings, but we did find a torn piece of paper that is a perfect fit for the top of the note left with Marie Downing's body. It was only tiny but it had one word printed on it: 'Loveless'."

"Loveless?"

"Yes, Loveless. L-O-V-E-L-E-S-S."

"And it was printed not handwritten?"

"Yes, printed."

"Could it be from headed stationery?"

"Possibly, and I've got my guys looking into all the

possibilities. We've found a Love Road in Lowestoft, a Love Avenue in Dudley and even a Loves Lane in Trowbridge but nothing with Loveless in it."

"Perhaps it's something to do with the bullying, suggesting she was loveless as a first draft for the suicide note?"

"It's a possibility...but why printed not handwritten?"

"You're right, Pete." Luke paused for a second. "Do you think you could do me a favour?"

"If I can, I will."

He explained what had happened with Angie Johnson. "The thing is," he said, "regardless of what her partner shows me tomorrow, I need to find out if she met anyone, perhaps their competitor for the government contract, when she stormed out of Filchers last week. Do you think you could see if there's any CCTV footage that might help?"

Pete sighed. "Okay," he said. "When was this?"

Luke gave him the date and time Angie was last seen and hung up. Almost immediately the phone rang and he looked down to see Helen's name on the screen.

"Hi Helen," he said. "Are you okay?"

"I'm fine," she said, her voice shaking a little. "It's Sam. She's vanished."

It took less than ten minutes for Luke to get to Sam's apartment. Fortunately, he hadn't seen any traffic cops en route, but two officers were at the front door of the house when he arrived, in what appeared to be a heated conversation with Helen.

"Thank goodness you're here," Helen said. "These wee kiddies won't take this seriously."

The officers turned around and backed away slightly when they saw Luke towering over them. "Leave this to us, sir," the slightly older of the two said, though this still only put him in his mid-twenties. Luke didn't recognise either of them.

"What happened, Helen?" Luke said, ignoring the officer.

"I was just telling these two," she said and gave them a withering look. "I was having a shower, came out and Sam was nowhere. She must have answered the door…"

"It's not your fault," he said.

"We can handle this, sir," the younger of the officers said.

"Look," Helen said, deliberately turning her back on the policeman and pointing at the pizza boxes strewn around the footpath. "I can't see any other signs of what happened."

"Hungry were you?" Luke said.

"Well, yes but…"

"Four pizza boxes?"

Helen looked down at the boxes again. "That's odd," she said. "We only ordered two pizzas."

They heard the noise of an engine and a motorbike drew to a halt beside them. The rider dismounted, took his helmet off and looked down at the pizza boxes in shock. "Is she still here?" he said without looking up.

"Who?" Luke said.

"The lady I gave the pizzas to. I came back because I gave her the next delivery as well by mistake." He looked back to the ground. "Looks like she wasn't very pleased about it."

"No," Luke said. "I don't suppose you saw anything strange when you left did you?"

"Nah. I was running late so I was off pretty sharpish. That's probably why I cocked the order up." He pointed to the ground. "That'll come out of my wages that will." He grunted and got back onto his bike. "Nearly had a crash as well,' he said.

"What happened?"

"Bloody Hyundai came around the bend too fast. Almost caught me.

"A white Hyundai i20?"

"Yes, I think it was. How did you know?"

Chapter 40

The lights were still on so it had to be less than twenty-four hours since Angie had woken to find Emily locked in with her. Mac hadn't been back since then and the poor girl didn't seem to be able to stop herself shaking. She was traumatised, understandably so, but what bothered Angie most was that she seemed to still harbour feelings for him, despite everything he had put her through.

"He's mad," Angie said for the umpteenth time. "Absolutely raving bonkers. You have to see that?"

"I know, I know." Emily twisted the ends of her hair between her fingers. She dropped her voice to a whisper. "But he was so nice to me."

"He was sucking you in. You were groomed, Emily. He always planned to do this." She gave a sigh. "What concerns me is why he's taken us and what he plans to do next."

"Has he tried anything? You know, made any advances, or…" Emily swallowed, "…worse?"

"No," Angie said, "which in itself is odd. Don't get me wrong," she added quickly. "I'm pleased he hasn't, but why abduct us? He has to have a reason." She hesitated. "And why you and me? How are we connected? We both work for Filchers but there must be something else. Emily, what has he told you about himself?"

"Not a lot. He told me he'd been in a relationship but it hadn't worked out. She had been violent towards him."

"That's ironic," Angie said, recalling him slapping her across the cheek. "Did he tell you his surname, or where he lives?"

"He said his surname is Broadhurst and that he lives in the centre of Bath."

"Of course, both could be lies. Probably are. Did he say

anything about why he was called Mac? Whether it's short for something or a nickname?"

"No."

"What about work? Did he tell you what he did?"

"He told me he's a graphic designer."

"More lies I suspect."

Emily thought for a moment. "I first saw him in Filchers' reception area," she said. "We nodded hello, then a week or so later he was there again and we got chatting and he asked me out."

Angie considered this for a moment. "I wonder if he works for Filchers then?"

"Possible, but…"

Angie put out her hand to cover Emily's mouth. "Shush," she said. "Listen."

There was a scraping outside the door, the sound of something heavy being dragged along the ground. Angie hesitated, wondering if she should put the wig and stilettos on, but decided it would freak Emily out if she did. She took Emily's hand and pulled her next to her on the bed.

The sound became louder, and Angie realised she was holding her breath, anticipating the key in the lock or the sliding back of the vision panel. But after a few seconds, the sound became quieter, barely audible, and she realised it was moving to the left, to where she had heard that other woman, the one Mac had killed. The sound disappeared completely and Emily started to speak but Angie shushed her again. "It's him," she whispered.

Minutes passed, though it felt like hours. Then there was another sound, but this time there was no scraping, just the sound of footsteps, drawing ever nearer. Angie almost jumped out of her skin when there was a knocking at the door. The vision panel opened and she saw Mac's eyes staring in at the two of them.

"Hello ladies," he said in his sing-song voice. "How are you both this evening?"

They didn't say anything.

He shouted the next few words. "I - SAID - HOW - ARE - YOU?"

"Fine," Angie said quickly. "We're both fine."

"Good, good." The smile was back.

"Have you brought us food?" she said.

"No time tonight. I'm too busy I'm afraid. But I'll be back tomorrow and I'll bring some tasty treats." He paused and tilted his head to one side. "Say thank you, my darlings."

"Thank you, Mac," Angie said.

The eyes looked pointedly at Emily and Angie nudged her.

"Thank you, Mac," Emily said, her voice weak and trembling.

"Night night then," he said. "Sleep tight, make sure the bedbugs don't bite."

The vision panel closed and they heard his steps as he moved away.

Chapter 41

Luke persuaded the officers to file a missing person report. They refused to do anything further, and hardly listened when he told them about Marie Downing's murder and the possible link. They left in their car just after nine, leaving assurances that 'everything possible will be done to find your friend', though he knew they would file a report and that would be it.

He rang Pete who to his relief answered straight away. Luke was in no mood to talk to Janice again. It was the Hyundai i20 that was the clincher. Although the other officers had put it down to coincidence Pete was on the same wavelength. He and Luke knew they should assume it was the same car as the one used to abduct Marie Downing, which meant that Sam was in great danger. They also knew that they didn't have long to find her. Pete said he would go straight to the station and issue an alert for the car.

Luke rang Josh who insisted he would come to Sam's apartment. Maj didn't answer so he left a voicemail.

"What can we do?" Helen said.

"We wait for Pete to get things going. He'll instigate a house-to-house down this road, see if anyone saw the incident or the car. No point in starting ourselves, but we should look along the pavement, see if there are any clues other than pizza boxes." It gave Helen something to do, but he didn't hold out much hope for finding anything.

After ten minutes or so Josh turned up, his car a battered and ancient Renault Clio. "Any sign, guv?" he said. He was on edge and it showed.

"Nothing yet." He updated Josh on everything Pete had told him earlier, and what the Deliveroo driver had said about the Hyundai.

"What can I do?" Josh said. "Should I knock on doors?"

Before Luke could answer a police car drew up, followed immediately by a second. He recognised the two officers in the second car, having said goodbye to them less than an hour earlier. They were looking sheepish and didn't come over. After a few words with their colleagues, the four split up and made their way to different houses along the street.

"Helen," he said, "I suggest you keep looking along the pavement and in the bushes, and catch those officers before they leave, try to find out if they've located a witness. There's always a chance Sam might return too, though it looks almost certain she's been abducted." He turned his attention to Josh. "Josh, there's little you and I can do here but a couple of extra pairs of eyes on the road would be handy. I suggest we head south of the city since the car with Angie was seen heading up Wellsway. I'll take the roads around Odd Down and Combe Down if you scout around the villages between here and Radstock."

"Roger, guv," Josh said and started quickly back to his car.

"Drive sensibly Josh. We need to spot the car so there's no point in racing anywhere."

"I know, guv." He tried to smile but it bore only a vague resemblance to the real thing. "I'll be safe."

Chapter 42

Sam's eyes opened but she saw nothing. She tried to adjust her vision, tried squinting, but it was too dark. She raised her hand to her face but even her fingers were swallowed by the blackness. She felt her arm ache as she moved it and remembered the pain, and vaguely of falling.

The ground beneath her was cold and smooth. She was indoors, she could tell that much, but there was no sound. The room was either heavily insulated or remote or both. She felt in her pocket but it was no surprise to find her phone gone. Her wallet too.

Could it have been a mugging? But muggers didn't use hypodermic needles. And they didn't move their victims either. They stole and then fled. No, she had been taken by someone. A man, she was sure. He had been very strong, she remembered that much. And it had to be the man who took Angie. She was part of the team looking into her disappearance and Marie Downing's murder so that had to be the reason she had been abducted.

But if that was the case why hadn't he just taken her somewhere to kill her? What did he intend to do with her? He wasn't in the room, the deathly silence told her that much. But he could be back at any time. She needed to escape, and she needed to act quickly.

The effects of whatever he had injected her with were beginning to wear off. She had a headache, but nothing more. The room was warm too, so although the floor was hard it seemed like it had been prepared for her. She stood up carefully, wary lest the ceiling was low. She held her hands out and almost immediately felt a hard surface. Feeling around she realised it was a stone wall. She let herself be guided by it and stepped tentatively along. After a couple of paces, her knee bumped into something. It was soft but on a hard base. She put her hand out and realised it was a bed.

Which meant what? A bed in a room with a concrete floor and bare stone walls. And then it dawned on her. It was a cell. The man who had kidnapped her had prepared this, which meant he intended to keep her alive. Perhaps she should wait, find a way of overpowering him when he came back. It was an option, but first, she had to find out more about the room she was in, starting with locating the door.

It didn't take her long to find it. It was opposite the foot of the bed and was wooden, studded and rock solid. Sam tried pushing against it but it wouldn't budge. She felt around the edges and then across the face but couldn't find a handle. However, near the top, at about eye level in the middle, there was some kind of object attached. It was rectangular, perhaps twenty centimetres wide and half that in height, and protruded slightly. It felt like a sign, but surely, she thought, a sign would be on the outside not the inside.

With a start, she realised the outer edges were only a centimetre or so wide. They were cold to the touch, perhaps made of steel rather than wood, and within them was a recess with a plate which again felt metallic. What was more, the plate moved slightly at her touch. She tried pulling at the outer edges but they were securely attached to the door. It was the inside that was moving but it was flat so there was nothing to grab hold of. She tried to push and there was a sense of it wanting to slide downwards, although its smoothness made it difficult to get a decent hold. She pushed hard with her fingertips while trying to exert a downward motion. Nothing happened and she was about to give up when it suddenly moved downwards with a bang.

Suddenly there was light in the room, although it was

still very dim. She could see a table and chair alongside the bed and a bucket in the opposite corner. She looked through the opening. There were pinpricks of light in the far distance and she could see a crescent moon in the sky, but otherwise nothing.

Now what? The gap was too small to crawl through. She thought about calling out in the hope there was someone near who would come to her rescue. The risk was that her abductor was waiting nearby and would hear her. It might be better to spend time looking for other ways out, in the hope he wouldn't come back for a while. There could be a boarded window she could unblock perhaps, or a weakness in the roof. Yes, that would be the sensible approach.

She looked around the room but there were no windows. The ceiling was crisscrossed with metal bars beneath a substantial-looking metal roof.

She approached the door again. Bugger the risk.

"Help!" she screamed. "Is anyone there?"

Chapter 43

Josh tried to keep his speed down, conscious that he needed to look out for the Hyundai, but also keen to get properly out of Bath to the outlying countryside where he felt sure Sam would have been taken. Why he thought this he couldn't have said, but his gut told him she would be out in the sticks, somewhere where no one would be nearby to help.

He was at the top of Wellsway now, the park and ride on his left while the road continued as Fosse Way in the direction of Radstock. There was still a fair amount of traffic, and at one point a white car drew his attention travelling in the opposite direction. However, a quick glance in his rear-view mirror revealed it to be a low-slung sports car, certainly not an i20.

He decided to take the next right which was signposted to Timsbury. He took the turning and the road almost immediately narrowed and he was forced to slow down to twenty or so as it meandered slightly uphill. At least the car was behaving. It had been recently serviced but it was old and he didn't like the noise the gearbox made when he accelerated.

He reached a minor crossroads and on impulse took a right, which headed even further uphill between hedges that even his tiny Clio found it difficult to fit between. There were now no vehicles and he realised his mistake. He should have kept to the villages, not wandered off onto a road as little used as this one. He decided to turn around, head back to the more significant, if still minor, road and keep on that. Perhaps head towards Paulton then circle back and come into Bath from the east.

He spotted a field gate on the left with a flat area in

front which didn't look too pot-holed. Enough room to turn the car, even if it was going to require a seven or nine-point turn. He drove a few yards past it, changed gear and reversed back towards the gate. Then he rotated the steering wheel and went forward a few yards before repeating. At least he tried to repeat. But this time the gearbox decided it had had enough. With a crunch the stick returned to the neutral position and refused to move back to either first gear or reverse, no matter how hard he pressed the clutch.

"Shit," he said, and banged his hands on the steering wheel. "For goodness sake, Horatio, don't let me down now."

With a click the dashboard lights went off and the engine died. He put his head in his hands, then reached into his pocket for his phone. Of all evenings for the car to let him down this had to be the worst one. He brought Luke's number up and was about to click on the green button when he realised there were no bars showing.

"Fuck-a-daisy, fuck-a-daisy, fuck-a-daisy," he exclaimed, before getting out of the car, retrieving his coat from the rear and starting to trudge uphill.

Chapter 44

Sam was amazed when she heard a voice calling back to her.

"Be quiet!"

It had to be shouted to carry the distance, and it was brief, but it was nonetheless possible to detect a tremor in the other woman's voice. "Is that Angie?" Sam shouted back, "Angie Johnson?"

There was silence for a few seconds, then an answer came. "Yes. Who are you?"

Sam hesitated. She wasn't going to say she was a failed accountant now investigating missing people. Nor that she was in a newly formed Ethics Team investigating Angie for taking bribes. "My name's Sam," she said. "Sam Chambers."

"Someone else is with me," Angie shouted. "Emily Parker."

So she had been taken after all. "Do you know who's taken us?" Sam said.

"He calls himself Mac. We think he works at Filchers."

"When does he come here?"

"It varies. Once a day or once every other day."

"Have you tried to escape, or to jump him?"

"It's impossible. He always brings a weapon and the building is really secure. The doors came from a prison and are solid as hell."

They continued talking for a few minutes but it was difficult given the need to shout to be heard and they stopped after a while, agreeing to talk again later.

Sam sat back on the bed. What Angie and Emily didn't know was that this man Mac had already killed someone which meant their time was limited. They needed to move quickly. But how? Angie said she had tried everything. The ceilings were solid, the door only had a handle on the outside, there was no window, and Mac was always armed. It was all stacked against them.

There had to be a way. It sounded like the building Angie and Emily were in was identical to hers, so there was no way of escape by physical means. Which meant she or they had to fool Mac somehow, find a way of making him relax so that they could attack him when he lowered his guard. She had taken karate up as a hobby but perhaps she could use her skills against him.

It suddenly dawned on her that there was a difference between her building and Angie's. Angie had said there was a handle on the outside of the door. Which was no good to her because her vision panel was closed, but Sam's vision panel was open. Mac must have forgotten to latch it shut when he left. If she could reach the handle then perhaps she could exert pressure and open the door. She would need something strong though.

The hinges were on the left as she looked at the door which meant the handle had to be on the right and she guessed it would be about halfway up. She put her head up to the vision panel and tried to look down but the gap was too narrow for her head to go through and all she could see was the ground. She fetched the bucket and inverted it. Standing on it enabled her to reach her arm through. She stretched down as far as she could but felt nothing. The distance between the panel and the handle couldn't be more than a metre so she must be almost there. She tried again, stretching as far as possible. Still nothing.

She looked around the room. It was dark, but no longer pitch black, and her eyes had grown accustomed to the limited light on offer. There was a desk and chair but neither would fit through the panel. She looked up at the metal beams running between the walls. They were certainly strong enough but much too strongly fixed to be removed without tools. She sat back on the bed. There was nothing else. She'd have to wait for Mac to return and try to jump him. Make him relaxed. Perhaps she should try to seduce him? Lie back on the bed when he came in and…

The bed!

She jumped off and pulled the mattress up. The bed base was metal, with six legs and three cross bars, one at each end and one across the middle. Between these cross bars were sprung wooden planks. If she could separate one of the legs then perhaps…

She went back to the door. "Angie," she shouted.

After a few seconds, the reply came back. "Yes."

"How does the door handle work? Do you push it down or pull it up?"

"Neither. It's like a tap. You have to turn it clockwise to open."

"Is there a key?"

"No. Just the handle. Have you got an idea?"

"Maybe."

Sam wished she had more light. She went back to the bed base and felt around the joins. The legs were held to the cross bars by nuts and bolts. Most were tight but there was play in the one at the foot of the bed on the left.

The head of the bolt was notched to take a screwdriver and she needed to find a way to hold it still while turning the nut. Her eyes fell on the bucket. It had a metal handle which might just be thin enough to work. She brought the bucket over and inverted it so that the handle was across the notch. Then she tried to turn the nut but it was too tight and the handle kept slipping out. She wrapped the duvet around both hands and tried. Again it slipped. On the third try she was lucky. The nut started to turn and by holding tight and exerting pressure she managed to keep the bolt from moving with it.

This is going to work, she thought. The duvet was causing problems now though, its hold on the nut too imprecise. She removed it and grasped the nut with her fingers. The edges were tight and she yelped when she felt it cut into the end of her finger. She ignored the pain and pressed the nut as hard as she could between her thumb and index finger. Slowly, ever so slowly, she managed to force it to move some more, then after a few seconds something gave and the nut became easier to turn.

Once the nut was removed there was a clatter as the leg supporting it fell to the floor. She picked it up and gauged its length. It was around thirty centimetres long with a curve at the top where the crossbar had been attached.

She took the bucket back to the door and inverted it again. She stood on it and pushed the leg through the vision panel and down towards where she thought the door handle would be. Sure enough, there was a ping as the metal bar hit something. She turned the bar to try to push the bent end under the end of the tap but it kept sliding off.

After a few minutes, her arm started to ache. She pulled it back through the door.

There was a knocking, a rat-tat-tat that made her jump with shock. Then a man's voice, very faint but she could hear his words and they chilled her to the bone.

"Hello, my darlings," he said. "Maccy's back."

Although it was faint, she thought she recognised his voice.

Chapter 45

Luke would never have dreamt white cars were so popular. He cursed as yet another white Hyundai passed him, pulling out of the pub car park in a manner that would have made him pull them over if he had been a traffic cop. It was an i10 though, and he watched it go, hoping that his reading of the driving was wrong and that the car's occupants got home safely without injuring themselves or anyone else.

He was worried sick about Sam. They had so little to go on, hoping as they were that he or Josh or one of the police on duty would happen upon her abductor's car. He had tried ringing her mobile, but it had gone straight to voicemail. He knew Pete Gilmore would kick off a GPS trace but the phone would no doubt turn up in a bin somewhere, discarded near to her apartment.

They needed some luck. If he'd learned anything from his years in the police, it was that the unexpected was often what led to a breakthrough. Something would come out of the blue and that would be it, victim found and attacker arrested. How he wished for that piece of good fortune now.

But he'd also learned that you could make your own luck. He needed to mull over everything they had learned about Marie and Angie, about Emily for that matter because she too could have been kidnapped. There was a clue somewhere, there had to be. Something that linked them all and would lead him to their kidnapper or to the place where he had hidden them. He reached the turning for Southstoke and decided on a quick sortie into the village before retracing his steps.

His phone rang. It was Pete.

"Pete," he said, "What have you got?"

"We've had a piece of luck. Found Angie Johnson on CCTV after she left Filchers last week. She was in the city centre and it looks like she may have gone into the Salamander. And before you ask, we've tried ringing the pub but there's no answer. An officer's on his way there now but it may be closed up for the night."

Luke looked at the dashboard clock. It was almost midnight. "Are you sending someone to the landlord's home?" he said.

"We, uh…"

"What is it, Pete?"

"We don't seem to have his address."

"For fuck's sake."

"Or his mobile number. Cock-up Luke. We've got his name and nothing else." There was silence for a moment before Pete continued. "I'll let you know if our officer finds anyone there."

Luke hung up and turned the car around. Bugger the Hyundai, he thought, they had a decent lead now and he wasn't going to let it pass. He wished he could blue-light it. Heaven help any traffic cop who decided to pull him over when he was in a mood like this.

It took him less than five minutes. He screeched to a halt on Wood Street to find an officer peering through the window of the Salamander. He turned when he heard Luke get out of the car.

"Good evening, sir," he said and Luke recognised him immediately. PC Crabtree was one of the more reliable officers.

"Hello Crabtree," he said. "No joy?"

"Nothing sir, and I can't see any contact numbers anywhere." He indicated the notice on the front door. "Shut at eleven today so I guess the staff left a while ago."

"Crabtree," Luke said, "Do a PNC search for the Salamander. See what comes up."

"Sir, you can't…"

"I'm not ordering you, Crabtree, it's just a suggestion."

Crabtree smiled. "Right sir, got you." He tapped away at his phone. "As you'd expect, sir, the Salamander comes up a number of times. Most recent was a brawl last November."

"Any mention of the staff?"

"Not on that one. Just a minute." He tapped away at the phone again. "Here's one. Last June. Customer refused to pay and it was a barman who called it in."

"Is his number there?"

"I can't give you his number, sir."

Luke took his phone out of his pocket and opened his contacts. He looked up at the officer. "Crabtree," he said. "His name and number please."

Crabtree sighed. "Colin Jennings," he said. "07505 443189."

"Thank you." Luke dialled the number. It was answered after a few rings.

"Hello." The man sounded sleepy.

"Sorry to disturb you, Mr Jennings," Luke said. "Do you still work at the Salamander?"

"Yes but..." he yawned, "it's gone midnight and you woke me up. Can't this wait?"

"I'm sorry sir, but the police are investigating a woman's disappearance and we have discovered she was in the Salamander on the afternoon she was last seen. It was on Thursday the third. Her name is Angie Johnson. If you weren't there on that date perhaps you could give me the landlord's name and number."

"Okay, just a minute."

The phone went silent and Luke heard him tapping on his phone. After a few seconds, he gave Luke the landlord's name and number.

"Thanks," Luke said and was about to hang up when Colin spoke again.

"Actually, I do remember an Angie around that date. She was in a right state, that's why I remember her. I think she'd had a bad day at work."

"That'll be her. Do you know what she did when she left? Did she call a taxi?"

"No, she got a lift home I think. There was a guy in the bar who took pity on her. They left together."

"You didn't catch his name did you?"

"Not his full name, but I remember he said to call him Mac and she found it hilarious for some reason."

"Thank you, Mr Jennings."

"No problem. Are you in the CID then?"

Luke hung up.

Chapter 46

Josh tried waving his phone in the air, twisting it, spinning it in a figure of eight. He turned it off and then on again. Nothing, zilcho, nada. Surely, he thought, there would be a signal as he went further up the hill. He looked back down at his car, about fifty yards behind him now and barely visible in the faint moonlight. At least it wasn't raining.

Something wet hit his ear. He looked up to see clouds starting to block the moon from view. "Shittedy-shit," he said, and pulled the zip up on his Barbour before folding the collar around his neck.

Another fifty yards and the rain was coming down hard. He reached a second gate and at the end of the field a farmhouse, side on to the road. There were no lights that he could see but then the owners were probably asleep. Clearly, the gate wasn't the main entrance and he decided to walk on until he found it.

It was around the next bend. A sturdier gate this time, and behind it was a track winding its way up to the front of the house. He bent down and saw tyre tracks. This was the main entrance then. Great. He would wake the owners up so that he could call for help. He needed to be out there looking for Sam, not wasting his time on a back road in the middle of nowhere.

As he drew nearer to the house he was disappointed to see that it wasn't going to be occupied. It looked like there had been a fire, and some time ago at that. The right-hand side of the roof was gone and the ground-floor windows were boarded up. Just his luck. He walked the last couple of paces to the door, stared at it for a while, then turned around to go back to the road.

He had only gone a few paces when something he had

seen in his peripheral vision made him stop. He returned to the front of the house, turned the light on on his phone and directed it at the sign he'd half-spotted to the right of the door. It was half-covered with ivy which he scraped back.

"Bloody hell," he said, as he read the house name which was picked out in large capital letters.

'LOVELESS FARM'

Chapter 47

Sam heard the man knock again, then the sound of a door opening. He said something but she couldn't make out the words. She assumed he had gone inside.

She had to get out before he came to her building. Standing on the bucket she pushed the metal bar through the vision panel and down to the right, trying to get some kind of purchase on the handle. Again it slipped and she cursed quietly to herself. It had to work, had to.

She pulled the bar back in and looked at it for a second. The curve at the end wasn't long enough, that was the problem. Think, Sam, think. How could she lengthen it with something solid enough not to fold over? The bolt, she thought. If she wedged that in with cloth of some sort perhaps…

She got down onto the floor, retrieved the bolt and looked at it for a moment in the pale light. It was long, about eight centimetres, so it might work. Hell, it had to work. She reached for the duvet and used the bolt to tear into it, then her teeth to rip across to separate a piece of cloth away. She poked it into the hollow bent end of the bar then screwed the bolt into it. After a few seconds she was happy. She tugged at the bolt gently and it held. It wasn't ultra tight but with any luck it would do.

And she needed luck.

She stood on the bucket and listened at the vision panel. Nothing. She pushed the bar through and down, hoping and praying that it would work this time. It clanged against the handle and she held her breath, hoping the sound hadn't carried. After a few seconds she twisted and felt the handle turn slightly, then almost fell over as the door started to open.

Quickly she pulled her hand free. She was shaking but elated. It had worked. She pushed the door open and stepped out. It was raining and she heard large droplets clanging on the metal roof of the buildings. She looked to the right and saw another door, slightly ajar, twenty or thirty yards away. Again she heard a muffled voice.

She hesitated, trying to decide what to do. She had escaped and she had a weapon, the metal bar, and the element of surprise. The question was whether to go on the attack or hide. If she slid around the corner she could wait for him to come to her building and close the door after him so that he was locked inside.

The voice grew louder and she realised he was leaving the building Angie and Emily were in. She had to act now before he saw her.

Chapter 48

Luke tried to ring Josh but there was no answer. He needed Josh's notes so that he knew precisely what was said in the interview with Angelica Reid. There was a clue there somewhere, he knew there was. Angelica had said something about problems at big school causing difficulties for her at Filchers. He'd been amused by it because Josh had seemed to think 'Big School' was an adult term for secondary school, rather than an expression only children used. And there was also something Helen had said about Marie Downing wanting an assistant. It was linked in some way but what was it? He rang Helen.

"Hi," she said. "Have you found her?"

"Not yet." He paused for a second before continuing. This was the clincher. If he was right they had him. He didn't want to ask a leading question though. He needed her to volunteer the information so that he could establish once and for all that he was right. "Have you ever had any dealings with senior Filchers management?"

"A fair bit, yes, but why…"

"Humour me, Helen." He paused for a second. "I don't mean run-of-the-mill meetings. Have you ever fallen out with any of them for any reason?"

"To be honest, I wasn't very happy when Edward Filcher told me I was joining your team."

"Anything else?"

"There was something. It's a bit embarrassing though."

"Please tell me, Helen. It could be important."

"If you must know it was the menopause."

"The menopause?"

"Yes. I've had on-and-off trouble for years, and a couple of months ago I had one of my mood swings and lost my temper in a meeting. The next day the Head of HR called me into his office and I lost it again."

"The Head of HR. You mean James McDonald?"

"Yes, but I apologised and he was fine about it. Gave me a warning and that was it." There was silence from the other end. "Are you there, Luke?" Helen said.

"Didn't you tell Sam and Josh that Marie Downing had a run-in with James because she wasn't given an assistant?"

"Yes."

"And," he mused, "Angelica said that she went to the Head of HR because they wouldn't move her to a morning shift."

"You think he's the connection?"

"More than the connection. I think he's our man."

Chapter 49

Josh looked at his phone for the umpteenth time. Still no bloody signal. He glanced up at the house. It was dark and foreboding but deserted. And yet Marie's so-called suicide note had been printed on headed stationery which must have come from here. Which meant what? No one lived here and hadn't for a while. Unless there was someone living in the grounds, perhaps in a caravan or an outbuilding.

He walked around to the back of the building. There was an enclosure with stone shed-like structures forming a 'U' shape. They too looked dilapidated, doors either hanging off or completely absent. It looked to him like horses had been kept there at some point, but a long time ago.

He stepped away from them and went back to the front. He could just about make out his car at the far end of the field, but there were no outbuildings anywhere in eyesight. Reversing his steps, he saw that the track to the farmhouse curved around the stables and then further up the hill. He followed it and bent forward against the rain. As he did so he noted there were tyre tracks here as well.

The rain was almost torrential and he could barely see more than a few yards. He pulled his collar tighter against his skin. His shoes were covered with mud and it was hard going. He had to see what was up there though, for Sam's sake. He looked up again and there was a brief respite in the almost horizontal rain. Through the drops he could see a pair of low buildings standing at the top of the hill, separated by a few yards from each other. No lights were visible but he needed to check them out just in case.

Chapter 50

Sam stood pressed to the side of the building, rivulets of water running from her hair, clothes soaked. She was shivering, whether because of the cold and wet or because she was scared, she didn't know. Probably both. She held the metal bar up, ready to bring it down if he appeared. It had only been a few seconds since she had heard him but it felt like he should be at her building by now.

Unless he knew she had escaped.

She turned, suddenly afraid that he was behind her, but there was nothing. Where was he? The noise of the rain was so great now that he could be inches from her and she wouldn't hear him. How long should she give it before she came out? A minute passed, then another. The rain lessened slightly, but still she heard nothing. She inhaled deeply, raised the bar higher above her head and stepped around the corner. No sign of him. He had vanished. She looked behind her again. Still nothing.

Then she heard the noise of an engine and a pair of headlights came on, their powerful beams piercing the driving rain. She squeezed against the building, fearful the lights would pick her out. They seemed to be moving away and she realised he was reversing. The car moved forwards again and to the left. She didn't know why but he was leaving.

She ran to the other building. "Angie, Emily, are you okay?" she shouted.

"We're fine," Angie said.

"Where's he gone?"

"He forgot our meals. He's gone to get them and said he wouldn't be long."

Sam looked down at the door. It had the same type of

handle as her own. No lock so with any luck… She twisted and the door opened at the first attempt. Angie ran into her arms and she looked over her shoulders to see Emily. She was lain across the bed, sobbing.

"What happened?"

"He hit her," Angie said.

"Come on. We need to get out of here."

Chapter 51

Luke needed to get a handle on where James McDonald might have taken Sam. He had his mobile number but he didn't want to spook him. However, his wife or partner might have some idea of where he might have gone, perhaps to a holiday home or a lock-up. He needed James's home number and he knew a man who would have it.

Luke could hear music and laughter when the phone was answered.

"Who the ruddy hell is this?"

"Mr Filcher," Luke said, "It's Luke Sackville."

"Ah, yes." Filcher burped then said, "One of my staff, ex-police, very with it. Needs my help." Luke realised he was talking to someone else. "I have to deal with this," Filcher continued. "Can you move away, uh, what was it…"

Luke heard a woman's reply. She sounded very young. "It's Gemma," she said.

"Yes, of course it is. Be there in a swish, Emma."

"Gemma," she corrected.

"Indeed. Over there, dear. This is very important. Go on, shush, shush." His tone changed. "What is it, Sackville?" he barked.

"Have you got James McDonald's home phone number and address?"

"Yes."

Luke waited for a few seconds. "Can I have it?"

"Why?"

"It's urgent, Mr Filcher. I haven't the time to explain now."

"I'll be there in a minute."

"What?" Luke said, then it dawned on him that Filcher was talking to someone else again.

"Yes, Ian," Filcher said, "a double. The Lagavulin 12-year-old." There was a pause. "Or the 16-year-old. You choose."

"Mr Filcher?" Luke said.

"Sorry, what, yes, McDonald's number. Here somewhere. Is this for work reasons, Sackville?"

"Yes sir."

"Righto." He read out James's contact details.

"One more thing?" Luke said.

"What now?"

"Is James married?"

"Yes." Filcher hung up.

Luke looked at the address: it was in Nettleton, a village about twenty minutes away. He would have liked to go there in person but couldn't afford to waste time. No, he needed to ring and follow up by visiting if necessary.

A woman answered and there was a tremble to her voice. "Hello," she said.

"Is that Mrs McDonald?"

"Yes." She paused and it was clear she was struggling to hold herself together. "Are you…are you her husband?"

"My name's Luke Sackville," Luke said. "I'm from Filchers' Ethics Team and I'm trying to track James down."

"Oh," she said, before adding, almost under her breath, "Ethics. That's ironic."

"Do you know where he is?"

"With her, that's where. He thinks I'm stupid, but I found a hotel receipt in his suit last week. He told me he'd stayed over because he worked late after a conference but who does he think he's fooling? There are taxis aren't there? And besides it's a hell of a posh place to stay over on your own."

"Which hotel was it?"

"Widbrook Grange."

He knew the hotel. It was an old country estate set in several acres just outside Bath. Unlikely that he would have taken Sam there but perhaps he had somewhere nearby and used the hotel because it was close.

"I rang Widbrook Grange tonight," she sobbed. "A couple of hours ago. There's no James McDonald booked in but they have got a Mr Ronald.' She paused, then snorted again. "Wait until I catch him. I'll tell him where to stick his golden arches."

Chapter 52

Widbrook Grange was signposted off the main road between Bradford-on-Avon and Trowbridge. As Luke headed down the drive he was surprised to see fairy lights strung across at regular intervals every twenty or thirty yards.

In front of the main hotel building there was a large wooden sign emerging from a barrel, rustic and somewhat quirky. 'Welcome to the Bash' it said, and below that 'Pam and Frank - hitched at last'. There was music and the sound of drunken singing coming from another building across the courtyard.

He walked into the lobby where a vicar stepped towards him and held out a silver tray holding five or six flutes of champagne. "Champagne sir?" he said. "Grotcham or Peakes?"

"Pardon," Luke said.

"Which party are you with? Grotcham or Peakes?"

Luke was saved from answering by a voice behind him.

"Is that you, Luke?" He turned to see James McDonald, also dressed as a vicar. "What the hell are you doing here?" James continued. He was on edge and looking around nervously.

"I know what you've done," Luke said.

"You do, but what? I mean, why..." He paused for a second and wiped his forehead with his sleeve. "Luke, I know you're in charge of Ethics but surely this is outside your remit."

A woman in her mid-thirties walked into the lobby behind them. She was swaying slightly and dressed in a black skirt split to the thigh and a cream blouse that revealed an ample cleavage. "Come back and dance with me darling," she said. "Your tart awaits you."

"Oh god," James said and put his head in his hands. "Oh god, oh god, oh god."

"Who's he," the woman said, wagging her finger in Luke's direction. "Is he a private detective?" She giggled before adding, "Is he a dick?"

"No, Soph," James said, his voice slow and flat. "He's one of my work colleagues."

"I need to have a word, James," Luke said.

"I know." James sighed. "Soph, go back in. I'll be there in a bit."

"Okay," she said, before smiling and cocking her head to one side. "I'll be waiting."

Luke gestured to a long green sofa at one side of the room and they sat down. James turned nervously towards Luke. "What do you want?" he said.

Luke was exasperated. He had reached the wrong conclusion but he owed James an explanation before he left. "I didn't come to talk to you about your affair," he said.

"You didn't? But then why are you here?"

"I put two and two together and made five. I'm here because Sam Chambers has gone missing."

"That's awful, but what's it got to do with me?"

"We also found out this evening that the man who took Angie Johnson calls himself Mac and…"

"I see." James almost laughed with relief as the penny dropped. "So you're not going to tell Paula about…" he indicated the door through which Soph had just left.

"No, James. Sorry to disturb you." He stood up.

"That's okay," James said, the relief still apparent in his voice. "And good luck with finding Sam."

"Thanks. I'll leave you to get back to the party."

"Just a second," James said, grasping Luke's arm. "I do know a Mac. Could be a different person of course but…"

"Who?" Luke said.

"He's a graphic designer. I met him through one of my

colleagues, and then used him for an internal campaign we ran."

"What's his name?"

"To be honest, I don't know. I only met him a couple of times, and I only know him as Mac. We paid him through his company." The corners of his mouth turned up slightly.

"What is it, James?" Luke said.

"Nothing really. I was remembering the story Mac told me about his company. Apparently, he'd been a farmer of all things before moving into design, but his house burnt down so he had no option other than to find another source of income. He named his company after the farm."

"What was its name?"

"Loveless Designs."

Chapter 53

The noise and the lights took Josh by surprise. He jumped sideways and threw himself to the ground, the mud and heavens knew what else squelching beneath him. He lay on his front, as still as possible, afraid to look up in case the car's beams bounced back off his eyes. Something at the back of his mind was telling him that this only happened with cats. He shook his head. Concentrate Josh, concentrate.

The engine noise increased as the car drew nearer. He breathed in, wondering what to do if it stopped, but before he could decide it was past him, flicking him with water and dirt as it came within inches of his face. He looked up to see the tail lights disappearing around the stables and clambered to his feet.

He looked down at his Barbour, a Christmas present from his parents. It was filthy. "Buggery buggery," he exclaimed before bending his face down and inhaling. The smell was unmistakable. He was covered in cow shit.

The man had gone, but who knew for how long. He could have Sam with him in the car, but if that was the case there was nothing Josh could do about it. No, he had to hope she was still in one of those buildings at the top of the hill.

He stepped forward, slow squelch after slow squelch. After a few steps he heard a crunching bang, the unmistakable sound of metal hitting metal. It was behind him and some way off. He wondered for a moment what it was, then it dawned on him. Horatio had fought back. His trusty Clio had blocked the escape and saved the day.

Josh half ran, half-stumbled back to the stables then followed them to the side of the farmhouse. Sure enough, he could see a light on the other side of the field gate where he had left his car. He couldn't see clearly through the rain but the beam looked too high, as if the car was upside down or on its side.

He decided to go straight to the cars but halfway there realised his mistake. The farmhouse might be long disused but the field certainly wasn't. With every third or fourth step he felt his foot sink as he stepped in yet more cow shit, each one delaying him for a few seconds, unwilling to let him go.

He listened for sounds as he got nearer, for crying or screaming or worse, but there was nothing, just the incessant beating of the rain. He clambered over the gate and took everything in. The Clio, to his surprise, had fared relatively well. The other car, and he could see now it was a white Hyundai, had toppled to its side, the bonnet screwed up like tin foil and the driver's door thrown in the air.

He walked tentatively over to the open door, afraid that there might be some bloody mess of a human slapped against the windscreen, but the seat was empty. With a start, he turned around and looked at the ground, in case the driver had been thrown out when the car rolled over. Again nothing.

He heard a splash, just about audible through the wind and rain. He stepped out onto the road in time to see a grey shape disappearing around the corner where the main entrance to the farmhouse lay.

"Well done, Horatio," he said, tapping the Clio's bonnet. "England expects that every man will do his duty."

Chapter 54

Sam and Angie supported Emily between them. Mac had hit her across the leg and she was finding it impossible to put any weight on it. She had one arm around each of their shoulders and was hopping forward but it was slow progress. The hill was steep and it was several hundred yards down to the farmhouse, beyond which there had to be a road and perhaps some traffic.

"Do you know where we are?" Sam said.

"No idea," Angie replied. "He said we were remote but nothing else."

"We have to find the road. Locate the nearest house and get the owner to call the police."

"What if he comes back while we're looking?" Emily said. "We're hardly getting anywhere and it's my fault. You need to leave me, go on to call for help then come back. He's bound to be a while."

Sam considered this. It was true that she and Angie would make much more rapid progress on their own, probably covering four or five times as much ground as they could with Emily. But there was nowhere to leave her, the pigsties a definite no-no. They had to plod on, slow as it was, and hope that their remoteness meant he would be a while. "Come on," she said in what she hoped was a cheery voice. "We're out and he's gone. Now all we…"

Something charged into her. The impact took her breath away and she fell back, the metal bar thrown out of her hand as she jolted against the ground. A body landed on top of her chest and Emily screamed. Sam felt hands around her neck.

"Get off her, Mac," Angie screeched and Sam could see her pulling at his arms, trying to wrestle him away. But he was too strong and after a few seconds Angie let go and pulled away.

Sam's arms were caught between their bodies. She tried to reach forward with her head, find something to bite, anything, but his grip was too firm. He pressed tightly around her neck, his fingers almost piercing her skin. Breathing became more difficult and she felt a flush come to her face. It was difficult to focus her eyes.

She heard another scream, but it was Mac this time. He rolled to the side and she sat up, her breaths coming in short gasps. Angie stood above them both, the metal bar held above her head.

"You bastard," she said and swung down to hit him again, but his hand was up before the bar met its target. He grabbed it and twisted. She was forced to let go and he stood, panting, the weapon held triumphantly in his hand. Angie moved towards him but he raised the bar and she was forced to stop. She put her arm around Emily and looked down at Sam who was on her knees now, hands around her neck. "I tried," she said.

"Get back up there, you bitches," Mac snarled, gesturing to the buildings at the top of the hill.

If we all jump him we might stand a chance, Sam thought, but how could she communicate this to the others? And then there was Emily's leg. She was in too much pain for her to be able to be of any help. She looked at Angie, but Angie had eyes only for Mac, her face a picture of hate.

"Okay," Sam said as she got to her feet. Angie looked at her and she gave a slight nod, hoping Angie would catch on.

"I helped the three of you," Mac said. "I saved you from death. And then you do this. I was wrong to save you. You deserve to die, all of you."

Emily screamed again.

"Shut the fuck up!" he shouted.

Emily took a step back onto her bad leg and fell into

the mud as it gave way. Before Sam or Angie could move to help her Mac swung his arm and the metal bar came crashing down on the side of Emily's head. Sam gasped as she saw blood gushing from an open wound just above her left eye.

"Leave her," Mac snarled, gesturing with his arm. "Go."

Sam moved towards Emily. "But she's…" she started to say

He swung the bar above his head again. "I said, go." He said it slowly and deliberately and there was no mistaking his intention if she didn't obey. With one last look at Emily, she and Angie trudged up the hill towards the pigsties.

Chapter 55

Josh moved as quickly as he could but his Nike slip-ons were absolutely useless in gaining traction. He could see thirty or forty yards ahead but there was no sign of the man from the car, who was doubtless wearing something more appropriate, hiking boots or wellies perhaps. He extracted his right foot from one particularly soft pile of bovine excrement and put it down again onto something much more solid.

He yelped, lifted his foot and took a pace backwards. Looking down he saw it was a woman's body he had stepped on. She was on her side, not moving, hair covering her face. He bent forward and pushed the hair to one side. He could see now that that it wasn't Sam. He looked up, fearful that the man he was chasing might appear at any moment, then back down. It must be Angie or Emily, he thought then looked again at her face. It was Emily.

Blood covered the side of her head, and he saw that there was a three or four inch gash across her temple. He felt for a pulse and was relieved when he found one. She was out for the count but breathing, thank god. She needed medical attention though. If she stayed out for long in this weather she would deteriorate fast.

He wanted to go on, to rescue Sam before the man did to her what he had done to Emily, or worse. But he had to take Emily somewhere first. She would at least be dry if he put her in the Clio. It was downhill all the way so he should be able to manage her. Once she was in the car he could, for the third time for goodness sake, make his way back up the hill to find Sam. He had a wheel wrench in the boot too. He could grab that.

With new determination he stood either side of her

head and put his arms under her back. He lifted her so that she was sitting up. He had to be careful now and support her with…

"Josh."

He yelped and dropped her.

"Shit," he said, as her head slapped onto the ground.

"Josh, it's me," Luke said as he materialised from the gloom.

Josh breathed a huge sigh of relief. "Thank god all bloody mighty," he said, then words tumbled out from him in a stream. "It's Sam," he said, "she's …" he gestured up the hill, "and the man, he hit the car…" he waved his arm down to the road. "Well he didn't hit it but his car did." He pointed at the body on the floor. "This is Emily. She's conscious but cold and wet. What if she gets hypochondria?"

"Calm down, Josh," Luke said. "You mean hypothermia."

"Yes, that one."

Luke took his coat off and put it on top of Emily. "You stay here with her, Josh. Wrap yourself around her to keep her warm until the police arrive. I rang them on the way here so they shouldn't be too long." He looked up the hill to the two stone structures. "He must have been keeping them up there," he said, half to himself. "Somehow Emily got away, which means Sam and Angie may have as well. "

"What are you going to do, guv?"

"Sort him out," Luke said. "Once and for all."

Chapter 56

Seeing the way Mac had treated Emily made Sam fear for their lives. If he got them to the pigsties they were done for, and being locked inside them would be the very best they could hope for. She held her hand out and grasped Angie's before tentatively looking around. Mac stood a few yards behind, watching their every move and too far away for them to rush him. He smiled at her, but it was a shambles of a thing, almost a leer. Then the corners of his mouth dropped and he started mumbling. She could make out the odd word.

"Should have killed...told me...not too late...do it now...or later..." Suddenly he stopped and called out, loudly and clearly now, "Stop, both of you."

They stopped and turned, still holding hands.

"Over there," he said and gestured to a clump of trees some fifty yards to their left.

Sam squeezed Angie and slid her finger across her palm, hoping her message was clear. She ran to the left and sure enough Angie ran right. Mac looked from one to the other, then screeched at the top of his voice. "I'll get you." He raised the metal bar above his head and ran after Sam.

"Go, Angie," Sam said under her breath. She was running along the side of the slope and it was difficult to grip the surface. She was sure he was gaining on her but pressed on, the trees only a few yards away. Perhaps she could find a branch to defend herself with, or he would trip on something, or...

Her legs gave way as metal crunched into her calf. He hissed with triumph and swung it up above his head. At the last moment she managed to twist away and the bar slammed down inches from her face. It embedded itself in the ground but he tore it out, lifted it again. He was about to bring it down for the second time when movement caught his eye. He turned to see Angie bearing down on him, her eyes blazing.

"Angie, no," Sam shouted. She reached out and managed to grab his ankle. He hesitated, turned, snarled and then fell back as something hit him hard in the temple. He stumbled back and looked up but someone was on him now, someone a lot bigger than Mac.

The man punched him once, twice, but Mac snarled and fought back. He was stronger than he looked and managed to land a hefty blow which made his assailant leap back. Sam saw then that it was Luke.

Mac crawled away, got to his feet and ran towards the trees.

Then disappeared.

She saw Luke follow tentatively before stopping. She limped up beside him, Angie close behind. He held out his hand for them to stop and they held hands again as he stepped tentatively forward. After a few paces he signalled for them to join him.

They stepped to his side and Sam saw that they were on the edge of a sheer drop, the land falling away almost vertically in front of them. The rain was heavy but she could make out Mac's body some fifty feet down. It was contorted, his face looking into the rain, his legs splayed at an unnatural angle.

Luke supported Sam as the two of them and Angie made their way back to Josh. He was lying beside Emily, cradling her body to keep her warm. He looked up when they drew near.

"Where is he?" he asked.

"Dead," Luke said, then raised his head as he heard the sound of sirens. "Wait here." He headed off towards the farmhouse. When he rounded the stables he saw several sets of blue lights and three men heading towards him, led by a figure he recognised.

"Pete," he shouted. "Thank goodness you're here."

Luke gave him a brief account of what had happened and Pete pulled out his airwave radio.

"Tell the paramedics to bring a stretcher and blankets," he said. "They'll have to come through the field, there's no way past those two cars to get to the main entrance."

Chapter 57

Luke pressed the button, wishing there were three 'extra shot' buttons rather than one, and took the espresso back to his chair.

"Are you okay?" he said.

Josh looked up from his hot chocolate. "Fine, guv," he said, though he looked anything but. "Worried about Emily though."

A man in his late forties appeared at the end of the corridor. He was overweight, sweating and walking quickly, almost running. When he reached the nurse's station he stopped, disappointed to see there was no-one there.

Luke stood up. "Andy Parker?" he said.

"Yes."

"I'm Luke Sackville, from Filchers." He held out his hand. "We spoke the other day."

"Oh yes," Andy said, and shook Luke's hand absent-mindedly. "Do you know how Emily is?"

"We're waiting to hear. She's still unconscious and they've taken her for a CT scan."

"Oh god, is it…" He stopped as a nurse came into view further down the corridor.

"Mr Parker," she said.

He nodded. "Is she going to be alright?" The words came out in a rush.

"She's still unconscious but we've completed the scan and you can sit at her bedside if you'd like to."

"Of course," he said, and followed her back down the corridor.

As he left, Sam came into view. She was supporting herself with crutches and the bottom half of her leg was encased in plaster. She limped over and sat beside them.

"No news on Emily I take it?" she said.

"Not yet," Luke said.

"What about Mac?"

"As yet we don't know what Mac's real name is or why he did what he did. Normally in cases like this there's some kind of sexual motive, but there's no sign of that being the case. Revenge would be an option, but you've never met him and neither has Angie Johnson. It's different with Emily given they had some kind of a relationship, brief as it was, and the police will be keen to talk to her when she regains consciousness." He exchanged looks with Sam, and could see that she appreciated that it was an 'if' rather than a 'when'.

"Angie said he made her wear a blonde wig and high heels," Sam said. "Could that be some kind of sexual fantasy?"

"It's possible, but he held her for several days without sexually assaulting her, and there were no signs that Marie Downing had been raped. No, I think it's more complex. Hopefully it will become clearer when we find out more about him."

He stepped away and rang Pete Gilmore.

"Gilmore."

"Any news, Pete?"

"I can't share…"

Luke didn't allow him to finish. "You can trust me, Pete. I'm hardly the sort to blab to the press."

Pete sighed. "His wallet was in his pocket and it had his driving licence in it," he said. "Mac's real name is Malcolm Smith and he lives in Combe Down. We're at the house now."

"Keep me in the loop will you?"

"I'll do what I can."

Luke looked at his watch. It was ten past three. "Why don't you two go home," he said. "I'll stay here and let you know if there are any developments or if Emily regains consciousness."

Or if she deteriorates, he thought.

Josh yawned. "I think I'll do that, guv," he said. "I'm not much use here anyway. "

"I've told Angie she can stay with me," Sam said. "Helen's returned to her house and Angie can hardly go back to her cheating boyfriend which means she's more or less homeless. The police said they'd bring her here as soon as they've finished questioning her, so I'll wait for her then we'll head off." She grunted. "Not sure we'll get much sleep though."

"What time shall we meet tomorrow?" Josh said, then added, "uh, I guess I mean today."

"We still have to ask Angie about Project Iceberg and Bannermans,' Luke said, and held his hand up as Sam started to protest. "I'm not suggesting we do that today, but we should at least get together to talk about next steps. We need to bring Helen and Maj up to date too. Let's meet in the Ethics Room at ten."

The others agreed, but Luke had no intention of going home. He was going to Combe Down. He rang Pete as he walked to the Beemer and cajoled the address out of him before heading off, wishing again that he could blue light the journey.

Chapter 58

"I'm sorry but you can't go in there, sir," the young officer said.

"Please tell DI Gilmore I'm here," Luke said. He looked up at the house. It was terraced, Victorian probably, and not much more than a two-up two-down. He spotted a curtain move in the upstairs window next door. The press would be there in no time, he thought, the squirrely bastards able to spot a potential scoop almost before it happened.

Pete appeared at the front door. "It's okay, let him in," he said grudgingly.

"Found anything?" Luke said, as he joined him in the narrow hallway. He looked around. It was flamboyantly decorated with swirling wallpaper and a deep red carpet. The lampshade was as near to a chandelier as you could get in such a tiny space.

"There are signs that someone else has been here," Pete said. "Two unwashed wine glasses in the kitchen which we've sent back for fingerprinting."

"Anything that links him to the women he kidnapped?"

"We found a blonde wig similar to the one he made Angie Johnson wear. Nothing else of significance, but there is something I'd like you to take a look at." He started up the stairs. "We found it in the bedroom."

At the top of the stairs was a miniscule landing, with two doors leading off. The door of the room nearer the back of the house was open and Luke could see it was a small bathroom. Pete opened the other door and they entered a bedroom, again vividly decorated and certainly not to Luke's taste but otherwise unremarkable. It was a small room but squeezed into it were a double bed, single wardrobe and a table and chair.

Pete passed him a pair of blue nitrile gloves and gestured to the table on top of which was a large notebook. Luke put the gloves on and walked over. He could see now that it was an A3 sketch pad. The cover was unadorned. He turned to the first page. It was covered in black and white drawings which looked to have been done in charcoal. He had to admire the skill of whoever had drawn them, presumably Malcolm Smith, aka Mac, but the subject matter was bizarre.

They were sketches, almost doodles, rather than finished pieces of art. In the centre was a stylised woman's head, with long hair and her mouth open. It was impossible to say what age she was meant to be but she was angry, her brows furrowed. Encircling her face were drawings of men, perhaps of the same man, all facing her and all naked, but with no genitalia. They were bent in different positions, some backwards, some forwards and one sideways at the waist. Their eyes were slits and their lips turned down in a parody of absolute misery.

He turned the page to reveal a second charcoal drawing, and this one was more complete. It portrayed a tall slender woman in an evening dress and high heels. She too had long hair but there the resemblance with the woman on the first page ended. This woman was smiling.

"He's only drawn on those two pages," Pete said. "Angie Johnson said that Smith told her she was kind and gentle. I think," he gestured to the drawing, "that this is his ideal woman and he was searching for her. Perhaps Marie wasn't the right one so he took Angie, but she was't good enough so he moved on to Emily then Sam."

"It's possible," Luke mused. He turned back to the first set of sketches. "But it makes me wonder who this woman is. These," he gestured to the male figures, "are presumably meant to be him, suffering because of her."

"Could be his mother," Pete said. "Perhaps she abused

him as a child."

"Then I would expect drawings of children around her face, not grown men."

"I'm not sure it matters, Luke. Something caused Smith to abduct these women but I don't think we'll ever get under his skin and understand his true motivation. He was twisted and psychopathic and it could be as simple as that."

Chapter 59

Luke woke and looked at his alarm clock. It was just gone nine which gave him enough time to shower, dress and be at Filchers in time to meet the team at ten.

He got into the shower and let the hot water cascade over his head and body. It had been five when he got to bed, high on adrenaline and not expecting to sleep. But it must have been only minutes before his body succumbed. Towelling himself down he thought about what they might be able to achieve after the events of the night before. It wasn't as if they could schedule any meetings. His phone rang. It was Sam.

"Are you and Angie okay?" he said.

"We're fine," Sam said, "But I think I know who's behind the Project Iceberg problems."

"Who?"

"The Head of Marketing, Arthur Bloomsbury. Angie told me he was asking her all sorts of questions about the ins and outs of the deal, claiming it was to ensure he was ready to run a campaign on the back of winning the bid. She found it a bit odd, but thought nothing more about it."

Luke wondered if what Rob Talbot had found was something to do with Bloomsbury. "Shit," he said.

"What is it?" Sam said.

"I forgot, I'm seeing Rob Talbot at ten. I'll have to go Sam. Tell Helen and the others I may be a few minutes late."

Seeing Rob was less urgent now that Angie had been found but he still had to investigate the bribery allegation and whether she was implicated, much as he didn't want to.

*

It was nine fifty when Luke pulled up outside Rob Talbot's apartment. He rang the buzzer, expecting an immediate, if gruff, reply but there was nothing. Exasperated, and wondering if he should have gone straight to Filchers, he pressed the buzzer again. Still nothing. He was about to return to the car when the door opened to reveal a slight and viscerally thin middle-aged woman who stared up at him in shock.

"Get away," she screamed and stepped backwards.

He saw that she had blood on the sleeve of her coat and on her hand. "Are you okay?" he said, gesturing to her arm.

She looked at her arm then back up to him. "I'm fine," she said, her voice trembling. "This isn't mine. I saw the door was open." She gestured behind her and up the stairs. "And he didn't answer so I went in." She put a hand to her mouth. "I saw him then, lying on the floor, not moving. He was staring at me and there's blood, god so much blood." She started to sob. "I was so scared, I ran." She took a deep breath. "He might be alive, I didn't check."

"Have you got a phone?" She fumbled in her pocket and pulled out her mobile, hand shaking. "Call 999 and wait here."

He raced past her, taking the stairs two at a time. There were drops of blood on the first-floor landing and the door to apartment 2B was partly open. He pushed it wide to reveal a body on the floor, Rob Talbot's body. There was blood on his shirt, and it looked like he had been stabbed more than once. His face was unmarked but his eyes were open and unseeing. Luke felt for a pulse but knew there wouldn't be one.

He returned to the woman at the front of the building. She hung up as he emerged. "Are the police on their way?" he said.

"Yes, and an ambulance. Is he…" Her voice was still shaky and she was unable to complete the question.

"Yes, he's dead. Did you see anyone go in?"

"No," she said. "I heard Rob letting someone in though, probably about an hour ago."

"Did you hear the other person say anything?"

"No, I'm afraid not. I guess it must have been…"

"His murderer. Yes, I think so."

Chapter 60

It was eleven before Luke got to Filchers. He was surprised to hear laughter as he approached the Ethics Room, and walked in to hear Josh regaling the other team members with the many reasons, mainly related to cow excrement, why he was never ever going in a field again.

They all looked up at him and their smiles drained away when they saw the expression on his face.

"What's happened?" Sam said. "Is it Emily?"

"No," Luke said. "She's still unconscious but stable. It's Rob Talbot, Angie Johnson's partner."

"What about him?" asked Helen.

"He was murdered last night." There was a collective gasp. "He was stabbed. On the surface it looks like he disturbed a burglar."

"Home invasion," Josh said.

"Indeed, Josh," Luke said, before continuing. "Of course, it could be a coincidence and not connected to Angie's disappearance. However, I'm inclined to think, and apologies here if I stray into police jargon, that that hypothesis…" He saw Josh reach for his pad and pen. "…is a load of bollocks."

Josh put his pen down. "Have CSIs been in?" he said.

"Yes, Josh," Luke said. "SOCOs, as we call them in the UK, are in the apartment now. There were no signs of a struggle so Talbot either knew his assailant or he was surprised. The killer appears to have run off without taking anything of value. Talbot's wallet, with about £200 in it, was left, as was his Breitling watch."

"Cool," Josh said. "Was it a Duograph?"

Luke shut him up with a glare. "The police think the burglar panicked and that's why he didn't steal anything.

However, he may have been there simply to kill Talbot or else looking for something of importance."

"Do you mean sentimental value?" Sam said.

"Possibly," Luke said. "But more likely an object that would reveal something the killer wanted kept a secret."

"Could Mac have killed him?" Helen said.

"We can't be certain until the post-mortem, but I doubt it. With what we saw of his behaviour with you and the other women this was not his modus operandi."

"M-O," Josh said.

Luke ignored him. "This killing," he said, "was very different from Marie Downing's murder which was planned and was made to look like suicide." He gestured to the whiteboard. "Helen, could you…"

"Of course," she said and stood up to add a post-it above Rob Talbot's photo. She wrote 'Murderer?' on it then drew a line connecting them.

"Helen," Luke said, "Can you draw a dotted line between our murderer and Angie please?"

"In my view," he went on, and he was speaking to all of them now, "this puts Angie in danger again. If I'm right and Rob Talbot's murder is not a coincidence then his killer could be after her next." He looked at Sam. "Or you Sam."

"Do you know if the SOCOs have found anything of interest yet, guv?" Josh said.

"Several sets of fingerprints," Luke said, "but it's too early to say if any of them will be useful. Yours and mine will be among them of course. Pete promised me an update later and the post-mortem is set for this afternoon."

Luke sat back on his chair and looked up at the whiteboards Helen had created. She'd done a good job with what they had but they needed more information, particularly on Marie Downing. Other than the bullying accusations they knew almost nothing about her.

They knew much more about Angie Johnson but he needed to talk to her as soon as possible to see if she had any idea what Rob Talbot's murderer might have been looking for at the apartment. The killing could be linked to the bribery accusation, which put Arthur Bloomsbury in the spotlight. But if that was the case, what was the connection with Mac given Mac had also taken Marie, Emily and Sam, none of whom had had anything to do with Project Iceberg?

He was convinced the abduction and killings were all linked but how? Neither Mac nor Rob Talbot's killer had seemed to gain any sexual gratification from what they had done which, in his experience, left money, love, revenge or a combination of the three to be the most likely motive.

His phone buzzed and he looked down to see Pete Gilmore's name on the screen. "Hi Pete," he said. "Any progress?"

"Not really. Looks to me like he was killed this morning, possibly not long before you called on him in fact. The post-mortem will confirm that of course. It could be a home invasion gone wrong."

"So you think it's a coincidence?" Luke said, and he couldn't keep the doubt from his voice.

"Luke, I know you don't believe in coincidences…"

Luke broke in before Pete could continue. "You know full well I don't." He was in full DCI mode now, voice raised, hackles up. "There's got to be a connection, has to be." He stood up and walked towards the whiteboard. Rob Talbot's name was there and arrows connected him to Angie and Olivia but that was it. He needed more information. "When's the post-mortem?" he barked, eyes still on the whiteboard.

"I can't let…"

"When is it, Pete?"

"Luke, this is a separate incident. I'm letting you know as a courtesy. There's no connection to Malcolm Smith let alone Filchers, so…"

Luke interrupted again. "Of course there's a bloody

connection." He paused and lowered his voice, tried to control his rising anger. He spoke his next words very deliberately and slowly. "I need to be at the post-mortem."

He heard Pete sigh. "I'm sorry Luke, but you know I can't let a civilian attend."

Luke grunted and hung up. "Josh," he said on his way out. "I want you to go to Sam's apartment and fetch Angie. I want her here where she's safe."

"Roger, guv."

"Sam, Helen and Maj, take a good look at the whiteboard and adjust it in light of what happened last night and this morning. This case is far from over."

Chapter 61

"I can't believe she's let you in again," Pete said.

Luke shrugged. "She insisted," he said. They were sitting at either end of Sally Croft's sofa. "Any more news on Rob Talbot?"

"SOCOs are still there." Pete looked at his watch. "Barry Statham's taking the lead. He said he'd ring me at noon with an update."

"What do you think happened?".

"Whoever broke in didn't realise the victim was in and panicked."

"Was the murder weapon found?'

"Yes, it was next to the body on the lounge floor. Paring knife taken from a block of knives in the kitchen."

"Any sign of a struggle?"

"Loads of them," Pete said. "Lamps knocked over, TV smashed. I'd say the assailant must have been injured as well."

"Do you think it might have been staged to make it look like a burglary gone wrong?"

"Could be," Pete said.

The door to the examination room opened and a figure beckoned to the two men. Clad from head to toe in goggles, face mask, lab suit and surgical gloves it was only the pink hair that was the giveaway. "Gentlemen, how lovely of you to visit me again so soon," Sally said. She removed the goggles and winked at Pete. "Anyone would think you were stalking me, Inspector Gilmore." She paused for a response, but aside from an audible swallow Pete just stared back, his lips slightly apart.

She adopted a more serious tone. "Please go upstairs," she said, "and prepare yourselves. It's a bit of a messy one."

She turned and both men made their way up to the viewing gallery. The smell, as ever, was intense. It was reminiscent of a hospital but mixed in with the aroma of antiseptic was the sweet sickly odour of death.

Through the glass Luke saw Sally's assistant Nina standing next to the examination table, notepad in hand. Sally walked to the other side of a linen-covered shape, still in one piece he was pleased to see, and without another word swept the covering back to reveal a naked and bloodied corpse, the head shaved but the body untouched.

"As you can see, gents," Sally said, looking up at the gallery, "I've already cut away his clothes and done a preliminary external examination."

"Cause of death?" Pete said.

"At the moment I'm thinking one of the knife wounds. I've counted sixteen so far. There's a lot of blood so I might find more when I clean him down." She gestured to the left thigh. "There are two here, the others I've found…" she waved her hand around the man's abdomen and stomach, "…are here. All at the front." She pointed at two near the victim's left nipple. "I'd say one of these killed him."

"How long has he been dead?" Luke asked.

"I'd guess three to five hours, so that puts the killing in the early hours of this morning. I'll know for certain when I've spliced and diced."

"Anything else of note?"

"Not at the moment. But who knows what excitement the next hour or two might bring. Do you want to stay?" she said.

It took Pete less than a second to answer. "No," he said, "but thanks for the offer. We need to go."

"Right you are." She removed a long scalpel from a block on a metal table next to the body, held it to the light then bent over Talbot's head. She looked up and smiled to herself when she saw that the two had already left the gallery.

Luke removed his mask and looked over at Pete as he closed the door. "Please ring me when SOCOs are done," he said.

"I told you, Luke," Pete said. "You're a civilian now and…" He stopped and held his hand up when he saw the expression on Luke's face. "Look, I'll ring you, I promise, but I won't be able to share everything."

"Thanks, Pete. I think I'm going to stay for the post-mortem."

"Fine. Rather you than me." He gave a little shudder. "We'll speak later."

Sally's goggles were off when Luke re-entered the viewing gallery and she was sitting on a chair next to Talbot's body. Her eyes twinkled when she saw him.

"I thought you'd be back," she said. "You're expecting something, aren't you?"

"I have a suspicion," Luke said.

Sally leant over the corpse and used the scalpel to cut across the crown of the head, from the bony bump behind one ear to the bump behind the other. She handed the scalpel to her assistant.

"Pass me Bobby please," she said, before adding for Luke's benefit, "it's a craniotome but I think Bobby the Brainsaw is more descriptive." Nina passed her an electric implement that looked like a dentist's drill. Sally leant over one end of the cut, flicked the on switch and sawed through the skull before peeling back the flap that had been created. Luke didn't know which bothered him more, the screeching sound of metal against bone or the thought that this was a man's head being ripped apart.

Sally examined the brain carefully from all angles before making the cuts necessary to remove it from the skull. She passed it to Nina. "Standard thickness," she said, then looked up at Luke. "If there are blood clots or tumours I have to point them out." She gestured to the many cuts on the abdomen and smiled. "Although if he has any I suspect they are not what killed him."

Once Nina had completed the cuts Sally examined the exposed slices. "Nothing," she said. She returned to the body and made a long incision down the front of the abdomen. One by one she removed the internal organs and passed them to Nina. Luke stepped right up to the glass when she cut away the stomach.

"I thought that might be where your interests lay," she said. Rather than pass the stomach to her assistant she carried it to the cutting table herself. Luke watched carefully as she cut into it and started separating items of semi-digested and non-digested food, all of which were sloshing around in a kind of noxious gruel which almost made him heave.

"This is certainly unusual," she said. "I've only seen this once before." She indicated the inner walls of the stomach lining. They had a strong greenish-blue tinge. Sally used her index finger and thumb to open Talbot's mouth. Nina moved to her side and shone a torch inside. "Here too," Sally said. "There's colouring to the tongue and the mucous membrane around the mouth."

"What does that mean?" Luke said.

"It means, dear Luke, that I was wrong earlier. The knife wounds weren't what killed him. Our man here was poisoned, then stabbed immediately after death."

"You said you've seen this before?"

"Yes, it was an overdose of dextropropoxyphene which women used for pain relief. It hasn't been available for over a decade though, and I'm inclined to think our murderer used copper sulphate which is much more readily available. You can buy it over the counter or from amazon or eBay without any prescription. I'll know for certain when we get the blood results back."

"Could it have been given to him dissolved in a drink?" Luke said.

"Yes, but it has a strong smell and taste so it would have to be a strong black coffee or something similar."

The espresso Luke had been looking forward to was suddenly a lot less appealing.

Chapter 62

Angie buzzed Josh into the apartment.

"What is it?" she said when she opened the door. She was still in a dressing gown and her hair was wet so he guessed she had just had a shower.

"Can I come in," Josh said. "I've got some news and I think you should sit down to hear it." He followed her into the lounge. She sat on the sofa and he sat on the armchair opposite.

"He is dead, isn't he?" she said.

"You mean you know?" Josh exclaimed. "How did you find out?"

She gave him a quizzical look. "I was there, Josh. I saw his body. We all saw his body. He didn't survive that fall did he?"

"Oh, I see. No, I mean…"

"What?"

"I mean…" Josh hesitated. "Yes, Mac is dead, but, the thing is…" He cleared his throat. "…so is Rob Talbot."

"Don't be silly." She smiled, but it faded when she saw the expression on his face. "You're serious? But how, where?"

"He was stabbed repeatedly at your flat."

"God, that's awful. Could it have been Mac?"

"We don't know when he was killed. They're doing the post-mortem now. The police think it might have been a robbery and Rob disturbed them. The guv, I mean Luke, doesn't believe in coincidences so I guess it has to have been Mac."

Angie stood up. "Well thanks for letting me know, but I'll be okay." She attempted a half-smile. "Rob and I had split up so I can cope."

"No, no," Josh said. "Luke says you have to come back to Filchers with me."

"But Mac is dead. He can't harm me now."

Josh hesitated before answering. "The thing is, Angie, if it wasn't Mac then your life could still be in danger from whoever he was working with. Luke wants you where he knows you'll be safe."

"Okay. I'll need to…" She gestured to her dressing gown.

"Yes, of course."

She stood up and walked to the bedroom door. "What about clothes?" she said.

He looked at her and raised one eyebrow.

"I mean should I pack some?"

"Oh yes, of course." His cheeks turned a subtle shade of pink. "Gotcha. Yes, definito."

She shook her head and went into the bedroom.

Josh ordered the taxi while Angie dressed.

"It was Luke who found your ex," he said, as he buckled his seat belt. "They'd arranged to meet this morning because Rob said he'd found something which might help track you down. Any idea what it might be?"

"Not really." She was quiet for a few seconds. "We were meant to be going to Tuscany. Do you think it could be that?"

"I don't think so," Josh said. "We knew all about that trip and had already spoken to your hotel in Florence."

"I kept my bills, payslips and so on in a metal file box. I wonder if there was something in there he thought might be relevant. I can't think what though."

"Could it have been something to do with Project Iceberg?"

"No, I didn't keep anything from Iceberg at home. Physical papers are kept at Filchers in locked cupboards and Rob wouldn't have been able to access my emails or online storage." She thought for a minute longer before continuing. "There is some Filchers correspondence in the file though, personal stuff but not related to bids or anything like that."

"Could it have been that?"

"Possibly. It was all to do with a guy who was stalking me online. I managed to find out who it was and Filchers had a word with him. They wouldn't discipline him though, let alone sack him, which really irritated me but he did stop and to be honest, I'd almost forgotten about it. It was last summer so eight or nine months ago now."

"Do you remember his name?"

"Oh yes. His name is Dale Cartwright."

Chapter 63

Sam read the message, astonished that Dale Cartwright was trying to make contact. He'd been pleasant looking, and for a few seconds she'd even thought him attractive, but his overt misogyny had upset and horrified her.

But then again, she was in the Ethics Team. Malcolm Smith, aka Mac, was the kidnapper and killer they had been seeking so they, and hence she, needed to be investigating other unethical conduct. If she took Dale up on his offer it would give her the chance to show initiative and prove her worth. All he was doing was inviting her for a coffee and he couldn't try anything on, or nothing nasty at least, if it was in a public place. She could subtly probe about Marie and try to find out if there were other Filchers' employees he might have been assaulting or worse.

She texted back a thumbs-up emoji with the message "See you in the canteen in ten minutes."

"What was that?" Helen said.

Sam decided she would keep this meeting under her hat for the time being. "A friend of mine asking to meet up for a coffee. She's in the canteen now. Do you mind if I pop out? I'll only be half an hour or so."

"Of course not," Helen said, her focus already back on the whiteboard where Maj was updating the Iceberg team members' post-its.

Sam grabbed her crutches and stepped outside the room. She limped slowly down the corridor, trying to decide what the best approach would be. She could flirt or act dumb and see what happened next, but that in itself might be unethical and qualify as some kind of 'honey trap'. Perhaps she should be honest and announce she was there as an Ethics Team member because of what the video had shown. But if she did that he might just get up and leave and she wouldn't have achieved anything.

She was so deep in thought that she didn't notice the steps behind her until they were only a few feet away. When she did pick up on them she felt a shudder go through her body, her mind transferred back to her apartment, to the feeling of faintness and weightlessness when Mac had stabbed a needle in her arm.

She stumbled and almost fell. An arm grabbed hers and held her up.

She turned.

"Oh," she said. "It's you."

Chapter 64

Luke's phone rang and he smiled when he saw his daughter's photo on the screen.

"Hi darling," he said. "Did you speak to the old grump?"

"I did," Chloe said.

"Well?"

"He agreed to me changing the article."

"Brilliant. How did you persuade him?"

"I did as you said. I watched a YouTube of him speaking about boat migrants and praised him for his performance. It worked a treat."

"Well done, Chloe. Did you ask about your grandmother?"

"I tried to, but all he would say was that she was having precautionary treatment but that it was probably nothing to worry about. I tried pressing but he wouldn't say any more."

"Well, thanks for trying. I don't suppose he asked about you and how you were getting on?"

Chloe laughed. "Not a chance."

Luke hung up and turned his attention back to his laptop. He had googled copper sulphate and what he found confirmed everything Sally Croft had said. Buying it was easy, no prescription needed, no proof of anything in fact. And it wasn't just through pharmaceutical companies. Sally had been right, you could buy it on Amazon or eBay, no questions asked.

He walked into the Ethics Room to find Helen at the whiteboard while Maj was on his laptop. Josh and Angie were at the table deep in conversation.

"Where's Sam?" Luke said.

"She popped out to meet a friend about twenty minutes ago," Helen said. "Said she wouldn't be long."

"Okay, I want to update you all on the post-mortem but let's give Sam five minutes. Sorry, Angie, but the findings are confidential, plus it's your ex, so I'll have to ask you to leave while we go through what the pathologist found."

"That's fine," Angie said.

"But I don't want you going far."

"It's okay, I can wait outside." Her phone rang and she looked down at the name on the screen then stood up. "Actually," she said, "I'll step out now. I need to take this."

Luke waited for her to close the door. "I'll tell you more when Sam returns but it definitely wasn't Malcolm Smith who killed Rob Talbot," he said. "We know the time of death now and Mac, as he called himself, was dead by then.'

"Guv," Josh said. "It may have been Dale Cartwright. Angie told me she was stalked online by him last year. There were letters about it which may have been what Rob Talbot had found. And he's also linked to Marie Downing and…"

Luke cut him off. "Dale Cartwright's not the killer," he said.

"How do you know?"

"I can read people," Luke said. "Put it down to experience. Cartwright wasn't lying when we asked about the murder, I'm convinced of it."

"How can you be so sure?"

"Luke's a truth wizard," Maj said.

"What?" Josh said. "You mean like Harry Potter?"

"No," Maj said.

"I'm very good at reading body language that's all," Luke said.

"It's a bit more than that," Maj went on. "Sorry Luke, but when I knew I was going to be working for you I did a bit of googling. First up was the Oliver Penman case and I found an article describing how another man was in the frame until you viewed a short video of Penman's interview. Apparently, you spotted a series of oddities in his responses that led to a separate line of enquiry and ultimately to his arrest."

Josh's mouth opened. "You are like Harry Potter," he said.

"No, Josh," Luke said. "I'm a bit more attuned than most people to facial expressions and the like, that's all."

"Then," Maj said, "I looked at earlier cases and one of them led me to a study by Oxford University in which you were identified as one of only six known truth wizards in the UK."

"Okay, okay," Luke said, holding his hand up. "I may be a bit unusual but back to the point - and you can stop gawping now, Josh - if Cartwright's not our killer then who is?" Josh started to answer, but Luke held his hand up. "You've made me think, Maj," he said. "There was someone I talked to and I thought the conversation was odd, but…" He looked at his watch.

"Helen," he said, and there was a new sense of urgency in his voice. "Can you check Angie's all right please?"

Helen nodded and went to the door. She opened it and looked around. "She's not there," she said.

"Josh," Luke said. "Give Angie a ring. Maj, call Sam. We need to get both of them back here immediately."

"What is it?" Helen said.

"I think I know who killed Rob Talbot," Luke said. "And if I'm right then Sam and Angie are in great danger."

"No answer," Josh said.

"The same for Sam," Maj added.

"Right," Luke said. He stood and walked to the door. "Josh and Maj, you go to the canteen and see if either of them is there. Helen, you stay here in case they return. And all of you, keep in touch."

"Will do, guv," Josh said. "Where are you going?"

"I'm going to see if James McDonald is in today."

Luke raced down the corridor, ignored the lift and took two stairs at a time to the Executive Floor, almost barrelling into Glen Baxter when he emerged at the top.

"Watch it!" Glen exclaimed.

"Where's James?" Luke said.

"In with Filcher. Why…"

But Luke was already gone. He ignored Filcher's secretary when she stood to try to stop him and pushed the door open. James and Filcher were sitting opposite one another across the desk. Both looked up when he walked in but it was Filcher who spoke first.

"What do you mean by this, Sackville?" he snarled and stood up. "Get out of my office." He pointed to the door. "This minute."

Luke heard Gloria open the door behind him.

"Shut up, Filcher," Luke said, and the emphasis he put behind the three words made Filcher sit down again.

"If this is about last night," James said.

"It's not," Luke said. "This is much more important than your love life."

Filcher looked up at this. "Hey, what…"

"I said shut up," Luke snapped, his eyes still focused on James.

"James," he continued, "you told me that you met the man who called himself Mac through a colleague."

"That's right."

"Was it Caroline Klein?"

"Yes, but how did you know?"

Luke ignored the question. "Do you know where she is?"

"Not right now, no." It was his turn to stand up. "I know she can be difficult at times but this really is out of order."

"She's our killer," Luke said.

"Gloria," Filcher said. "Call security."

"They're here," she said.

Luke turned to see Glen Baxter standing behind Gloria, fighting unsuccessfully to keep the smirk from his face.

"Listen, Sackville," Filcher said, "I know about Mr Talbot. In fact James and I were just discussing what to do about Angie Johnson given everything that's happened to her. However, I've spoken to the police, the real police that is, on the phone and they've confirmed he was killed by a burglar. So this fanciful nonsense about one of our best HR managers being his killer. Really." He looked over at Glen. "Baxter, get him out of here and escort him from the building."

"Wait a minute," James said. He addressed his next comments to Luke, ignoring Baxter who now stood at Luke's side, and Filcher who was harrumphing to himself in his chair. "You're convinced of this aren't you, Luke?"

"Yes James, totally convinced."

"Come with me then. I think I know where she may be. You can explain on the way."

Luke vaguely heard Filcher saying "And let that be a lesson to you" as he and James left his office.

Chapter 65

Angie wasn't sure this was a good idea but there was no harm in seeing what the Head of HR had to say. She could always say 'no' after all. Caroline Klein was a couple of paces ahead and walking briskly, looking over her shoulder every few seconds to ensure she was keeping up. They reached the end of the corridor and she held the door open for Angie to go through. She was immediately met by iron steps going down.

"Why are we going to the basement?" Angie said. "I thought his office was on the Executive Floor?"

"James has an office here," Caroline said as she closed the door behind them. "We use it for sensitive meetings like this. The company want to make you a generous offer in light of everything that's happened. We'll forget about what you did on Project Iceberg…"

"I didn't do anything wrong."

Caroline ignored her. "…and in exchange you sign a non-disclosure agreement. That's all there is to it. Now hurry, we can't leave James waiting for much longer." At the bottom of the stairs they went through another door and entered a soulless corridor. "Left here," Caroline said.

It was the first time Angie had been in Filchers' basement and it was certainly a lot less fancy than the floors above ground. There were strip lights every few metres, but it was dim despite them. The lack of a ceiling meant the grey ducting for power cables was visible above her head and the walls and floor were similarly bare and grey. The place looked cold and, given the lack of heating, felt cold too.

She was vaguely aware of the basement being where the security team were based, and someone had once told her housekeeping used it. Plus she guessed that air conditioning units, emergency generators and the like were probably down there. But she would never have dreamt that it contained special meeting rooms.

"This is it," Caroline said as they approached a door with a metal sign saying *'Warning - Do Not Enter'*.

"Ignore the sign," she added with a half-chuckle. "We use it to keep people away."

Caroline removed a key from her briefcase and unlocked the door. She stood back and Angie pushed the door open, prepared to say hello to James McDonald who she assumed would be sitting waiting for him.

The last person she expected to see was Sam, her eyes wide and a cloth stuffed into her mouth.

She stared back for a split second before it dawned on her what was going on. She turned in time to see Caroline's arm swinging down, a hammer in her hand. Angie tried to grasp it but the other woman was too quick and she was thrown backwards as it slammed into her left temple. She put her hand to her head, felt blood oozing from the wound, and fell to her knees.

Caroline took a step towards her, a glint of triumph in her eyes. Angie wanted to speak, scream, react, fight but her body wouldn't respond. She was unable to move, her head wound generating a pain such as she had never felt before. She tried to look at Caroline, but her face was moving in and out of focus.

Her eyelids started to close and she tried to resist but they were having none of it. Inexorably the gap between them grew smaller and smaller.

Angie toppled forward and her body crashed to the floor.

Chapter 66

Luke followed James towards the stairs.

"Where do you think she is?" he said.

"My best guess is the HR Depository. It's a room in the basement where we lock away sensitive files and Caroline spends a lot of time there." James shook his head. "She likes to look at people's references and other background information. It gives her material to confront them with if they've lied or exaggerated in their applications."

Luke sensed the disapproval in James's tone. "Have you had problems with her?"

"I've had a few complaints over the past couple of months, most recently by your team member Sam, but I put it down to pressure of work and Caroline's abrasive personality. She tends to rub people up the wrong way, but she's a hard worker so I've been putting off confronting her. I can't believe she's actually killed someone though. She has a temper but that's shocking."

"Rob Talbot wasn't the victim of a furious assault," Luke said, "even though it was made to look that way. His murder was planned down to the last detail. The only thing she didn't allow for was the effect the poison she gave him would have on his stomach."

"Have you any idea why she did it?"

"He had something he thought would help locate Angie Johnson. I believe it was a letter from HR after she was stalked by Dale Cartwright. It was probably way over the top in what it said about Angie's reaction to him not being sacked or even suspended."

"I wouldn't have authorised anything like that."

"I'm not saying you did. I think Caroline let her temper loose in that letter and then, when she discovered Angie still had it, decided she had to get it back. She also found out that Rob Talbot knew its importance and took the decision that he had to die."

"And you really think she might do something to Angie Johnson?"

"Or Sam. My team are looking for them both now. Hopefully, they'll message me to say they've turned up but we can't afford to wait. There's no doubt what Caroline is capable of."

They reached a door at the bottom of the stairs with a sign which read *'Housekeeping And Security Only'*.

"Through here," James said.

Luke followed him through, and they were greeted almost immediately by two more doors, one to the left and the other to the right. James grabbed the handle of the door to the left and pressed it down but it didn't move.

"That's odd," he said. He tried again then moved back from the door and pointed at the door plate. "There's no lock."

"It can't be bolted because the handle won't move," Luke said. "There has to be a lock fitted that's only usable from the other side."

He walked to the other door and tried the handle. Again it didn't budge, but this time there was a keyhole.

"Can you open this door, James?"

"No, but all there is behind it is a storage room for housekeeping's mops, buckets and so on. There's no corridor like there is behind the other door."

Chapter 67

Caroline was pacing from side to side, breathing heavily.

Sam was worried about Angie. She was still unconscious but, like her, now tied to a chair, arms bound behind her back. Her head was bent to the side, blood still seeping from her temple. They sat next to each other, facing the door.

The room they were in wasn't big, ironically about the same size as the room Malcolm Smith had put her in. Ducting cables ran across the top and the walls were unadorned breeze blocks. There was a single fluorescent tube near the top of the wall to her right which flickered slightly. Set against the wall to her left were two grey metal filing cabinets, each about six feet high and four feet wide. The only other furniture was a small table, which Caroline had pushed against one of the filing cabinets, and the two chairs she had tied them to.

Without preamble, Caroline marched over and ripped the cloth from Sam's mouth. Sam gasped and took a deep intake of breath. She worked her jaws in an attempt to relax them.

Caroline moved to Angie and lifted her head upright. There was no reaction and she let it drop back to her shoulder.

"She has to hear this," Caroline said. "I need her conscious."

"She needs medical help," Sam said. "You have to call someone."

"She'll need more than medical help when I've finished with her."

"You can't…"

Caroline punched her in the face and Sam heard a bone

crack in her nose. She felt blood forming in her nostrils, then drops running down to her lips. She tried to spit them away, and wrestled with her hands to try to free them, but they were too tightly bound.

"You deserve everything you've got coming to you," Caroline went on. "You tarted up bitch." She bent to her briefcase and pulled out a tightly wrapped carrier bag. She unfolded it and pulled out a short kitchen knife which she waved in front of Sam's face. The end of the blade was covered in dried blood. "I want you to suffer for what you did to me," she said, then nodded her head to Angie. "Her too."

"I didn't do anything," Sam said.

Caroline ignored her and lunged forward. Sam screamed as the blade sank two or three inches into her left arm just above the elbow. Caroline pulled the knife out and wiped the freshly bloodied end on her thigh before lunging forward again, aiming for her right arm this time.

"What about Mac?" Sam said through tears of pain.

Caroline withdrew her arm. "Mac?" she said. "Who's Mac?"

Sam gritted her teeth. She had to keep the woman talking, had to buy time. "Malcolm Smith," she said. "The man who took us."

"He calls himself Mac does he, the idiot. Malcolm's a useless fool. I told him to kill all of you and make it look like suicide or an accident. But he decided to let you survive and now he's let you escape, the idiot."

It dawned on Sam that Caroline didn't know Smith was dead.

"So now I've got to deal with you myself," Caroline said.

"Why are you doing this? Neither of us has hurt you."

Caroline gave a half-laugh. "You sound like my mother. She didn't lay a finger on me but she was always putting me down, telling me I wasn't good enough, that I was useless. I swore to myself I would never let anyone undermine me like that again."

"Listen, Caroline. What happened to you in the past is awful but Angie and I haven't undermined you."

"You've argued with me, you've gone to my boss about me, you've done everything you can to make me look bad."

"You must see that's not true."

Caroline leapt forward and put the tip of the knife to Sam's throat. She moved her face closer so that their noses were almost touching. "You and your friend are going to disappear," she whispered so quietly that Sam could barely make out the words. "There's a furnace two rooms away and you'll both be burnt to ashes." She giggled.

"We'll be missed."

"For a short while, until they find out about your lesbian affair and your plans to elope together."

Sam heard movement as Angie raised her head and slowly opened her eyes.

"Good, good," Caroline said.

It was Angie's turn to scream.

Chapter 68

Luke threw his shoulder against the locked door but it didn't so much as budge.

"We need a battering ram," he said. "The police will have one." He took his phone out of his pocket.

"There's no reception down here," James said.

Luke looked down at his phone, and sure enough there were no bars. He opened the door to the stairs and hurled himself up. As he turned the corner at the top he collided with Glen Baxter for the second time that day. The Head of Security stood back and smirked as two men emerged from behind him, each grabbing one of Luke's arms.

"Sorry, Luke," Glen said, though his face betrayed his true feelings. "Mr Filcher says you're to leave. Dave, Carl, take him to the front door and throw him out."

"She's got them," Luke said as they started to manhandle him towards the exit.

"Wait a minute, boys," Glen said. "Who's got who, Luke? Is this one of your fanciful theories?"

Luke knew Glen from old and what made him tick. "This is your chance to show Edward Filcher what you're made of," he said.

"What do you mean?"

Luke could tell his interest was piqued. "You can save them. Caroline Klein has taken Angie Johnson and Sam Chambers to the basement but the door's locked."

"Which door?"

"The housekeeping and security door."

"Now I know you're lying," Glen said. "That door doesn't lock." He nodded to the two men to take Luke away.

"Wait, Glen," Luke said. "There's nothing to lose. Go

down and try the door yourself. It will only take a moment. James is down there and he can show you."

Glen grunted. "Hold him there, guys,' he said, and headed down to the basement.

Chapter 69

"Why did Malcolm Smith do what you told him?" Sam said.

"It was the way we were," Caroline said. "Our relationship was based on it."

"It all makes sense," Angie said. She was bleary-eyed but now fully conscious. "The blonde wig, the heels, the stuff about liking gentle women."

"What do you mean?" Caroline snapped.

"You were the dominatrix and he was your slave. That was your relationship wasn't it?"

Caroline lunged forward with the knife again, this time at Angie. It struck her in the thigh and she gasped as it sank in.

"Malcolm's dead," Sam said.

Caroline returned her attention to Sam. "Rubbish."

"He died last night. He fell off a cliff and broke his neck on the rocks at the bottom."

Caroline shrugged. "What if he did? He was useless anyway. I told him to kill you all and yet here you are."

"Why did you want him to kill Marie?" She thought she knew but needed to keep Caroline talking.

"She complained about me to James when I refused to give her an assistant. I can't have that." She paused and looked at Angie. "You were the same. You went to him when I refused to do anything about Dale Cartwright after you claimed he was stalking you online."

"What about Emily?" Sam said.

"She asked for a bigger pay rise when she was promoted and seemed to think James could help when I said nothing could be done."

"And those were your reasons?" Sam was gob-smacked. "You wanted them killed because they complained to

James? Me too?"

Caroline shrugged and lifted the knife again.

"They'll link him to you," Sam said, the words coming out in a rush. "You'll be caught so you might as well give up. If you stop now you'll be an accessory to Marie Osborne's murder but nothing more."

"What about Rob?" As soon as she said it Angie realised her mistake.

This time Caroline went for her face.

Sam hurled herself sideways and her body smashed into Caroline's shoulder. The knife flew from her hand, nicking Angie's cheek before clattering to the floor. She exerted downward pressure to keep Caroline from getting up but her hands were still tied. The other woman started twisting and pushing and she realised she wasn't strong enough to resist. Caroline was almost out from under her when Sam felt pressure on her back as Angie fell onto her, the three of them in some kind of devil's embrace, the joint weights of Sam and Angie keeping Caroline from getting up.

Sam knew they couldn't hold this position for long. Her arm, her broken leg, and doubtless Angie's thigh as well, were agony. It was only a matter of time.

Angie screamed and fell away. "She bit me," she screamed.

Sam tried to keep the pressure on but with her arms tied she had no leverage. Caroline pushed her to one side and scrambled on all fours towards the knife which had come to rest in front of the door. She picked it up and Sam could do nothing but watch, tied as she was to the chair. She looked over at Angie but she was similarly constrained.

Caroline stood up. "No more talking," she said, waving the knife in front of her, the blade at eye height. "I've heard enough from you two."

Chapter 70

Glen reappeared on the stairs. "Let him go and call the police," he said. The men released Luke and he raced down. "You were right," Glen said as they reached the locked door. "I hadn't realised there was a lock on the other side but there must be. I wonder why?"

"We can worry about that later," Luke said impatiently. "How do we get in?"

"That's easy."

"What?"

Glen gestured to the right-hand door. "We'll use that one." He nodded his head knowingly then tapped the side of his nose. "There's a door at the back of the housekeeping room. The corridor runs from there all the way around..." he indicated the locked door "...to this one."

"And," he said triumphantly as he raised a set of some thirty or forty keys clipped to his belt, "one of these unlocks it." He raised them in the air. "I'll start with the one at this end."

Luke had visions of Glen slowly working his way through the complete set. "It's that one," he said, pointing to one of them.

"It might be, but..."

"Try it first. It's the only cross key."

"The only what?"

"Just try it."

Glen slotted it in and it connected then turned smoothly before clicking. He pressed the handle and the door opened outwards. Luke barged past him and found himself in a long narrow room. On both sides were shelves filled to the brim with boxes of hand towels and cleaning products, but what drew his attention was the door at the far end with mops leant against it. He threw the mops to one side and pressed the handle. To his relief it was unlocked. He pulled it open to reveal a corridor that stretched some forty or fifty meters before bending left, presumably when it reached the end of the building.

He ran as fast as he could, hoping he wasn't too late and conscious of the other two men not far behind. When he rounded the corner, he found himself in another, shorter corridor which again bent to the left at the end. Halfway along it there was a door on his left. He slowed down.

"Not that one," James called out. "First door around the corner."

Luke raced on and sure enough there was another door only a few yards after the bend. He stopped, panting, as the two men drew up beside him.

"Here," James said, passing him a key.

Luke grabbed it, took a deep breath and unlocked the door. There was resistance as he lowered the handle and pushed but he put all his weight against the door and it flew open. Caroline was propelled backwards. Beyond her he saw Sam and Angie, both lying sideways on the floor, tied to chairs and covered in blood.

"Are you all right?" he said.

"She's got a knife," Sam shouted. "Be careful."

He stepped towards Caroline who had fallen to the floor and was on her hands and knees facing away from him.

"Stand up slowly," he said.

She lifted her hands from the ground and raised herself to a standing position, still facing away.

"Now drop the knife."

She turned, her face a picture of hatred, and leapt at his stomach. He dodged to one side, grabbed her arm and twisted it behind her back. She yelped in pain and the knife fell to the floor.

"It's over, Caroline," he said. "The police will be here soon."

She tried to wriggle free but he had firm control of her arm. She was breathing heavily. "They - deserve - to - die," she hissed.

Luke shook his head. The sooner this woman was locked up the better.

Chapter 71

Filcher drummed his fingers on the table. "I can't afford to wait all day," he said. "When will the blighter be here?"

"Any minute," Luke said.

"You're not going to tell your police buddies about any of this, are you?"

"No, Mr Filcher, I won't tell them."

"Need to keep it internal. Confidential. Hush hush. Can't afford to let this kind of thing out there. Bad for the reputation."

Luke nodded.

"He's been here a long time," Filcher went on. He shook his head, then lowered his voice almost to a whisper. "A fellow Master Mason, who would have believed it." There was a knock at the door. "Enter."

James McDonald opened the door wide and gestured for the man with him to go in first.

"Sit down," Filcher said. He looked pointedly at Luke who stood up, allowing Arthur Bloomsbury to take his seat. James followed him in and stood next to Luke.

"What's he doing here?" Arthur said, pointing at Luke. "I thought we were meeting about share options."

Filcher shifted uncomfortably in his seat. He looked directly at James. "Tell him, James,' he said.

"We know about your deal with Bannermans," James said.

"I don't know what you're talking about." Arthur started rubbing his forehead vigorously and almost spat the next words out. "I had nothing to do with it." He sat back in his chair and folded his arms tightly across his chest. "That Angie Johnson woman betrayed the company," he said. "I've never even spoken to their Bid Director, Danny

Oglethingy. Ask him for yourself."

"You're right," Luke said.

"There you are then," Arthur said.

"But you have spoken to Charles Avery."

"Charles?" Filcher said and stood up. "What's he's got to do with it?"

"Don't worry, Mr Filcher," Luke said. "This is nothing to do with the Lodge."

"What, eh, I…"

"Sit down."

Filcher sat down and Luke turned back to Arthur. "We know all about the deal you and Charles struck. About the money he offered you in exchange for allowing Bannermans to front the deal and take the lion's share of the revenue."

"Nonsense," Arthur said. "Charles wouldn't…"

"He's admitted it. All of it. Two hundred thousand pounds is a lot of money."

Arthur's mouth started to open and close.

"I'm here to offer you a way out," James said. "Early retirement and a full pension in exchange for your silence." He placed a document on the table in front of Arthur. "You need to sign this and keep your word. If anything gets out to the press we have the power to stop your pension immediately and cancel all of your share options."

"I've served this company for over thirty years," Arthur said.

Filcher stood up. "Yes, Arthur,' he said, his words deliberate and forceful. "My Uncle trusted you and your betrayal sickens me, it really does. Sign the document." Arthur looked briefly at Filcher then bent to the table, picked up the pen and signed his name. "Now get out," Filcher shouted.

Chapter 72

It was six pm on a Friday and the Saracen's Head was buzzing. Luke picked up his and Josh's drinks and turned away from the bar to find DS Grace Cooper smiling up at him. He put one of the drinks down and took the offered hand.

"Great to see you back, sir," she said.

"Thanks, Sergeant."

She smiled and made her way back to her group. Several of them nodded their heads to him and he raised his hand in acknowledgement. She was right, he was back. Okay, he wasn't a policeman any more, but he was working and he was adding value. That was what mattered. He took the drinks over to the table and passed Josh his Thatchers Haze. Sam was already halfway through her prosecco while Helen cradled a gin and tonic and Maj a pint of lime and lemonade. An odd team, Luke thought, thrown together but god had they been effective. He'd had teams in Avon and Somerset with more ability on paper but bugger all in reality.

"Penny for them, guv," Josh said.

"I was thinking about letting you go…" Luke said, but couldn't keep it up when Josh's lips turned downwards, "… on a detecting course."

Josh's smile returned in an instant. "Seriously, guv?"

"Seriously." He looked around at the others. "We have the makings of a really good team here. You've all proved your worth and I'm very proud of you."

The others looked down at their glasses for a few seconds. It was Sam who broke the silence. "Have you heard how Emily's doing?" she said.

"They believe she'll make a full recovery," Luke said,

"She's going to be in hospital for a few more days but it's looking promising."

"That's great news."

"Guv?" Josh said. "How did Caroline persuade Rob Talbot to let her into his apartment?"

"I don't think we'll ever know. We know how she poisoned him though. Any guesses?"

"Made him a blue curaçao cocktail."

"No, Josh, she didn't make him a blue curaçao cocktail. SOCOs found traces of baking soda in Talbot's apartment."

"She baked him a cake?"

Luke shook his head. "Interesting idea, but no. Copper sulphate is distinctive because of its colour and because it tastes metallic. Baking soda is known to neutralise metallic tastes. So all she had to do was add copper sulphate and baking soda to a strongly coloured drink like black coffee."

"I didn't know baking soda did that," Sam said.

"To be honest I didn't until the pathologist told me," Luke said. "We've all learned a lot over the past couple of weeks."

"I've certainly learned a lot about abductions and kidnapping," Sam said.

"…and broken legs and knife wounds," Maj added.

"You must be missing your old job though, Sam," Helen said. "It must have been so much more exciting, adding numbers up and stuff."

"Sometimes I got to multiply them together," Sam said.

"But seriously, Luke," Maj said. "It's been great having even a small part in…" He stopped and gave a little chuckle.

"I don't think it's particularly funny," Sam said, gesturing to the plaster encasing her leg.

"Sorry Sam, I'm not laughing at you." Maj turned to Luke. "I nearly forgot. I asked around and the wife of one of the Security team has seen Glen on stage. He does only have a small part though." He was still grinning as he clicked a couple of times on his phone. "She took a photo."

He passed his phone to Helen, who gave a little snort and handed it on to Sam.

"I see what you mean, Maj," Sam said with a smile.

"That," Josh said in disgust as he took the phone from her, "is something I never want to see again." He threw it to Luke as if it were a grenade with the pin out.

Luke looked down and a smile grew on his face. "This," he said pointing at the screen, "is the mother lode. Please can I have a copy?"

"I'll send it over," Maj said.

"By the way, what was the name of the show?"

"The Chippenmales."

After the laughter had died down, Helen said, "Right, the drinks are on me."

"Nonsense," Luke said. "Edward Filcher's paying for the next round."

"That doesn't sound like him," Helen said.

Luke tapped the side of his nose. "He doesn't know yet."

Acknowledgements

I have to start by thanking my wife Penny who has given me endless support and encouragement. Not only has she given me the space and time to write, edit and promote this book, she was also my first reader and, being an ardent reader of crime fiction series, gave me some great constructive feedback.

After editing for Penny's comments, I was lucky to have six tremendous beta readers whose feedback was invaluable. My sincere thanks to Lauren Cooke, Denise Goodhand, Keith Innes, Sarah McKenzie, Irene Paterson and Marcie Whitecotton-Carroll.

My final feedback before completion came from my daughter Abby Davies. She is a brilliant writer (you should check out her latest novels 'Arrietty' and 'Her No.1 Fan' if you're into psychological thrillers), and it was with trepidation that I hit the send button! Luckily, she thought the book was okay but, again, her feedback was brilliant.

And now to three people who aren't even aware they helped me! Barry Hutchison (aka JD Kirk), Gordon Smith (aka Alex Smith) and Dave Gatward (aka David J Gatward) are all writers of crime fiction series. If you haven't read their books (featuring DCI Logan, DCI Kett and DCI Grimm respectively) then you really must check them out. I love their writing, but it was a YouTube video of the 3 of them talking about the benefits of self-publishing that persuaded me to give it a go. So thanks, guys!

Thanks also to Aubrey Parsons for doing such a fantastic job narrating the audiobook, to Olly Bennett for the excellent cover design, and to Roger Wilkins for two things: (1) letting me include him in this book, and (2) his awesome cider.

Last but not least, thanks to you the reader. I love your feedback and reading your reviews, and I'm always delighted to hear from you so please feel free to get in touch.

Thanks for reading my debut novel. I would really appreciate it if you could leave a review on Goodreads and Amazon.

Want to read more about Luke Sackville and what shaped his career choices? 'Change of Direction', the prequel to 'Taken to the Hills', can be downloaded as an ebook or audiobook free of charge by subscribing to my newsletter at:

sjrichardsauthor.com

Book 2 in the series raises the stakes for Luke and his team when MI6 asks for their help

BLACK MONEY

December 2023

Order your copy now

ABOUT THE AUTHOR

Let's get one thing straight: my name's Steve. I've never been called 'SJ', but Steve Richards is a well-known political writer hence the pen name.

I was born in Bath and have lived at various times on an irregular clockwise circle around England. After university in Manchester, my wife and I settled in Macclesfield before moving to Bedfordshire then a few years ago back to Somerset. We now live in Croscombe, a lovely village just outside Wells, with our 2 sprightly cocker spaniels.

I've always loved writing but have only really had the time to indulge myself since taking early retirement. My daughter is a brilliant author (I'm not biased of course) which is both an inspiration and - because she's so good - a challenge. After a few experiments, and a couple of completed but unsatisfactory and never published novels, I decided to write a crime fiction series as it's one of the genres I most enjoy.

You can find out more about me and my books at my website:

sjrichardsauthor.com

Printed in Great Britain
by Amazon

45769301R00169